Pride Publishing books by Rae Marks

Hart Consulting
Sweet Hart

Hart Consulting

SWEET HART

RAE MARKS

Sweet Hart
ISBN # 978-1-83943-978-0

Interior text design by Claire Siemaszkiewicz
Pride Publishing

Published in 2021 by Pride Publishing, United Kingdom.

Pride Publishing is an imprint of Totally Entwined Group Limited.

SWEET HART

Dedication

To my friend Jean, who challenged me to keep writing, and to my husband, who believes in me when I don't even believe in myself.

Chapter One

Brayden

"Look, kid. I got nothing to tell you."

Bray pulled his gaze from the full lips he'd been watching as the man in the doorway, Sam, gave a flat refusal. He took a deep, calming breath and willed away his body's response. Maybe he needed to back up a little and explain the urgency of the situation. He didn't have a lot of time to find Mase, and this Sam guy was his best bet.

The guy blocking the doorway would be hot if his eyebrows weren't pinched together so tight and his big, full lips weren't turned down. Hell, he was still hot, even in full intimidation mode.

Sam's honey-blond hair was longer on top and styled high. His groomed beard was just a few shades darker than the hair on his head and hinted at the tiniest bit of red highlights. Bray lowered his eyes again to Sam's lips. Both were plump, but the top lip was a little fuller than the bottom one. That was rare, in Bray's experience, but sexy as hell.

The tic in the jaw next to those lips brought Bray back to the matter at hand. He looked up into Sam's cinnamon-brown eyes as he considered his options.

"I know you're working with Mase and I have to find him. I'm—"

"I don't know what you're going on about, but I have shit to do."

Sam tried to close the old, paint-chipped door in Bray's face, but Bray stepped forward, using his foot as a doorstop. He wouldn't give up that easily. Bray needed to untie his tongue and keep on task, no matter how sexy the guy was.

"Please, I don't have a lot of time. I just need to talk to him."

"Look, kid—"

"I'm not a kid. I know he's pulled some crazy stunts since he got kicked out—"

"You don't know shit, *kid*. If you just got kicked out of the military and you're looking for camaraderie and a job, forget it."

As soon as Sam said the word 'military', Bray breathed a sigh of relief. Sam swore under his breath. So the guy definitely knew his brother. Sam flexed his huge biceps as he crossed his arms. His head dipped to one side as he leaned forward. Bray swallowed then a tiny breath escaped his lips as he imagined the man before him leaning in to steal a kiss. Was this guy Mase's boyfriend? If so, his brother was one lucky bastard.

"Move your foot. Like I said, kid, you don't know shit," Sam ground out through clenched teeth.

"Just tell me what's going on. Is he okay? If he'd returned any of my emails over the past two and half years, maybe I'd know more about what was happening."

"You think I can help you?"

Bray gave one sharp nod of confirmation. Sam blew a breath out between his lush lips and dropped his arms to his sides. The crease between his brows eased a bit as he seemed to really look at Bray for the first time. He looked over Bray's head down the hallway for a moment before coming to some kind of decision.

"What's your name, kid?"

"Bray, Brayden Hart."

There was a pause. Bray assumed it was Sam digesting Bray's last name, Mase's last name.

"Well, I'm sorry, but I got nothing for you, Mr. Hart."

"How'd you know I was in the army?"

"You got it written all over you, from your close-cropped cut to your military stance." The guy rolled his eyes and shook his head. "I've got things to do, kid, so do you mind moving your foot—or do I need to move it for you?"

Bray wet his dry lips as he contemplated his choices. He could call Max for another favor, but if he went that route, he'd need this part to be believable.

"I can just sit out here and wait until he comes home."

"You'll be waiting the rest of your life, kid."

"It's Bray or Brayden, and I think you have a really good idea when you'll be talking to Mase again."

Looking over Sam's shoulder, Bray took in the shit-hole apartment with its dingy brown carpet and walls so old that the wallpaper was peeling at the corners along the ceiling. A ceiling with tiles that had different-sized brown rings, a sure sign of water damage. Was this how Mase was living now? The thought made Bray's gut twist uncomfortably.

If Mase needed money… Bray shook his head. Mase would never be the one to reach out, which was exactly why Bray was standing in the hallway that smelled like piss mixed with broccoli farts. Unless the inside of the apartment smelled better, he didn't see how anyone could even think about putting a morsel of food into their mouth in this place.

If by chance Sam did talk to Mase before Brayden could get to him, he had to figure out a message most likely to get a response. Would Mase come home or even return a call if he knew the truth? *Probably not.* Bray bit his lip as he waffled. He didn't like lying, and he especially didn't like lying to family. He wasn't sure he'd ever be able to forgive his father for his 'little white lie'.

"When you see him, tell him Nickel needs him. Tell him it's looking like it might be life or death."

Both those statements taken separately were absolutely one hundred percent true. Nick might deny he needed their older brother, but he and Bray were twins. Bray knew they both required all the support they could get.

When Mase heard those statements together, Bray knew what he'd assume, and he'd have to apologize for it later. For now, he decided it was the best route. He had a feeling Sam would repeat those statements verbatim to his brother.

"Nickel?" Sam asked.

"Nick, my twin."

"Twins? There're two of you running around wreaking havoc?"

"Nick wreaks more havoc and we're not identical, so there aren't exactly two of me."

Sam's only response was a raised eyebrow.

"So you'll tell him?"

"I'm sorry. There's no way I can help you," Sam said with the shake of his head.

Even though Bray was anxious, he hesitated before lifting his foot. He needed Sam to think he was reluctant to leave. Sam was only a couple inches taller than Bray's five-foot-eleven-inch frame, but he hunched down a little, so they were eye to eye.

"I can't help you," Sam said again.

Bray swallowed as energy began to hum under his skin at the man's direct stare. He couldn't be lusting after his brother's boyfriend. Wetting his dry lips one last time, Bray nodded and lifted his foot. The two men stared at each other for a moment longer, until the sound of a baby screaming somewhere down the hall had Bray turning his head. Before he could even suck in another breath, the door in front of him slammed shut and the lock snicked into place.

With a dejected sigh, Brayden looked at the door for another minute. Guilt had his stomach tightening into knots. He couldn't afford to stand around, though his hesitation to leave would probably work in his favor in case Sam was watching through the peephole.

When he pushed open the door of the building a few minutes later, Bray sucked in some of the fresh air. He didn't even care that his clothes immediately glued themselves to his body with the humidity Florida was famous for. He was just glad to be out of the stench that had pressed down on him inside the apartment building.

After one last glance at the second floor, Bray walked down the sidewalk toward the parking lot. As soon as he was in his rental car, he dialed Max's number.

"How'd it go?" Max said.

"He wouldn't even admit he knew Mase."

There was silence on the other end. Max had warned him against making contact with Sam. He'd suggested following him until he led Bray to Mase, but Bray didn't have that kind of time.

"So, it looks like you were right," Bray admitted.

There was still silence on the other end of the line.

"Look, Sin. I still need help."

Bray always struggled calling his friend by his pseudonym. Even though it stood for Super Intel Nerd, calling a nerdy guy like Max, Sin seemed funny to Bray.

"Next time listen to me. You've now ruined the advantage of surprising him."

"Fine. Can you find out where he's going?"

"Of course I can."

Bray could hear the light click-clack of Max tapping on the keys of his laptop. Putting the phone on Bluetooth, Bray started his rental and pulled out of the parking spot behind Sam's apartment building.

"Where's he going?" Bray asked as he pulled out onto the street.

"I have him traveling out of Miami to Kiev tomorrow with a stopover in Munich."

Bray tapped his fingers on the steering wheel. This had just gotten a lot more complicated and expensive than he'd anticipated. Was Mase undercover or was he in trouble? If he was in trouble, Bray wanted to be there.

"Looks like I'll be heading to Kiev," he sighed.

"I'll book you a flight that stops over in DC. I've got something I want to give you if you're going to Kiev."

"I just have to check out of the hotel. Give me a couple of hours to get to the airport."

Max disconnected the call without saying goodbye, but it didn't surprise Bray at all. Max was always on to the next problem.

Chapter Two

Sam

"So that's Mase's little brother?" Brody said through Sam's ear mic.

"Yeah, his bro." That from Ax, who chuckled at his own joke.

Sam almost snorted, but he couldn't seem to pull his gaze away from the gorgeous man taking up his doorway. After all, everyone called Brody 'Bro'. There was irony in that too, since Brody wasn't a bro. He was the sweetest guy Sam had ever met. The guy's handle in the army had been 'F-Bomb', but only because the kid didn't swear.

"He's adorable," Colt purred through the mic.

Even though he knew it was a joke, Sam found his gaze flicking to the door down the hall where Colt, Ax and Brody were cooped up doing surveillance. Sam was off his game today and the blond in front of him was responsible. He'd never expected Mase's family to get entangled in their op.

"Better get him out of here and quick, Magnum. Your mark is T-minus eight minutes," Ax said.

Sam wanted to roll his eyes at his call sign. He hadn't used it in years, but Colt and Ax had of course started using it as soon as they'd found out what it was. Colt went by Reaper. Ax's call had been Loco. It wasn't exactly fair that Sam got the name of a cheesy eighties TV character. *Damn mustache.*

Sam leaned in and told the kid again that he couldn't help him. Brayden Hart kept licking his lips and it was making Sam's pants tighter than he liked. It was probably a nervous habit, but it kept drawing attention to his perfectly formed mouth, not to mention his razor-sharp jaw.

Sam usually dated guys his own age, but Mase's little brother was ringing all his bells. *All the more reason to get him out of the way.* Brayden had no idea what he'd just stepped into.

After a few more delay tactics, Brayden finally moved his foot from blocking the door. It was a good thing too, because the stench in the hallway was pretty unbearable. It also gave Sam a minute to let his body calm down before he had to meet with some pretty serious homophobes. The last thing he needed was a tent in his jeans.

As soon as he closed the door, Sam went to his laptop. He opened it and watched the security cameras located throughout the building.

"One of you needs to tail him to make sure we're the only ones who know he was here."

"Be more than happy to follow that ass—" Colt started.

"Bro, you follow him. And make sure you're the only one following him."

"Sure thing, Sam," Bro replied.

"Did you know they were twins? Can you imagine if they were identical?" Colt groaned.

"Kid looks smart enough not to fall for your bullshit," Ax said.

Someone snorted and Sam assumed it was Bro, since it was only his three back-ups in the apartment down the hall, and no way was Colt going to laugh at a joke at his expense, even if the guy was a man-whore.

Sam hadn't known they were twins. He knew Mase had two younger brothers but not much beyond that. They tried to leave the past in the past. But two guys who looked like that kid? No one in their right mind would be able to resist putting that in their spank bank.

Sam watched as Brayden stood in the hall and stared at his closed door. Normally he'd be completely turned off when someone pushed back as hard as Brayden had. He could respect it, sure, but to have it turn him on was disconcerting.

Mase's kid brother had made it seem brave. The desperation in those pretty blue eyes had Sam actually considering opening the door back up to comfort him…Brayden Hart.

Shaking his head, Sam leaned over the computer and watched as Brayden finally turned toward the stairs. Bro had already made his way down the fire escape and was getting into the car he and Colt were driving.

Leaving Brayden in Bro's hands, Sam closed out of the security footage, shut his laptop and hid it in the cubby he'd built under the kitchen sink. Everything was in place for the deal today. Tomorrow he would head to Ukraine to make a deal that would put them on the right track.

"They're here," Colt's voice came through Sam's earpiece. "Over and out."

Sam left his earpiece in, knowing it couldn't be seen with the naked eye and couldn't be heard unless Colt or Ax took themselves off mute and blasted music loud enough to burst Sam's eardrums. Blowing out a quick breath, he walked away from the door so they'd hear him approach it when they knocked. It was showtime.

* * * *

Sam relaxed back into his seat as the pilot announced the final descent into Kiev. He gave a disgusted snort as he looked over at his traveling companion. Ax was fast asleep and had been almost since he'd buckled his seatbelt. If Sam hadn't woken him up when the last flight had landed in Munich, Ax might have ended up in China.

At home in Virginia it was still the middle of the night, but in Kiev, it was almost eight a.m. Sleep had eluded Sam on the flight from Miami. Every time he closed his eyes, he'd heard the entreaty in Brayden Hart's voice. He kept seeing the plea in those bright blue eyes. *'Life and death'*, he'd said. Mase would want to know if his little brother was dying, so Sam had to find a way to tell him.

Brayden showing up had Sam tempted to call this whole deal off. He had no idea how Brayden had found him or how he'd tied him to Mase, but the fact that he'd been able to had Sam going up his chain of command. Jazz Thibodeaux, his direct superior, had told him to go full speed ahead. The Kiev deal wasn't really related to Miami.

As his partner on this op, Sam had discussed with Ax the potential threat to their cover that was Mase's little brother. Of course, Colt and Ax had teased Sam about being jealous and wanting to keep Bray for himself. Sam had rolled his eyes and prayed no one saw how fucking true that was.

From what he'd been able to find out, the kid was almost twelve years younger than him. The last thing Brayden Hart wanted was an old asshole who had to be in control in order to let go at all. He didn't want to deal with Sam's issues. Sam didn't even want to deal with his own issues. It was why he only had sex when he couldn't hold out anymore. Plus, from what he knew of Mase's family, the kid was probably straight as an arrow.

Leaning his head back, Sam looked at the ceiling of the plane. He trusted Jazz, would trust him with his life, *had* trusted him with his life. But something felt off. He'd known Jazz for fourteen years, almost as long as he'd known Mase, but Jazz hadn't seen the determination in Brayden's eyes. That kid was trouble with a capital T, and not just because he'd distracted Sam for a minute. He was trouble because he'd walked into the situation yesterday totally blind to the dangers he might face.

Luckily, Bro had followed him all the way to the airport and Brayden had caught a flight to DC. The fact that the link between him and Mase was so easy to find made Sam's skin itch. Jazz had said he'd look into it, but Jazz had his own problems.

Another French trafficker was putting out the word that Jazz was stepping on his toes. That shit was bound to happen. If anyone found out who Jazz really was…

They needed to make sure their intel was secure, and as soon as he got back to the States, Sam would figure out how Mase's little brother had found him. Until then, he'd have to rely on his team to look into it while he furthered their cause.

As soon as he walked into the airport, Sam felt eyes on him. Figuring it was Oleksiy Kozak and Ruslan Andreiko's men checking him out, Sam continued at a leisurely pace toward the baggage claim.

"You feel it too?" Ax asked.

The side of Sam's mouth kicked up. Ax had good instincts. In the year he'd been on the team, Ax had proven to be a valuable asset and Sam hadn't once regretted giving him the opportunity. Their team was still coming together, but they had a great foundation.

"You don't think it's Kozak's men?" Sam asked in low tones.

Ax answered with the slightest shake of his head and that caused a crease to form between Sam's eyebrows. With Mase's little brother crashing their party in Miami, they would take every precaution.

"I'll get the luggage," Sam said. "You get the car. We'll see who they follow. Either way, we lose them."

"You're the boss," Ax said as he walked off toward the car rentals.

Sam could still feel it. If two people were following them, they would have divided as well, so Sam couldn't be sure if they were both still being followed until he met back up with Ax.

After getting their supply bag, Sam took his time strapping his carry-on to the larger suitcase. He pretended to struggle as he covertly looked around for someone he'd consistently seen through the airport. He couldn't pinpoint anyone, but he still knew he was being watched.

Taking a chance, Sam pulled his luggage into the restroom. Keeping his eyes trained on the reflection of the door in the mirror, Sam went to the sink and washed his hands before heading back out into the airport. He slowly looked around and finally spotted someone. They guy was wearing a hoodie, so only the outline of his back was visible. His phone was in selfie mode. That wouldn't be so strange, except the guy's face wasn't in frame—only the people behind him were. Feeling his phone buzz in his pocket, Sam pulled it out to look at the text from Ax.

I'm clear. Got the car. Be at the curb in less than 2 minutes.

Sam made his way in a wide circle around the guy to try to see him from the front. Just when Sam was about to glimpse his face, a girl approached the guy and he turned. Sam took advantage of the distraction and strode quickly out of the door.

Ax already had the trunk popped open and was back in the driver's seat. Sam tossed the suitcases in, closed the trunk and slipped into the back seat. Before the door was even latched, Ax was pulling away from the curb.

"Did you lose him, or do you think he got our plates?" Ax asked as he pulled into traffic.

"I lost one, but keep an eye out. He was talking to someone else, so not sure what was going on. I slipped out while he was distracted, but if there's one—"

"There could be more. Do you think he's one of Kozak and Andreiko's men?"

"Not sure."

Sam was set to meet with Oleksiy Kozak and Ruslan Andreiko in a few hours' time. They were high-level men in the Ukraine mafia and they dealt in both drugs and people. Sam had been working with the Kozak on the drugs side, but the people side of things was the ultimate goal.

Sam looked up and met Ax's eyes in the rearview mirror. Ax shook his head. They weren't being followed.

Chapter Three

Brayden

"Excuse, please," a woman said as she patted Bray's arm.

Bray shook her off, but by the time he looked back to where Sam had been, he was gone. He turned in a circle as he tried to locate Sam again.

"Excuse, please," the woman said again.

"Sorry. I'm waiting for someone."

Bray reached down to grab the handle of his carry-on, but his hand only grasped air. He turned in a circle again, this time looking for his suitcase. It was gone and so was the woman. Bray quickly patted his abdomen and blew out a relieved sigh when he felt his passport, wallet and extra cash in his money belt. Like a true tourist, he turned his backpack around so he was wearing it over his chest.

He was in over his head. He knew it, but he couldn't give up. Admitting defeat, Bray unlocked his phone and dialed Max. When there was no answer, Bray left a message.

"Sin, you were right. I need back-up and there's no one I'd rather have at my back than you. I've already had my luggage stolen and I haven't even left the airport, not to mention I lost my mark while my bag was being snatched. Please call me back."

Bray disconnected the call and headed toward the sign for car rentals. He couldn't exactly follow Sam in a taxi. It wouldn't be the first time he'd driven in a foreign country, but it was the first time he was in a foreign country without the US Army watching his six.

He didn't imagine himself naïve, but he hadn't known how much back-up he'd need. Bray wasn't a covert operator like Mase, but he'd have to manage on his own somehow.

Since he'd lost Sam anyway, Bray walked into the bathroom to use the head. As he finished using the urinal, Bray zipped up his pants. Before he could turn to leave, his arm was twisted behind his back. Rather than fight, Bray simply sighed. This day couldn't get much worse.

"Your wallet," the guy behind him whispered in his ear.

To bring the point home, he poked Bray in the back with a knife. The thick hoodie he was wearing offered good protection, so Bray took a chance and threw back an elbow. The guy behind him grunted.

There was a loud ripping sound as Bray swung around and flung out his arm to get the guy's throat. His attacker dropped the knife and grabbed his neck, but another guy stepped toward Bray.

Before the second man reached him, Bray kicked out with his leg and caught the guy in the chest. As the second attacker stumbled back to try to keep his balance, Bray followed, kicking again until the attacker landed on his ass.

As he headed out of the door, the first guy jumped him from behind. Bray dropped all his weight and was trying to crouch down to throw the guy, but his backpack was in the way, so he only succeeded in getting the guy on top of him.

A group of men entered the bathroom and tripped over the heap Bray had made of himself and the first attacker. Rolling to his side, he popped up into a crouch position with his fists ready, but everyone was still trying to get themselves straightened out. Bray slipped through the fray and headed back into the airport.

Keeping an eye out behind him, Bray took out his phone and tried calling Max again. He reached under his backpack to make sure he hadn't lost any of his valuables in the fight. If he had, he'd most likely keep walking unless his passport was gone.

"Need help again already?" Max asked without even a 'hello'.

"Did you get my message?"

"I haven't checked my voicemail yet. Let me guess. You lost him."

"Lost Sam, lost my luggage, lost my dignity."

"Your dignity?"

"Apparently I look like an easy mark. A couple of guys tried to mug me in the bathroom."

"If they got your luggage, maybe you *are* an easy mark."

"Thanks." Bray rolled his eyes but still looked back to make sure he wasn't being followed.

"I figured this would happen. I'll send you the hotel where he's registered."

"You have zero faith in me," Bray grumbled as he got in line at the car rental agency.

"I have plenty of faith in you. You're an eternal optimist. It's what I like about you. You're just not trained as an operator."

Bray didn't argue, because Max was right and this 'op' proved it. It seemed like everyone was two steps ahead of him. He just had to do his best to get to Mase and to try to get Mase to agree to come home, even if it was just for a visit.

"I also rented you a car. I'm texting you the confirmation number."

"Sin, you're the best. I have a feeling I'm going to need more of your help over the next few days."

"I have no doubt. Just use the coins I gave you. It'll make both our lives a lot easier."

"I will."

Bray reached down to feel his money belt again. The whole airport experience was making him paranoid, but he was relieved when he felt the two large coins Max had given him.

It gave him a little security to have someone like Max in his corner, especially when it sped up the process of getting the car. Bray hadn't lost too much time. Max had even been thoughtful enough to text him Sam's room number.

When Bray pulled up to the valet stand, he was hesitant to hand over his keys, but this wasn't the type of hotel where someone parked their own car.

Bray took off his ripped hoodie and stuffed it into his backpack as he walked into the hotel. When he looked up, he stumbled to a stop to avoid running into a group of men. They all turned to look at him and Bray saw they were talking to Sam. Sam's frown went from confused to fierce within a heartbeat.

The man standing next to Sam leaned in to whisper something in his ear. Sam's nostrils flared and his eyes narrowed. It wasn't that Bray was expecting a warm welcome, but he also hadn't expected to literally run into him either.

"Your boyfriend?" one of the guys in the group asked.

Sam looked at the guy who'd spoken for a long moment before his gaze flicked back to Bray. He could see the moment Sam made a decision.

"You got a problem with that, Sergiy?" Sam asked.

Sergiy looked around at everyone in the group. He curled his lip in disgust, but he shook his head. Bray knew that a lot of people in Ukraine were homophobic. He hadn't exactly planned to broadcast his sexuality, but if it tied him to Sam, he was game.

Sam pushed through the group, grabbed Bray's bicep and pulled him toward the elevator. Bray followed with only a glance over his shoulder. The guy who seemed to be with Sam closed his eyes and rubbed his forehead as if he were stressed, or maybe getting a headache.

"Listen, kid. You're in way over your head here. You have zero clue what the fuck you just waltzed into. I know what you want, but I can't help you. The only thing I can do is keep your ass alive and the only way I can do that is if you fucking listen to what I say."

Bray tried not to swallow his tongue as he felt Sam's warm breath caress his ear. He willed his dick not to respond. Now was *not* the time.

Though he wouldn't call himself a natural follower, the idea of being told what to do had never done it for Bray until now. Images flooded his brain as he pictured Sam doing just that. Sam telling him where to sit, how to move, when to come.

Bray gave his head a little shake. He needed to focus.

Chapter Four

Sam

"Don't fucking shake your head at me," Sam ground out. "These are not the kind of people you spring a plus-one on. I'll do what I can to help you on all fronts, but you have to stay here and wait for me to come back. I have a meeting I can't reschedule."

"Will he be there?"

Sam closed his eyes and willed his temper to cool. He should have known it was Brayden following him at the airport. The kid was tenacious. Sam would normally respect him for that, but Brayden was going to get himself killed. Mase had always acted like he was dead to his family. The man before him, risking his life just to *talk* to Mase, proved that wasn't the case.

They'd lost Brayden at the airport, yet somehow he'd found them. Sam was going to find out exactly how he'd done it when he got back from his meeting. *What kind of tricks did the kid have up his sleeve?*

He was also going to kick Ax's ass. Sam was sure he hadn't expected Sergiy to hear him teasing Sam about Brayden. Ax had a sense of humor as dark as his hair. The dude lived up to his call sign. Ax was loco. But this time he'd taken it too far.

When Brayden had come bumbling into Sergiy's band of goons, Ax had leaned in and said "Fuck. Looks like your boyfriend followed us." Sergiy had sure picked up on that one word, 'boyfriend'. It was no secret that Sergiy and a few of Kozak's other lackeys were homophobes, but Sam hadn't given it much thought until now.

Kozak and Andreiko knew he was gay, otherwise they would have offered him women at each visit. He couldn't risk bribing one of Kozak and Andreiko's women to keep his lack of erection a secret, so he'd elected to tell the truth about his sexuality.

They seemed not to care as long as his money arrived on time. Sam wasn't sure that was true of Sergiy. Now it was up to him to make sure things didn't get FUBAR—fucked up beyond all recognition.

Sam had been whispering in Brayden's ear, because one never knew who was listening in a hotel lobby. He pulled back a little to look Brayden in the eye. Big mistake. Sam was immediately drawn in as he noticed tiny gold flecks highlighting the blue of his irises.

Brayden licked his lips. And of course that had Sam's gaze moving to his mouth. His grip tightened a little on Brayden's arm as he pictured those lips stretched around his cock. Sam struggled not to jerk Brayden forward and taste his tongue as it flicked out.

"Listen to me and listen good. Stay here. Go up to my room." Sam passed Brayden his key.

When Brayden took it, Sam reached up and grabbed his other bicep so Brayden couldn't look anywhere but at him. The kid smelled good, almost sweet, like fresh-baked cookies or something. He couldn't exactly put his finger on it, but he found himself taking deeper breaths to inhale the scent.

When he looked over Brayden's shoulder, Sam saw Sergiy muttering to himself. Ax leaned forward and said something to Sergiy that had him straightening his shoulders and shutting his mouth.

Sam leaned in and whispered in Brayden's ear, soft enough that he knew no one would hear. Brayden's surprised little intake of breath had the hairs on the back of Sam's neck standing on end.

"There's an extra gun taped under the desk in the office of my suite. I assume you know how it works. Keep it in your hand while I'm gone and don't open the door to anyone but me. My room has a private elevator, so I'm not sure how you planned to get there, but we'll discuss that when I get back. We'll discuss a lot of things when I get back."

Sam straightened from the man and his intoxicating smell. Brayden looked Sam in the eye for a long time before finally nodding slowly. Sam hadn't known he was holding his breath until it came out in a quiet, relieved whoosh.

He wasn't sure why he cared so much. The only thing he could come up with was that this kid was Mase's little brother. Even though Mase's family had turned their backs on him, he wouldn't want any harm to come to his sibling. Sam would make sure nothing happened to Brayden…for Mase.

"I don't know what you thought you were walking into, but you just became my arm candy. Hope that doesn't bother you," Sam said. "Don't say your brother's name in the hotel room."

Sam leaned in and pressed a small kiss to Brayden's mouth. His lips were soft as velvet. When he gasped, Sam was so tempted to take just a little taste. He came to his senses at the last minute and pulled back. Brayden's eyes were wide with shock as Sam turned and walked past.

Ax kept shooting Sam glances as they walked to the valet. Sam shook his head. Ax might have taken it as 'don't talk now' or 'no, I don't forgive you.' Sam didn't care. It was a little bit of both.

As they reached the door of the hotel, Sam looked back. Brayden was still standing there, facing away from them, his hand over his mouth. If he was straight, the kid was probably mortified—maybe even disgusted. If he was gay or bi… Sam didn't even want to finish that thought.

As soon as they were closed in their own car, Ax opened his mouth, but Sam shook his head again.

"I checked the car. It's secure," Ax said. "They only bugged the suite. I don't think they had any way of knowing what car rental agency we'd use."

Sam kept his gaze out of the window.

"Look, Sam. I'm sorry, okay? I didn't mean for Sergiy to hear."

"You should have kept your mouth shut. Now we've got an innocent civilian involved."

"Not exactly a civilian. Either way, I'm sorry. I fucked up, okay? If there's anyone who wouldn't want to pull an innocent into an op, it's me."

Sam was still pissed, but he knew that was true. Ax had his own cross to bear when it came to innocent family members stumbling into a shitstorm.

"It doesn't matter how we got here. The kid ultimately got himself into this, but we're going to make sure he gets out. He's Mase's baby brother. He gets out of this without a scratch on him if we can pull it off."

"Copy that." Ax nodded as he followed Sergiy and his men into a more industrial area of Kiev. "You want me to drop you off and circle back to the hotel?"

"It doesn't matter what I want. I need you to stay with me. We can't blow this. It's been almost two years of work to get here. The kid will just have to learn to be patient. We'll get him on the first secure flight out of here."

"He'll just hop off in Munich or Paris or wherever and turn right back around."

"Not after I find out how he traced us. I'll put a stop to it."

Ax only responded with a shake of his head.

"I'll get the message to Mase somehow. The kid will just have to believe that I did it and head home. He just wants to make sure Mase gets the message."

"And if the message has Mase tearing out of here to be with his family?"

Sam puffed out a breath. What would he do if his family wanted to see him after all this time? If his family had been trying to contact him for years like Brayden had said he'd been trying to do with Mase?

It didn't really matter what Sam would do. It mattered what Mase would do, and Sam was worried he would want to tear out of here just like Ax said. But Mase wouldn't do that. No matter what he'd been accused of in the army, Mase didn't disobey orders. If his little brother was dying, Sam and Jazz would have to find an excuse for him to disappear for a while.

"I'm taking the battery and SIM card out of my phone," Sam said as he did just that. "I'm thinking that might be how the kid tracking me."

Ax was using a burner just for the current mission. There was no way he was being tracked by anyone outside the team, so he just nodded as he continued to drive.

"What did you say to Sergiy that had him clamping his big trap shut?" Sam asked as he pocketed the phone battery.

Ax chuckled and shook his head.

"He was muttering something about *pidaras*, so I told him the people who protest the loudest are usually the ones who feel the same inside. Shut him up pretty quick. Dude totally has latent tendencies."

Sam wasn't sure about that, but Sergiy sure was a homophobe. It was pretty common in Ukraine, from what Sam had seen. Yet another reason a guy like Brayden, who was almost pretty with his pink, heart-shaped lips, needed to head home as soon as possible.

Chapter Five

Brayden

After memorizing the license plate of Sam's car, Bray walked back through the lobby. His lips still tingled. He'd stood there in a daze for a moment after Sam had walked away, but belatedly remembered he needed a method to track him.

Bray pulled his phone out of his pocket. He already had Max's number pulled up before he even got to the room. His first order of business was the gun.

It took Bray a minute to find the office. He quickly crawled under the desk and found a Glock 22 taped under the drawer. Sitting at the desk, he tested the weight of the weapon in his hand.

He pulled out the magazine to check the rounds. He opened the chamber to verify that it was empty then slid the magazine back home and set it on the desk before dialing Max.

"Are you lost?"

"No. Stop teasing me. I found Sam, but he's sure not happy I did."

"Big surprise."

Bray rolled his eyes. He sat back in the chair and sighed.

"Apparently I'm just... I think 'arm candy' was the term Sam used."

Max mumbled something Bray couldn't make out, probably a snide comment. His friend had become much more cynical since he'd begun working with the government.

"Can you find out where he went?" Bray asked.

"Do you know who he's meeting with?"

"No. I don't get to know any details. Arm candy, remember? I don't really care who he went to meet with unless..." Bray didn't finish, because Sam had told him not to say Mase's name.

"I know. Unless it's Mase."

"Exactly. If that's what's going on, I have to know."

Max was quiet for a long time.

"Please," Bray said.

"Bray"—Max paused to sigh—"why are you risking your own ass for someone who turned his back on you?"

"I love him," Bray said with a shrug.

"You are too sweet and forgiving for your own good, for anyone's." After another long pause, Max finally relented. "Let me see what I can do."

"Thanks, Sin. I'll text you his license plate. Not sure if his car has anything you can track, but it's probably a rental car."

"Send me what you've got."

Max hung up before Bray could respond. When this was over, Bray needed to spend some more time with his friend. He had a feeling Max was getting too isolated. He was losing a little bit of himself.

Bray knew how that felt. It was hard when someone only saw the bad side of humanity. Bray had been trying to decide if he wanted to re-up for another few years of active duty or move to the reserves. The problem was that he didn't know what else he wanted to do.

His bachelor's was in microbiology, as he'd done a pre-med track. He'd thought about becoming a nurse practitioner or a doctor, but after seeing blood in action, he really didn't want anything to do with it. He might be a coward, but he didn't want to be responsible for keeping someone alive. He'd done that using a gun. He didn't want to bear the same weight with a scalpel.

If he ever had to walk into a waiting room and tell someone that their loved one had died, Bray would die inside a little as well. Just like he had when he'd had to tell the parents of one of his friends that their child had died. It was nice to want to be a hero, but being one came at a very high price.

Bray considered calling Nick, but he didn't want to have to tell his brother he hadn't made any progress. He chuckled as he realized a theme. Bray didn't like delivering bad news. Then again, most people seemed to avoid it.

As he waited for Max to get back to him, Bray looked around the suite. He wasn't snooping as much as he was getting the lay of the land. The room was at least a few thousand square feet. It had a fucking kitchen with a formal dining room and the bathroom had black wallpaper.

It was worlds away from the shit-hole Sam had been in when Bray had found him in Miami. Bray had been worried Mase was destitute, but this had to be some sort of op. It was either that or Mase really had done what he was accused of and now he'd gone into business with the people who'd paid him to betray his whole team.

Bray shook his head. Mase wouldn't do that. Someone who walked away from their family rather than pretending to be what they weren't was someone who had integrity. His brother had said he was innocent and Bray believed him.

The tragedy was that they hadn't known he was being court-martialed until after it was over. It might have benefitted Mase to have his family sitting behind him in that courtroom, even if he would no longer let his family stand up for him in his daily life.

Bray had joined the army with the hope that it would bring Mase back into his life. That hadn't happened when they were both in the military and it sure as hell hadn't happened once Mase had been kicked out.

In truth, their time in the army had only overlapped by about a year. Before that, Bray had been going to school on an ROTC scholarship. After that—while Bray had been trying to contact Mase through military channels—Mase had been investigated, charged and sentenced.

Bray was staring out of the window when his phone rang. Expecting it to be Max, he answered. He was surprised it was his mother's voice that replied to his mindless "Hello." Then again, they tended to talk most mornings and he'd missed her call earlier. She was probably heading to bed.

"Hey, Mom."

"Hey, Bray, how's your mission going?"

"Not well."

Bray snorted at just how *not* well it was going.

"Did you find him?"

"Not yet, but I'm close."

"I don't like this. I don't like any of this."

Bray didn't have to respond. She knew he agreed.

"You better not be putting yourself in danger," she warned.

"I'm a grown man."

He wouldn't outright lie to his mom. He'd probably tell her all about his luggage and would-be mugging once he got home safe. Telling her now and worrying her would serve no purpose.

"The only reason I agreed to this was because I'd hoped you might finally be able to bring Mase back, so that he might finally hear us out and maybe even forgive us."

"I don't think it's going to be that easy if I can't even get him to talk to me."

"No one expects miracles."

Bray snorted again. His father sure as hell expected miracles.

"All right," she conceded. "Your father wants a miracle. It doesn't mean he deserves it or that he'll get it. He hopes, but won't be disappointed in you. He'll only be disappointed in himself."

"Thanks for the pep talk, Mom."

"When did my sweet boy become so sarcastic?"

"Sorry. I'm just… I want everything wrapped up in a pretty red bow. I want the happy ending."

"We all do. And if it is possible, I hope it happens sooner rather than later—for your father's sake."

"You're a saint," Bray said.

"No. I just believe in forgiveness."

"Love you, Mom. I'll let you know when I'm on my way home."

"Love you, Bray."

What would he do? What would he do if Mase still had no interest in being in his life? At least he and Nick had made amends. He had one brother, even if it still felt like something was missing.

Chapter Six

Sam

"How do you want this to go down?" Ax asked.

They pulled up to a fence topped with razor wire. This was only the second time Sam had been inside the compound, though he'd met with Kozak many times.

The driver of the car in front of them rolled down his window and entered a code into a keypad. As the gate slid open, Ax looked back at Sam in the rearview mirror.

"Nothing changes. We move forward as planned, with one small caveat. If either one of us gets Mase alone, we have to find a way to get the message to him about Nick. Brayden called him Nickel, so that's the best route. Brayden said, '*Nickel needs to see Mase and that it might be life or death.*'"

Ax gave a nod as he moved the car forward through the gate. They drove past a series of squat, square brick buildings.

"You think his kid brother needs a kidney or something?" Ax asked.

Sam shook his head at Ax's dark humor. The irony of that statement wasn't lost on him. As his cover, Mase was currently assisting with human trafficking, specifically the organ kind.

Ax pulled to a stop next to Sergiy's car. Sam took a deep, cleansing breath. He was dressed in a custom business suit, but he was still going into battle. When Ax opened Sam's door, his dark eyebrows were down in an intimidating scowl above his light-gray eyes, but he gave a quick wink as Sam stood from the car.

Sam would have rolled his eyes if it wouldn't have broken character. This was where Ax thrived. After shutting the car door, Ax was at his side, his arms loose, eyes assessing.

Ax wasn't quite as tall as Sam's six foot two inches, and Sam had a lot more upper-body strength. But Ax was a fighter—a good one—and Sam was glad the man had his back.

"This way," Sergiy said and walked into one of the buildings.

As they moved forward, Ax gave Sam a little shoulder bump. Sam's lips twitched. If Ax could have spoken freely, he would have said something like, 'What a douche.'

In Ukrainian, Sergiy told one of his men to take Sam to the conference room. Sam lifted his eyebrows as if waiting for direction. There had been no need so far to let them know he spoke Russian and Ukrainian.

With a flick of his wrist, Sergiy pointed to one of his men. "Follow him," he said before disappearing down a different hallway.

"Hands on the wall. No weapons in meeting," the man said when they entered an empty conference room.

Sam motioned toward Ax. "He'll stand so you'll see if he's reaching for his gun."

The man patted Sam down before telling him to sit. Ax went to the corner of the room that would give him the best vantage point, the one directly behind the seat Sam chose, and leaned back against the wall as if he didn't have a care in the world.

After a few minutes, the door opened. Ruslan Andreiko walked in with two men. Some tension left Sam's body when he saw that one of the men was Mase. He didn't let his eyes linger on Mase any longer than they had on the other guy behind Andreiko.

In the hallway, Sam heard raised voices. Sergiy was yelling in Ukrainian, "That's it? This is bullshit…" That was all Sam heard as Andreiko closed the door. A moment later, Oleksiy Kozak opened the door and slipped in.

"I hear your guard won't give up his weapon," Andreiko said as he relaxed back in his chair.

"I made the concession that he'll stand. You'll see if he's reaching for anything."

Andreiko's gaze flicked over Sam's shoulder. Ax was probably giving a smile or a wink or even both, but Sam just sat there, waiting. Andreiko asked Kozak if this was how he normally ran his meetings. Kozak shrugged.

In a low voice, Mase kept his eyes on Sam as he spoke to his bosses in Ukrainian. He told them Sam wouldn't be where he was today if he didn't understand at least part of what was being said. Both men turned to Sam, who didn't react at all.

Kozak and Andreiko looked at each other. They were powerful in Ukraine, which was probably where their overconfidence came from. On the world scene, they weren't even a blip. The people they reported to, though—that was who Sam was after. The trail that would lead back to the U.S.

The men were smart enough to shut up. Sam could have been pissed at Mase for giving up his advantage, but he wasn't. Mase was proving to his bosses that he had great instincts, that he had their backs, that he was cautious.

"Seems you have some interest in my side of this partnership, Mr. Wheeler," Andreiko said.

"The man I work for has friends with connections. He's looking to expand into other markets. If you can supply us and help us move our supply, this could help your business grow as well."

"We are already building contacts in America," Andreiko said.

"North America—and only the East Coast, at that. New York, New Jersey, Georgia and Florida combined aren't as bountiful as California. We also have a stronghold in Texas. I have contacts in both, as well as all the way up the West Coast and some of the Midwest. Business is booming in Ohio. I can guarantee I have better contacts in South America, Europe and Asia, not to mention Africa and Australia."

The two men looked at each other. Sam knew they didn't have any presence in Asia and they were looking to expand in the market that had little-to-no human rights laws.

"We have contacts in Europe, but we might be interested in expanding to Asia," Kozak said.

"You have contacts in Ukraine and France. I'm talking about all of Europe."

Andreiko snorted.

"I'm not biting hand that feeds me," Andreiko said. "Europe is expanding already with Clement. If you think crossing him is easy, you and Mr. Bernard will end up learning a hard lesson."

"I think we can agree to leave Europe out of it. We're in discussions with a couple Germans who can help us distribute through Europe."

Andreiko's nostrils flared. It was a bluff, but Andreiko had no way of knowing it. Mase had told Sam that the man was always complaining that the Germans had all of Western Europe and were now creeping into Eastern Europe. Mase ran his tongue over his top teeth. If Sam hadn't known the guy for almost seventeen years, he'd think Mase was pissed. But Sam had known him that long and knew that Mase was trying to keep from smiling.

Sam wondered if Brayden had any similar little tics.

That errant thought made Sam focus even harder on the task at hand. Distractions would cause mistakes, and mistakes would crumble the house of cards they'd built.

"Let me talk to Clement and see what he says. I don't think cutting him out all together is wise."

"We'll leave France alone for now and even Italy, but we already have Greece," Sam said.

Jazz, going by the name Lucien Bernard, had already taken over the market in Greece. They were trying to flush Clement out, forcing him to make a mistake and show his hand.

Clement used his connections and aristocratic heritage to insulate himself. And Sam wasn't green enough to believe that a few Ukrainian mafia bosses admitting to working with him would do any good.

They needed proof that Clement was a part of this underworld, just like they needed the names of the US citizens who connected this puzzle to the United States.

"Greece?" Kozak asked.

Sam nodded. Greece was a big market for drugs, which was Kozak's side of the business. Mase had also told Sam that Andreiko and Kozak had been arguing over how to handle Greece. Kozak wanted to unload drugs there, but Andreiko wanted to tap into the refugees who had been flooding to Greece. They'd be low-hanging fruit for the scams that traffickers used to rope people in.

"Monsieur Bernard has strong contacts there and has moved in. He's already got distribution networks working overtime. We need to get more supply into the country. He's also looking to move some human capital out of Greece. We're interested in partnering to use your distribution network."

"We're not DHL," Andreiko said.

"Maybe not, but working with us would be a lot more lucrative for you than competing with us. Besides, we can't supply the needs of the whole world simply from Greece."

"We already have an operation ready to go into Greece," Kozak said.

"And you think we're just going to back off and let you move in, especially when you have all these restrictions that will allow Clement to keep his foothold in France and possibly the East Coast?"

The light seemed to go on in Andreiko's eyes as he understood the bargaining chip. They'd have to decide if they wanted to keep Clement happy or if they wanted a boatload more money to expand their own business.

"It's an interesting offer, Wheeler. We'll have to discuss it."

And he'd have to talk to the people he was working for, the people whose names Sam and his team were desperate to uncover. Sam nodded and stood from the table.

"Please give us a few days to discuss your offer," Kozak said as he stood. "Is the hotel room to your liking?"

"It is. I can stay for a few days, but I have a meeting in Thailand in six days."

"It shouldn't take that long," Andreiko said as he too stood.

"Mason, can you show Mr. Wheeler to his car?"

The muscles in Sam's shoulders relax but he didn't change his stance. He counted to two before looking at Mase so they wouldn't think he knew who Mase was. Mase hesitated with a look of confusion for just a second. When Andreiko lifted an eyebrow, Mase agreed and waited for Sam just outside the door.

"This way," Mase said as he pointed in the direction they'd come from before the meeting.

"Isn't this usually Sergiy's job?"

Mase shrugged.

"Hope this isn't a demotion for you,"

"I'll get along."

"Your accent, it's American."

"So is yours," Mase shot back.

"Yes, but I'm just visiting. I don't live here."

"Does this conversation have a point?"

Another of Andreiko and Kozak's men walked past them going the other way.

"Not really. Just small talk. I mean, if I had a nickel for every ex-pat I've met in Ukraine, I'd only have a nickel."

Mase's forehead wrinkled in confusion.

"Isn't the saying, 'if I had a dime'?"

"No. I have a nickel, just one nickel, like I said. Then again, I wouldn't bet my life on it. I might end up with a dead nickel."

Sam watched Mase take a breath, but there was no other outward sign that he might be distressed. He scraped his top teeth over his bottom lip. It was a tell, but one that made it appear he was thinking. The anxiety didn't reach his eyes, but Sam knew the wheels were turning.

"A dead nickel? And you called me the ex-pat? At least I remember American clichés," Mase said with a shake of his head.

"I've never really liked clichés," Sam said with a shrug.

He had a feeling he'd be getting a call from Mase within the next four hours—as soon as his friend could get away and get a secure line. Sam would have to figure out a way to talk, even if he was in the bugged hotel room. He couldn't leave Mase hanging.

Chapter Seven

Brayden

Bray picked up his phone after the first ring. He'd been pacing back and forth in the office of the hotel room and had just looked at the screen for the fiftieth time when it rang.

"Please tell me you have good news," Bray said once he had the phone to his hear.

"I have decent news. I'm not a miracle worker. I was able to get in and watch where the car went via traffic cams. I have an idea where they went, but I'm not positive, and I don't think you'll be able to get in if I'm right about their destination."

"I have to try."

Bray jotted his phone number down on a piece of hotel paper and left it on the desk for Sam. Then he picked up the gun and the hotel key. His hoodie had been a loss after the attempted mugging, but he'd found another one in Sam's suitcase. After sticking the gun in the back of his jeans, Bray put the hoodie on and zipped it up. It was so big that it made him feel like a toddler playing in his older brother's clothes.

It smelled like Sam. Bray lifted the wrist cuff to his nose and inhaled. He pocketed the room key as he headed to the private elevator.

"You going to send me directions?" Bray asked as he pushed the button for the lobby.

"Already done. Do me a favor and be careful. I can track you, but I can't really get you help unless I call the actual military."

"I don't think I'll need the cavalry. I'm not going to try to bust in. I'm just going to scope the place out and see if he's there."

"All right. Just be careful."

Bray hung up without responding. He'd already told him he'd be careful. There wasn't much more he could say to ease his friend's conscience, because he wasn't going to turn around now.

Before the elevator reached the lobby, Bray took his wallet out from the money belt under his shirt. He slipped it into his front pocket as he headed for the valet stand.

He was looking at the directions on his phone when the valet pulled up with his car. He got in and was confused when the passenger door opened. The confusion dissipated when he felt the barrel of a gun press into his ribs.

"Hand over the phone."

Bray looked at the guy in his passenger seat. He was in a suit, which meant he probably belonged with the people Sam had gone to meet. Bray leaned against the seat and took comfort in the feel of the hard metal of the gun pressing into his back. When he didn't hand over the phone, the guy took it from him. Two other men got into the back seat.

His odds had just gotten worse, but they didn't pat him down, so he still had his gun. There was a little bit of an advantage to being considered eye candy.

"How did you get this?" the man in the front seat demanded.

Bray didn't answer.

"Go to the address on the phone."

The man rammed his gun harder into Bray's side and started talking in low tones with the men in the back seat. They were speaking what he assumed was Ukrainian, but he had no idea. Bray could speak Spanish, a little French and even some Italian, but no Ukrainian.

Following the directions on his phone, Bray drove onto the street. He turned when his phone said to as he listened to the men argue. One of the guys in the back pulled out his phone and made a call. The only word Bray even understood was Sam's name.

He hoped Sam was still at the meeting. He would be pissed, but Bray was ninety percent sure he wouldn't want Bray dead. He was just as sure the men in the car with him were looking for a reason to kill him.

Trying to keep a cool head, Bray started to come up with a plan. If it had only been the guy in the front seat, he would have been able to handle himself. It was the three-to-one ratio that made him nervous.

He needed to figure out if he should try to get his weapon as he got out of the car or if he should try to wait until it was a one-on-one situation. If he didn't draw the gun as soon as he had the chance, they might frisk him and take it away.

When the instructions announced his arrival, Front Seat Guy told Bray to pull into a driveway that was blocked by a chain-link fence. One of the guys got out of the back seat and entered a code into the keypad. The gate slid open and Bray drove through.

Front Seat Guy had him stop at the second building in the compound and told him to get out of the car. There were now only two of them. Bray didn't know exactly where the third guy was, but he couldn't see him in any of the car mirrors.

"Get out," Front Seat Guy demanded again.

Bray opened the door and slowly scooted to the edge of the seat. He reached back under his shirt with his left hand so the men in the car wouldn't see. It wasn't as smooth as it would have been if he'd been able to use his right hand, but he had the gun and he knew it was loaded. He could change hands when he took aim.

Twirling around, Bray ducked behind the open car door. Front Seat Guy told him to stand with his hands up. Bray made sure no one was behind him as he crawled around the front of the car. He didn't want to take fire, but the building wasn't close enough to dive for. Hoping the men in the car were still aiming their guns at the driver's-side door, Bray ran for the building.

Bullets pierced the bricks near his shoulder as he ran around the corner. He heard the men talking in Ukrainian as he edged his way along the wall. The buildings were all one-story cinder block boxes, so Bray silently climbed on top of a garbage can and scaled onto the roof.

Crouching low, Bray moved around the perimeter of the roof. Trapping himself with no way to run wasn't the best option, but he didn't know the layout, so he'd taken the high ground. He also had no idea how many men were in the buildings. He only had seventeen rounds in the Glock he'd taken from Sam's desk.

Scooting back, Bray moved to the farthest corner from where he'd jumped onto the roof. That would likely be where they came up, since that was the last place they'd spotted him. He had the low wall of the roof at his back and he kept his gun aimed forward. Eventually they'd start searching the roofs. He wasn't sure what he'd do then.

Boots crunched on the gravel below as shouts rang out. Bray kept his eyes front and tried to focus. Dog barks pierced the air as men continued to speak to each other in a language he couldn't decipher. He was trapped.

Bray desperately looked around the roof as he tried to form a plan. There were more than seventeen men on the ground. If he did go out with a fight, he'd have to try to get a new gun.

He was a sitting duck, but he'd gone with his instincts. He hadn't wanted them to take his gun. The men below would have the advantage of using the wall to shield them as they climbed up. Bray would need something more to protect himself.

The only thing on the roof not attached was an old grate of some sort. There was also a metal satellite dish, but he'd have to pull that loose, and it wouldn't be a quiet endeavor.

He'd just wrapped his hand around the grate when he heard it. He was speaking Ukrainian, but Bray recognized Mase's voice. His brother had yelled at him enough as a kid that he'd know the sound in any language. Mase was his only chance.

Bray turned his head slightly and tried to assess where his brother was. There were so many voices.

"What the fuck is going on?" Mase grumbled in English.

He sounded just below the ledge. Bray turned around and slowly moved forward enough to see down. It was Mase. That was the last thought he had before he heard a thump. He felt the roof reverberate and his head exploded in pain.

Everything went black for a moment as his shoulder hit the ground. Someone was yelling at him. Feet were kicking at his ribs. Bray's training kicked in and he curled up in defense and aimed the soles of his feet at his attacker.

Bray was able to reach for his gun and blindly fired off one shot, then another. He didn't want to hit Mase, but he didn't imagine Mase was the one currently kicking the shit out of him.

Somewhere in the distance, he heard Mase's voice again. He knew his brother would save him, so he let his body give out.

Chapter Eight

Sam

Andreiko and Kozak's reaction had been exactly as Sam had expected. He'd been able to chat with Mase, but that had been pure luck.

They were quiet as Ax drove them toward their hotel. Sam felt anticipation tingling along his skin. He shook it off. The last thing he needed was to look forward to sparring with Brayden Hart.

He'd delivered the message, so it was time to send the kid home. He'd never have to see him again. He should be celebrating.

"Seemed like Mase got the message," Ax said.

Sam nodded.

"You think Andreiko and Kozak will give him some PTO?"

"Ax, shut the fuck up."

"Seriously, though. If his brother needs him..."

Ax didn't finish the sentence, but Sam knew that if Ax's little brother needed him, the man would move heaven and earth to help him. Mase had that same integrity in him, but he hadn't spoken to his family. At least, he hadn't been in the all the time Sam had known him. Before that, Sam figured Mase had been extremely close to his family.

"We'll figure something out. I'm sure he can get thrown in jail or deported or even extradited for a 'crime' committed in the US. The possibilities are endless. We'll see what Jazz has to say if Mase asks for some time."

"I'd want a little more than 'some time' if Diego was dying."

"Brayden said possibly life or death. We can sure as hell hope that Nick will pull through whatever is going down."

Ax nodded, but his grim face said he was still putting his brother in Nick's place. As they neared the hotel, Sam put his SIM card and battery back in his phone. It was time to sit down and chat with Brayden.

* * * *

As soon as he stepped over the threshold of his hotel suite, Sam knew Brayden wasn't there. He rushed into the office anyway. When he found Brayden's note on the desk, he crushed it in his fist. Sam had pictured Brayden sitting by the front door ready to pounce on him. Brayden seemed like a smart kid, but leaving the hotel had been a very stupid mistake.

"He's not here," Sam said to Ax, who hadn't left the front door.

"Not too surprised. Kid's on a mission to find out who you're hanging with."

"We're heading back to Andreiko and Kozak. I don't know how the hell he found out where I was going, but he's going to tell me as soon as I beat his ass."

"Don't be too hard on him, boss. He's doing the wrong things for the right reasons."

Sam shook off that sentiment as they stepped back into the elevator. He opened his fist and looked at the little piece of hotel stationery.

"Aw, he made sure you could find him." Ax smiled.

Sam rolled his eyes as he pulled out his phone.

"I just hope we're not too late."

"Andreiko and Kozak won't kill him. They might use him as a bargaining chip now they know he's important to you, but they wouldn't kill him out of the gate."

"But how's Savage gonna react to seeing his baby brother 'questioned' by his associates?"

Sam used Mase's call sign just in case anyone overheard. Ax didn't need to answer. They both knew it might not end well. They might end up rescuing Mase for blowing his cover more than Brayden for being naïve. Sam dialed Brayden's number, but it went straight to voicemail.

"Let me use your burner. I'll try to track his phone so we know for sure where he is before we make any accusations."

Ax handed Sam his phone then strode back to the valet. Sam dialed through to get a secure line. When he heard the clicking, he entered his code. There was no guarantee that Jazz would be available, but this op was his current highest priority, so he needed to know what was at stake.

Sam was still waiting on the line when Ax jumped into the driver's seat. Sam slid into the back and Ax had the car moving as soon as Sam's door was shut.

Sam tapped on his leg. Slowly and purposefully, he straightened his shoulders and gently laid his hand on his knee. He was an operator of the highest caliber. He was an agent in a team that risked some lives every day, including his, in order to save others.

"You're like a virgin on prom night back there, boss."

Sam could only see the lower half of Ax's face in the rearview mirror, but he didn't even need the reflection to know Ax was smiling.

"If anything happens to Mase's brother and this whole deal goes south, we might all be without a job. Your wisecracks aren't helping."

"Mase won't blow his own cover."

Sam wasn't so sure.

"You sure you're tied in knots because he's Mase's little brother, or is it because you like him?"

Sam didn't even know the kid. Sure, he was tenacious, and Sam respected that. He was hot as fuck—but that shouldn't matter. What Sam kept coming back to was Brayden saying he'd been emailing Mase for two years.

When a hero was disgraced like Mase was, that was when people started walking away and forgetting they'd known you. It wasn't when people reached out and kept reaching out, hoping to open a dialogue. It wasn't like Brayden could have played a big role in what had happened to Mase as a teenager anyway. The kid had been, well, a kid when his brother had been kicked out.

"The line is secure. I'll connect your call," a voice said before more clicking and finally ringing.

"Don't tell me Andreiko and Kozak already folded. I wasn't expecting to hear from you—"

"No," Sam interrupted Jazz. "We have a little hiccup."

"You're trained to handle hiccups."

"Not like this. We could be heading straight to FUBAR. I told you Mase's kid brother came to visit me before I left. We followed him to the airport and he caught a flight to DC. Apparently that wasn't his final destination."

"He's there?"

"Yes, sir."

"How?"

"I was planning on finding out. I assumed it was my phone, so I disabled it. I told the kid to stay in the hotel, but I think he was still able to follow me."

"Think? You *think*? Where the fuck is the Fletch I knew in the army?"

Sam cringed at the name. He hadn't liked the nickname when he was in the military and he sure didn't like it now. It was worse than his call sign.

"The kid's a total surprise," Sam said.

"He shouldn't be. He's Mase's brother."

Sam snorted.

"Did you just leave the meeting? Where's Ax?"

"Ax is with me. I should have left him to guard the kid, but—"

"No. That would have seemed extreme to Andreiko and his men."

Sam's insides unknotted a little when Jazz agreed with his decision.

"So you don't know where he is?"

"No, but I do have his phone number,"

"The phone number he left you," Ax whispered.

Sam leaned forward, flicked Ax's ear and gave him a death glare. Ax smiled as he rubbed away the apparent sting.

"Give it to me. I'll track it."

Sam gave Jazz the phone number then waited impatiently for Jazz to confirm what he already knew.

"His phone is pinging at Andreiko and Kozak's compound," Jazz said.

"What if Mase's cover is blown?"

Sam's neck was tight with tension as he waited for his commanding officer to tell him to leave his best friend to the wolves. Sam closed his eyes. He'd never disobeyed a direct order, but he wouldn't leave Mase twisting in the wind.

"Get him out. Get Mase and his brother out by any means necessary."

Sam pulled the phone away from his ear to look at it. Not wanting Jazz to question his decision, Sam readily agreed.

"Yes, sir."

Ax pulled over. The guy had excellent hearing. Since they'd just been given the green light, Ax got out of the car while Sam finished up with Jazz.

"Report back within thirty minutes. I'll give you an hour before I start trying to get eyes on the situation."

"Yes, sir."

The trunk clicked open then banged shut as Sam looked at his watch. They were less than ten minutes from the compound. When Ax got back into the driver's seat, he handed Sam two guns, a few holsters and a knife. Sam had them concealed in seconds.

"We've got thirty minutes," Sam told Ax.

Ax pressed his foot on the gas and turned a corner on two wheels.

"Now you're in a hurry?"

"Now we have approval to do what we were gonna do anyway. This is gonna be fun."

Sam rolled his eyes.

Chapter Nine

Brayden

His head felt like it might fall off his shoulders. Bray groaned as he tried to lift his chin off his chest. Why was his chin on his chest? Had he fallen asleep? Even with his eyes closed, the room was spinning, so he didn't attempt to open them.

When he tried to lift his hands to his head, he realized they were tied to the chair he was sitting on. His ankles were tied too. Had he been captured? No. He was on leave.

Bray heard someone moving around in the room, so he tried to be still as he quietly assessed all the damage to his body. He had a splitting headache, his ribs hurt and the outer thigh of his left leg was sore as well.

He couldn't remember where he was. He was on leave trying to look for…Mase. He almost said the name out loud. He'd heard Mase's voice. Everything came barreling back to him like getting hit by a truck—

meeting Sam, following Sam, losing Sam, finding Sam and finally, finding Mase.

Was it Mase in the room with him? Bray couldn't be sure, so he remained still, keeping his eyes and his mouth shut. He just had to wait for Mase. That was what kept playing in his head until his chair jolted, shooting pain up from his knees to his hair.

"Wake up, faggot," someone said.

Bray opened his eyes and looked at the man, but his vision was a little blurry. There was no nausea, which was good. There was no real confusion either, once he'd realized where he was.

Bray recognized the guy. He'd been at the hotel earlier with Sam. He wasn't the one who had done all the talking—but he'd been there.

"Where's Sam?"

"You think your gay lover is going to come save you?"

"Where's your boss? Is he meeting with Sam?"

It probably wasn't the smartest move to remind the guy he was a peon, but Bray refused to take his bait. The guy narrowed his eyes.

"You think you're untouchable because you're gay-fucking that man? My bosses tolerate that faggot because his boss trusts him. If he didn't bring in so much business and money, they'd slit his throat. Or better, they'd cut off his dick."

Bray hoped that wasn't true.

"I bet he doesn't even realize you're missing" the man continued. "He's probably moved on to his next victim."

Bray swallowed past the knot of fear. He could be right. If he was too much trouble, Sam might just walk away. But Mase wouldn't. Mase would find a way to at least keep his brother alive. He may have gotten himself into this fix, but for all intents and purposes, Bray was an innocent bystander.

"I know Sam won't be happy." That was probably the truest thing he could say. "He may not have wanted me to follow him here, but he still wants me."

Bray attempted to smile but it hurt.

"You're disgusting."

"I could say the same to you. I'm not sure if you think what you're wearing is cologne, but the only thing you'll be attracting is dogs—and probably not even female dogs."

He stood and came at Bray, knocking his chair over. Bray felt hands close around his throat as the man's face blocked out everything else in the room. He opened his mouth to speak, but the door slammed open.

"Fedir," someone called.

Fedir backed off but only after a long hesitation. Bray turned toward the door and saw a large man blocking the entryway. He was imposing with his wide shoulders, dark hair and eyes. The man flicked his finger once at Fedir and Fedir jumped up and lifted Bray's chair from the floor so he was once again sitting.

The two men began conversing in Ukrainian. Fedir's tone voice was defensive as he most likely justified his actions. It was like listening to a child saying 'he started it'.

The man in the doorway jerked his head once, signaling for Fedir to leave the room. Fedir did just that, with no hesitation this time.

"It seems you're causing a lot of trouble for me today, Mr.…"

Bray didn't answer.

"Shall I just call you Sam's boy? You're quite young. I could call you Sam's little boy."

"What's your name?"

"I am Oleksiy Kozak. I've had business dealings with Sam for almost a year. Now, what shall I call you?"

"Bray. My name is Bray."

"I must apologize for Fedir. Unfortunately, there are many here who don't understand or do not wish to see the difference between a gay man and a pedophile. I've seen similar sentiments in South America, as I've spent much time there."

Even though he knew it was true that some people had those ideas, the thought was so offensive that it made Bray queasy. He hoped that didn't have anything to do with the mild concussion he was sure he had.

"I'm not a child. I'm twenty-six."

"You could pass for sixteen."

"Is what he said true? Would you slit Sam's throat if he wasn't worth so much money?"

"I am a businessman. I care about what he brings to the negotiation table. Our country is years behind America when comes to these things. People are getting rights in the law but no one wants to actually give it to them."

"That doesn't answer my question."

"Don't mistake my willingness to answer your questions. You have no power here. I feel guilt that you were beat by Sergiy, but you brought a gun."

"For protection. I wasn't going to breach your walls or your fence or whatever. If your men hadn't forced me onto your property, I would have just sat outside waiting for Sam."

"But then how would you verify he's not cheating on you?"

"I'm not a ninja. I can't leap over razor wire. And I'm not a hacker. I can't bypass your gate and security. I was just going to do what I could to make sure Sam was safe."

Oleksiy laughed.

"Even if you were these things, you would not breach our security."

"That's my point. It wasn't my goal. I just hoped… I don't even know what I hoped."

"Maybe you should find someone safer to love," Oleksie suggested.

"Who says I love Sam?"

"I believe you do. He thinks you follow because you don't trust him, but you are here to keep him safe. It's sweet."

Bray shook his head. He was attracted to Sam, sure, but there was no way he could be in love with the jerk. He'd only known him a little while, and…

Bray looked up to see Oleksiy laughing at him. Oleksiy only seemed mildly disgusted when talking about their big, gay relationship.

It didn't matter anyway, but Bray did need to stop denying being in love with Sam. It only benefitted Sam if Oleksiy thought Bray was head over heels. It would definitely explain his behavior.

"What happens now? Is this where you lull me into thinking we're friends, then you tell me to kill Sam in his sleep?"

"No. We are not friends and I won't ask you to kill Sam. He's been very useful."

"And still is useful if you want him alive."

"This is not a spy movie, Bray. Sam may be very important to you, but he is of little importance to me except for the connections he brings."

"And the money," Bray said.

"It's the same thing. In this business, connections are money."

There was a knock on the door before Oleksiy could say any more. He barked something in Ukrainian and the door opened. Fedir leaned into the room and said something that had Oleksiy rising from his chair.

"I'll be back in a few moments," Oleksiy said as he walked out of the room.

Fedir stepped in and closed the door. Bray sat up straight and raised an eyebrow at him. Fedir's lip curled in disgust but he didn't approach Bray. He leaned against the wall beside the doorframe.

It didn't seem smart to send the same guy back in to glare at Bray, but then maybe that was all part of the game. If they were playing good cop-bad cop, Bray could play along.

"Did you miss me?"

"I missed the chance to stomp all the air from your lungs," Fedir said through gritted teeth.

"That might have gotten you into trouble."

"If you think Mr. Kozak cares what happens to a little faggot like you, then you've lost your mind from the beating Sergiy gave you."

"It's better than losing my balls. This Kozak guy has you on a short leash. Are you guys secret lovers?"

Fedir straightened away from the wall, but the door opened before he could even take a step. Mase leaned in and said something to Fedir.

All the air puffed out of Bray's lungs. Mase looked so grown up. Bray had seen pictures of him in his uniform, but he'd had the military-issue haircut and clean-shaven face. His hair was longer now and he had a beard. His beard was a little longer and more unkempt than Sam's, but Bray thought it fit the character he seemed to be playing.

Mase's gaze flicked to Bray. He waited. Anticipation buzzed in his ears. He opened his mouth to say 'hello,' but Mase turned back to Fedir. There had been no spark of recognition. There had been no subtle sign that his brother knew who he was.

The disappointment had Bray balling his fists. His own brother didn't recognize him. Bray tried to pull air into his lungs. He'd hoped there would still be at least a fondness between them.

Bray barely noticed Fedir leaving the room. He looked down at his lap. He couldn't bring himself to watch his brother walk out of his life a second time. He didn't look up until the door clicked shut.

Chapter Ten

Sam

Sam was getting ready to dial Kozak's number when his phone rang. The number that popped up was from the States. He hesitated only a moment before answering.

"Hello?"

"Is this Sam?"

"Who the hell is this?"

"If you have to have a name, you can call me Sin. Is this Sam?"

There was annoyance in the kid's voice—as if Sam was the one holding him up rather than the other way around.

"Depends," Sam said. "What's this about?"

"It's about Bray. Shit. Did he give you his real name? I assume he did, considering who he's looking for."

Sin wasn't a name. It was a handle, but with the guy's bumbling, there was no way he was an operator. He had to be a tech guy, the ace up Brayden's sleeve.

"This is Sam."

"Bray's in trouble."

"No shit, Sherlock."

"I wasn't able to get a hold of him to tell him you'd already left that compound."

"That wouldn't have stopped him. He's not here for me," Sam said.

"Maybe not, but he's not a one-man army. There are at least forty-three men in that compound."

Sam was very interested to know how Sin had come to the figure of forty-three men. Sam would have guessed Kozak had thirty to forty men in the compound, but he had a feeling Sin *knew* there were exactly forty-three.

"We're already on our way back. I'd like to know how you got this number."

"Tell him to call me as soon as it's safe."

The line went dead. Sam pulled the phone from his ear and looked at it. After a moment, he programmed in the number Sin had called from. If he traced it, he had no doubt it would lead to a big dead-end, but he kept it anyway.

"Who was that?" Ax asked.

"A friend of Brayden Hart's."

"His guardian angel?"

Sam chuckled at the description, considering the caller's handle.

"Said his name was 'Sin', but he sounds about twelve, so who the fuck knows."

"Better make the call you need to make so they'll stop 'questioning' Bray and open the gate."

Sam didn't have Andreiko's number. Even if did, he would have called Kozak, because he already knew that Sam Wheeler didn't fuck around.

"Mr. Wheeler," Kozak said.

Sam had expected conceit or gloating in Kozak's voice, but it wasn't there. The man was all business. A bead of sweat trickled down Sam's neck, because he had no idea if that was a good sign or a bad sign.

"Where is he?"

"Your friend is here. There was apparently a miscommunication."

"Well, I'll be real clear then. We're pulling up to the compound. Open the gate."

"I'll send someone to meet you."

Sam was getting sick of people hanging up on him in the middle of a conversation. He threw his phone onto the seat beside him as Ax pulled up to the gate. Sam adjusted his suit to make sure his back-up weapon was covered, but he held the other in his hand. He wouldn't be submitting to a pat-down this time. Ax met Sam's eyes in the rearview mirror.

"Guess it's too much to hope for that Mase will be the one he sends," Ax said.

"I don't think our luck's gonna hold out for that," Sam tipped up his chin in the direction of the guy making his way toward them.

Their luck did hold a little, since the guy wasn't Sergiy.

"Sure would have been nice to know what we're walking into," Ax put the car in gear.

Ax pulled slowly through the gate. The guy tapped on the window. Ax unlocked the car and the guy slid into the back seat. Sam recognized him from earlier in the day. He'd been with Sergiy. Sam smiled and held up his gun as the man shut his door.

"You're one of Sergiy's lackeys."

"I'm Fedir. I'm no one's lackey. I work for Mr. Kozak."

Sam shrugged.

"You think your gun will do any good? Turn left here," Fedir told Ax.

"I'm pretty good with a gun."

"Then you might want to teach your little faggot to use one. He brought one here but didn't know how to use it. He got captured and only managed to get off a couple of shots. Pathetic."

"The real question is, did he hit anything?"

Fedir sneered but didn't comment. Brayden might not be trained for this scenario, but he was trained for combat. Sam tried to pop the bubble of pride that rose in his chest. Brayden hadn't gone down without a fight, even though he had probably been up against dozens of men.

"Maybe Brayden killed Fedir's boyfriend. He looks heartbroken," Ax said.

Fedir lunged forward, but Sam poked him in the ribs with his Sig. That had him leaning back really quick. Fedir may have calmed his temper, but when he looked at Sam, there was no less hatred in his eyes.

"I'm not heartbroken. I'm disgusted by faggots like you."

Sam smiled.

"I wonder if Kozak would care if my gun accidentally discharged?" Sam asked Ax.

"I bet they have cameras all over this place," Ax mused. "All I'd have to do would be to brake hard and it would look like I missed my turn."

Sam made sure his gun was cocked as he pressed the barrel to Fedir's temple. Fedir had to swallow twice before telling Ax to turn right. Sam kept his gun to

Fedir's head until they came to a stop next to the building Fedir had indicated.

"What I do in the privacy of my own bedroom doesn't affect how deadly I can be outside it. You'd be smart to remember that before you go around insulting people."

With a nod, Fedir opened the door, hopped out and hurried away. Sam wasn't sure he'd learned any real lesson, except that Sam was as dangerous as his bosses.

Sam un-cocked his Sig and slid it into the holster at the back of his waist. Ax got out and kept watch as Sam came around the back. Ax's hand remained at his back under his jacket. His hand was on the butt of his gun, Sam was sure. Sam's posture wasn't much different.

They stood by the car, watching each other's backs as they waited to see what was in store. A door banged open in front of them and Fedir appeared in the opening. He was a little out of breath as he stepped back outside, followed by Kozak.

Kozak looked back and forth between Sam and Ax. Fedir reached for the gun in his holster but Kozak stopped him. They went back and forth as Fedir quietly told his boss that Sam had held a gun to his head. Kozak snorted and told him to stop being a pansy, and that he might consider keeping his opinions about their clients to himself.

"Please come inside, Wheeler," Kozak said as he motioned Sam inside.

Neither Sam nor Ax moved. Kozak told Fedir to go inside. Fedir looked back and forth between all three of them before finally stomping away. Sam considered it a win that there had been no derogatory remarks as he'd done so.

Ax kept watch at the door as Sam made his way down the hall. Mase came around a corner, and Sam thought his friend would be a barometer so they might know what they were walking into. Sam relaxed a little until he saw Mase's face.

Mace wore a mask of indifference, but his blue gaze was shooting daggers, and they were aimed right at Sam. They'd known each other long enough to be able to read each other, and Mase was ready to take Sam down without the help of the Ukrainian mafia.

Sam's confusion must have been apparent, because Kozak looked back and forth between the two. Not knowing how to resolve any of this or what Mase's anger meant, Sam said the only thing he could think of that would excuse his long look at Mase.

"Where's Sergiy?"

Mase snorted but Kozak gave him a look that shut him up.

"Let's go in here to chat." Kozak opened a door.

Sam looked at Mase. The daggers were still in his glare and his nostrils flared in anger as he stared directly into Sam's eyes. Was Mase pissed at Sam because Brayden was there? Sam had done everything he could to keep the kid away.

"I'm not negotiating anything around Brayden. I want to see him now. There's a certain amount of trust that needs to exist between people who do business together."

"No negotiations. There was an incident we must discuss."

"What incident?"

Sam looked back at Mase as fear gripped his gut. Too late, Sam remembered he couldn't look at Mase too long, so he looked back and forth between Kozak and

Mase as if waiting to see who would crack first and tell him what had happened.

"Please, we will talk for just a moment before we take you to your friend."

Sam turned to Ax and motioned for him to join them. Kozak walked into the room, moved behind the desk and sat in the high-backed office chair. Mase stood against the wall behind him, his arms crossed over his chest, eyes narrowed.

Sam sat in the only other chair in the room. Ax settled behind him, his posture mirroring Mase's. Kozak leaned back in his chair and took a deep breath before he finally spoke.

"What you said before," Kozak said. "We do not give trust easily. You and I have been doing business for a year. In this business it takes longer than that to have any real trust."

"I trusted you when I walked into this compound. My bodyguard can only do so much to protect me. If all your men came at me at once, our chances of getting out of here would be slim-to-none. Yet you feel comfortable kidnapping my boyfriend."

When he said the last word, Sam looked up at Mase. The muscle in Mase's jaw ticked and his left eye looked like it was twitching. There was bad news on the horizon.

"Kidnapping is a strong word. We intercepted your…your friend while he was on his way here."

"Are you afraid he would have been able to breach your security?"

"No."

"Then why 'intercept' him? He's fairly harmless, just a little jealous."

"It wasn't jealousy that drove him here."

Sam's body went cold with fear, but he didn't lift his gaze to meet Mase's. That would have been too telling.

"Are you saying you know my boyfriend better than I do?"

"No. I'm saying I know what he said."

"What did he say?" Sam asked.

"He was coming here to make sure you were safe."

"What? He thinks he can protect me?"

Kozak chuckled. Sam belatedly realized that maybe Brayden had been talking about protecting his brother, not Sam. Either way, his surprised response worked in his favor.

"It appears you may not know your friend as well as you think you do, Mr. Wheeler."

"He knows I have Ax for protection."

"Maybe he knows about the trust you must put in the people you do business with. Maybe he's not as trusting with the man he loves."

"Loves?" Sam choked the word out.

He closed his eyes for a moment, because if he didn't, he wouldn't have been able to resist looking at Mase. Brayden must have really put on a show for Kozak.

"He said he was in love with you."

Sam shook his head to dispel the excitement that bubbled up at the thought of a sweet kid like Brayden Hart being in love with him. Then again, Sam knew that love wasn't all it was cracked up to be. When Sam didn't respond to the comment, Kozak changed the subject.

"The reason Sergiy isn't here is because of the misunderstanding,"

"What misunderstanding?"

"Ruslan and I told a few men to keep an eye on your friend. As I said, we don't trust easily. We wanted to make sure he was exactly who you said he was. Their directions were to follow, not to apprehend."

"What happens around here when men don't follow orders?" Sam asked.

Kozak looked at him for a long time before answering, "It depends on the order that wasn't followed."

"And this misunderstanding?"

"Your friend must have thought he was going to be harmed, because when they arrived here, he ran."

"And what did your men do?"

"It took a few moments to find him. Your man is resourceful. He made it up onto a rooftop with a gun, so my men went a little overboard."

Sam flicked his gaze up to Mase, who was running his finger along his lower lip.

"Not Mr. Mason," Kozak said quickly. "He's one of the only ones who kept a cool head. But Sergiy? Well, Sergiy always had a...I think you call it a short fuse? Anyway"—Kozak waved his hand—"Sergiy's fuse has worked for us in the past, but today he made the whole thing worse."

"Worse how, exactly?"

"He didn't realize what a delicate situation it was and got a little too physical while apprehending your friend."

Sam stood from his seat.

"He's fine. Nothing a few nights of good rest won't cure, but the same isn't true for Sergiy."

Mase mumbled something, but they all ignored it as they waited for Kozak to finish.

"Sergiy was shot twice, once in the foot and once in the thigh. We've advised him that his service is no longer needed. Next time, simply bring your friend. Even if he can't sit in on our conversation, at least we would know where he is."

"If story time is over, I'd appreciate it if someone told me where Brayden was. I need to see him for myself."

"Mr. Wheeler, Sam." Kozak stood and walked to Sam. "This truly was a miscommunication. I hope this won't affect our business dealings."

"I don't make promises I can't keep. And I'm sure as hell not promising anything until I see Brayden's injuries."

"Of course. This way."

Sam followed Kozak through a maze of hallways until he finally opened a door. At first, all Sam could see what the top of a blond head. Brayden had his arms folded on the table, his head resting on top of them.

He was angry as hell at Brayden for disobeying a direct order, and yet when Brayden's head popped up and their gazes met, Sam went weak in the knees with relief—the same relief he saw in Brayden's eyes.

Sam didn't like that it made him feel like a hero. He wasn't a hero. He also didn't like how his heart rate kicked up when relief turned to a look of adoration—even if it was good for their cover, even if it was probably just relief that the kid wasn't going to die there.

"Sam." Brayden sat up straight but winced as he did it.

Before he thought better of it, Sam took two strides and knelt next to Brayden's chair. Using gentle fingers, Sam lifted Brayden's shirt up to see a few bruises forming. He turned his head and shot a dark look at Kozak before quietly asking Brayden if he was all right. He answered with a nod but his eyes were downcast.

"I'm sorry, Sam," Brayden whispered. "You were right. I shouldn't have come."

Brayden looked over Sam's shoulder when he said the last part. Mase and Ax were standing outside the open door and Kozak stood just inside. Sam didn't know what had happened between Mase and his brother, but he knew it wasn't good.

Chapter Eleven

Brayden

When they'd untied his arms and legs, Bray hadn't been sure to be relieved or more frightened when they'd left him in the room alone. Had they wanted him to run so they could shoot him? He was sure he'd heard someone standing guard outside the door.

Then the door had opened again. When Bray had looked up to see Sam, he'd almost collapsed with relief. The concern on Sam's face had caused butterflies to flutter around his insides. He reminded himself that Sam was just playing a role, but Bray soaked up the attention.

When Sam had knelt beside him, whispered to him, touched him, Bray had wanted to throw his arms around the man, to fall at his feet. Sam could have just left him there to rot or be tortured or killed. He had no idea what Oleksiy Kozak and his men would have planned for him.

When he'd told Sam that he regretted coming, there had been curiosity in Kozak's eyes. Mase's gaze had been empty, lifeless except for a spark of anger, but Bray hadn't seen any brotherly love.

He wanted to scream. He wanted to rail at his brother. He wanted to punch him for not recognizing his own flesh and blood. Even if it had been years, they had the same eyes, their mother's eyes. Bray had their father's sharp, chiseled jawline. Mase had a masculine version of their mother's button nose. They were family. They were brothers.

"Let's get you out of here," Sam said.

He practically lifted Bray out of the chair by his arm. Bray winced at the pain in his ribs as he stood. When he looked up, he saw Sam send Kozak a sharp look. But Sam was gentle as a hummingbird when he lifted Bray's arm around his neck and wrapped his own arm around Bray's back for support.

As they walked down the hallway, they passed by a room with the door open. Several men were seated on couches and in chairs. They were joking and laughing about something. At one particular comment, Sam's body tensed. Someone said something about 'Wheeler's twink' but everything else had been in Ukrainian. Kozak reached past them and closed the door.

"Just men blowing off steam, Wheeler," Kozak said. "We've had good dealings. I hope that will continue. I think Ruslan will be open to working with you as well if we can get past this misunderstanding."

After a long moment, Sam gave one sharp nod.

"I'll speak with Bernard, but I won't hide this incident. As I said, trust is vital in this business."

Bray coughed so he wouldn't snort, then sucked in a breath as his body protested. Lying and being a hypocrite sometimes came with the territory, but Bray had never seen it so 'in your face'.

"Are you all right?" Sam whispered in his ear.

A shiver tickled its way down Bray's spine. He could only nod in response. Sam's bodyguard stayed behind them. It felt good to have someone at his back that Sam trusted, because Bray realized he already trusted Sam.

As they stepped out of the building, Sam slid his free hand under the jacket of his suit. Bray was even more relieved when he recognized the move. The bodyguard wasn't the only one armed.

Sam opened the back door of his car and helped Bray slide gently in. Bray was grateful Sam didn't ask him to scoot over but walked around the back of the car.

The bodyguard got into the driver's seat and started the engine. He opened his mouth to speak but Sam told him to wait. The guy rolled his eyes in the reflection of the rearview mirror.

Once the chain-link gate slid shut behind them, Sam seemed to relax as he slumped back against the seat. Relief overwhelmed Bray. Tears pricked his eyes as the reality of the situation hit him. His own brother hadn't had his back, but Sam, a total stranger, had.

"What the fuck were you thinking?" Sam burst out. "That was incredibly stupid. You could have gotten yourself killed. You could have gotten us all killed."

"I'm sorry," Bray said quietly without looking away from the window. "I had no intention of trying to get in. I just wanted to see if he was there. I got accosted as soon as I left the hotel."

He didn't want either of his companions to see how close he was to crying. No one responded to his apology. The tension in the car was suffocating.

"Fucking backward bigots," the man driving murmured.

"Ax," Sam scolded.

"Sorry. Not you, kid," Ax said.

Bray opened his mouth to say that he wasn't a kid, but he sure felt like one in that moment. He'd done something stupid and had almost paid too high a price for it.

"Those men," Bray said. "What were they saying?"

Both men were quiet for a moment, but their eyes met in the mirror.

"They were making fun of Sergiy," Sam finally said.

"What happened to Sergiy?"

"You shot him," Sam said.

"Oh. I didn't know who attacked me. He got me from behind. I also wasn't sure if I hit anything. I only got two shots off and they were blind."

"You're a lucky shot then." Sam shook his head. "You got him in the foot and in the thigh."

"They were making fun of him because he got shot?" Bray asked.

"No. Those assholes were making fun of him because he got taken down by a 'faggot'." Ax's voice deepened on that last word.

"You're gay?" Bray asked.

"I'm bi." Ax nodded.

The look he flicked over his shoulder at Bray seemed almost defiant before he turned toward the windshield and continued. "But these backward assholes think homosexuality is as bad as a pedophilia. Some people think the terms are basically interchangeable."

Bray nodded. He'd been to places like that while serving as well.

"How are your injuries?" Sam asked.

"Mostly just bruised ribs and a headache. He got a few good kicks in, but—"

The words dried up in Bray's throat as Sam slid his fingers through Bray's hair. In his head, he knew Sam was checking his scalp, but his body reacted as if it were a lover's caress.

"Lift your shirt," Sam commanded once he'd let go of Bray's head. "I want to check your ribs again."

Bray licked his dry lips before leaning back against the seat and lifting his T-shirt. Sam lowered his eyebrows when he took a closer look at Bray's abdomen. There were a few bruises forming. Sam gently prodded the tender skin and Bray sucked air in through his teeth at the jolt of pain.

"They're not broken," Bray said. "I've had broken ribs before. It's just the bruises. I was able to back away before he got too many kicks in."

"What you did was risky and foolish." Sam pulled his hands away.

"I had to see Mase. He didn't even recognize me."

"Oh, he recognized you," Sam said. "I think he blames me for your presence here. Maybe you played your role too well. You shouldn't have told Kozak you were in love with me."

"I didn't. He told me I was in love with you. I thought it was strange, but—"

"Fuck. The hotel room," Sam said.

"The hotel room," Ax confirmed.

"What did you say in the hotel room?"

"I called Sin and my mom called me."

Sam leaned back in his seat, closed his eyes and blew out a breath. Bray was once again on the man's bad side.

"Did you mention Mase's name?"

"No. I didn't say Mase's name."

"Not even to your mom?"

"I was careful. You told me not to, so I made sure I didn't. She asked me about my 'mission'. I told her it wasn't going well and not to expect miracles."

Sam nodded then asked, "Who's Sin?"

"A friend. One of my best friends and…he was helping me find you."

"So Sin's the ace in your pocket? He's how you trailed me to Kiev?"

Bray nodded but couldn't meet Sam's eyes. He hadn't realized the damage he could cause.

"So you spent that conversation asking for information on me? No wonder Kozak had men on you."

"I told him I didn't know who you were meeting with. I gave him your car information in case he could track you that way. He said he'd do what he could, but asked…"

"What?" Sam asked.

"He asked me why I was doing this, why I was searching for someone who… He asked why I was looking for my brother and I remember saying, '*I love him*'. If your room is bugged, then Kozak thought I was talking about you."

"So he thought he had inside info. I guess he did. I think we're in the clear, then. It appears Kozak has already listened to you in my room. If you'd said Mase's name, he wouldn't have been there today."

"He'd be dead," Ax said.

Bray shivered at the thought. He was hurt that his brother wanted nothing to do with him, but he still wanted Mase alive.

"At least you can follow some orders," Sam grumbled. "Call Sin."

"What? Why?"

"He called to tell me you were in trouble. We were already on our way to get you, but he seemed worried."

While Bray called Max, only to leave a message, Sam made a phone call too. He was speaking in French, but Bray understood most of what he was saying. It sounded like he was giving a report to his commanding officer. Ax pulled into the parking lot of a store and got out of the car.

"When we get back to the hotel," Sam said, "you have to be on all the time. You've put us in a precarious situation, so you're going to have to live with the consequences."

"Consequences?"

"Yes. You're now my 'boyfriend'. I assume you're straight, but—"

"Why would you assume I'm straight?"

"If you're not, Mase went through a whole hell of a lot of grief for nothing."

"I'm gay. So is Nick."

Sam looked down at the floor in front of him for a long time. "Does Mase know?"

Bray shook his head. "It's not exactly something you send in an email to your brother when you're trying to repair a broken relationship. He would never meet with me."

Sam sighed and looked up at Bray. As they sat for a moment, Sam seemed to come to a decision.

"We have to pretend to know each other pretty well. Mase's life is at stake, so we need to keep his name completely out of it."

"They called him 'Mason'. Is he using his own backstory?"

"He is, in a way. He's going by the name Drew Mason, whose background is that he was dishonorably discharged from the army, but for more serious crimes than the allegations Mase faced."

Bray nodded.

"So can you keep this up? Can you pretend to be in a relationship with me, all the while keeping your mouth shut to protect your brother? At least until I can get you safe passage back to the States?"

Bray wasn't sure what would happen if he didn't agree. He'd do pretty much anything to protect Mase, even if his brother didn't want him to. Pretending to belong to Sam wasn't a hardship. Bray wondered how far the pretending would go. His body lit up at the thought.

Chapter Twelve

Sam

Brayden nodded slowly. It wasn't like he had much of a choice. Sam's mind kept going back to the fact that Brayden was gay. He'd felt a strong pull toward the man from the moment he'd set eyes on him. But he'd been attracted to plenty of straight guys in his life.

He'd once thought himself in love with one. To be fair, Grayson hadn't been straight. He'd simply been so far back in the closet that he was probably in Narnia. Sam didn't like to think about that time in his life. If there was one thing he could scrub from his memory, it would be that year between the ages of sixteen and seventeen.

"Are you and Mase…?"

Sam had been so lost in his reverie that he'd almost forgotten what they were talking about. He looked at Brayden, expecting him to continue his thought. When he realized what Brayden was asking, he laughed.

"Mase is more a brother to me than my own brothers."

Sam could have bitten his tongue in two when Brayden's face fell. He would have done it too, if it would reel those words back into his mouth and prevent the look of shock and hurt in Brayden's eyes. Sam wouldn't have felt guilt, even a few days ago, but knowing Brayden had been trying to contact Mase changed his perspective on everything.

"I meant brothers-in-arms. It wasn't a dig at you. I've known Mase since boot camp."

"You and Mase were in boot camp together?"

Sam nodded as he thought back to those days. He'd finally found a purpose but had still been hiding who he was. He and Mase both had, which was probably why they'd bonded so easily. Brayden seemed so hungry for intel on his brother that Sam found himself wanting to give him some.

"I was coming in as an officer. I'd just graduated from college on an ROTC scholarship. Mase was fresh from high school, so we weren't even in the same barracks, but we bonded. We both applied for Ranger School as soon as we qualified. We helped each other through that too."

"So I guess he told you what my dad did?"

Sam nodded. He only knew a little, like Mase's parents had kicked him out and told him to stay away from his brothers.

"I know he had the same background as me. I don't know all the specifics. It didn't matter. We both lost our families because we were queer. We didn't get too much chance to talk about it anyway. 'Don't Ask Don't Tell' and all that bullshit was still around until we'd been serving for a while."

"Your parents asked you to leave?"

"My parents thought they were giving me a choice, just like your parents and Mase, but it's no choice. Pretend to be something you're not and die inside or leave. Parents are supposed to love their kids unconditionally. The only kinds of parents who gives their kids that choice are selfish, immature and unfit. They're worried their kid's sexuality is going to reflect poorly on them because they take credit for all their kid's accomplishments."

Ax opened the door and cut the conversation short. He threw a plastic bag into the passenger seat and started the car. Sam and Brayden both remained quiet as they made their way back to the hotel.

"You lovebirds work everything out?"

Sam gave Ax a glare. Ax lifted one hand from the steering wheel in surrender and probably apology, considering this predicament was partially his fault as well. The asshole still had a smirk on his face, though. Sam turned to find Brayden frowning as he gazed out of the window.

"So I guess we'll play this exactly like they think," Sam said. "You came here wanting to try to give me another person to watch my back. We'll go back and forth about it. I'll tell you that you can come to the next meeting since Kozak told me to bring you, but you can't be in on the actual conversation."

"Kozak said to bring me along?"

"He thinks we'll all be safer if we can have eyes on you, kid."

"You should probably stop calling me 'kid' if you're my boyfriend."

Sam had to gear himself up to use the kid's nickname out loud. It would feel too familiar, and Sam didn't get familiar. He didn't have boyfriends. He hadn't had anything even close to a relationship in years. He settled for the kid's full name instead.

"Brayden," Sam finally said.

"Only strangers call me Brayden."

Sam swallowed. "Bray."

"Should I call you 'master', since you call all the shots?"

There was a loud snort that came from the driver's seat.

"Sam is fine."

"Or Magnum," Ax suggested.

"Magnum?" Bray asked at the same time Sam said, "No."

"Absolutely not. That has ties to me."

"Just kidding, boss," Ax said.

"That's your call sign? Magnum?"

Sam shot Ax a look that said they'd be talking about this later, then nodded in answer to Bray's question. Ax already liked Bray if he was pulling him into inside jokes. Sam didn't like that the idea of Bray and Ax in cahoots had his stomach gnawing with…he didn't know what exactly.

"Like a three-fifty-seven?"

"No. As in P.I." Ax barely got the words out before he started to laugh.

"I get that too," Bray said with a serious nod.

"Get what?"

Bray shrugged like it was obvious as he said, "Well, you can probably pack a punch like a three-fifty-seven, but with the mustache I get the P.I. vibe, even though you have a beard."

Ax was very loudly trying not to laugh.

"You sound like a pig choking," Sam told him.

At that point, Ax stopped trying to hold it in and just guffawed. Sam had a powerful urge to smack him on the back of the head, but he kept his hands firmly in his lap.

Bray gave him a somewhat naïve smile, as if he were simply enjoying Ax's merriment. The corner of Sam's mouth kicked up a little when Bray started laughing at Ax's laughter.

"You sure do pack a punch," Ax said through his laughter.

"Shut the fuck up, Loco," Sam groused.

"Loco? Your call sign is 'crazy'?"

"Better than 'Magnum'." Ax said. "What's your handle, kid?"

Bray's eyes widened but he kept his mouth shut.

"Oooh, it's worse than Magnum?" Ax teased.

"Magnum is a cool handle," Bray said.

"And your call sign isn't," Ax guessed. "Hmm, are you out to your team? Is it 'Sugar Britches'?"

Ax chuckled at his own joke while Bray turned red from the tips of his ears to the neck of his shirt.

"Did I get it on the first guess?" Ax glanced at Bray.

"No," Bray grumbled.

Ax was obviously close—or at least in the same vein.

"What about 'Sugar', because you're so sweet?" Ax guessed.

"Right thought, wrong word," Bray said. "My handle is Sweet, as in Sweet Hart."

"Oh, man. That *is* worse than Magnum." Ax laughed.

Everything was all fun and games until they walked into the hotel room. Ax headed off to his room on one side of the suite while Sam led Bray to their room on the other side of the suite. *Their* room.

If Bray were any other guy—hell, if he were himself but not Mase's brother—Sam might be looking forward to spending a few nights in the same bed with him. But he was Mase's brother. And though the kid was fully responsible for getting himself tangled up in this mess, Sam was still responsible for his safety.

That meant that no matter how attracted he was to Bray, he would keep his hands to himself. With Kozak and Andreiko listening in, they at least had to pretend something was going on between them. Chances were that once they heard any type of kissing, Kozak and his men would fast forward—or they might listen to every damn second.

"Where's your luggage?" Sam asked when Bray only brought in a backpack.

"I…um… I kind of got mugged at the airport."

"Mugged?"

"Yeah, it's why I'm wearing your hoodie. Mine got cut up a little when I was fighting the guys off."

Sam sighed.

"Don't get all huffy. I'll give your hoodie back. I just needed it to cover the gun."

"Bray"—Sam didn't like how easily the name fell from his lips—"where did you even get a gun?"

"It's one of yours." Bray smirked, playing his role perfectly.

"And the muggers. Did they hurt you too?"

"No. They jumped me in the bathroom, but some other guys interrupted while I was trying to fight them off."

Bray took a coin from his pocket and began playing with it. He walked around the room before setting his backpack on the dresser.

"Well, it's not like you need clothes while we're in the hotel room, but tomorrow we'll have to go buy you something to wear. I'd prefer you don't look like a high school student if I take you to my next business meeting."

"I don't look like I belong in high school," Bray grumbled.

"College then," Sam conceded.

Bray shrugged as he unzipped his backpack.

"Don't act like I'm the bad guy here," Sam said. "You knew I wanted you to stay home. I knew this could be a risky trip. Legally speaking, homosexuality is recognized here, but socially speaking, it's a dangerous thing to be in Ukraine."

"I could have pretended to be your bodyguard too."

Sam smiled at the thought. "Bray, you're adorable, but you are *not* a bodyguard."

Bray turned at looked at Sam. After a moment, he lifted his mouth in a shy smile.

"I really didn't mean for all this to happen," Bray said. "I just wanted to see where you go. I wanted to make sure you were okay."

"And what about me?" Ax was standing in the open doorway. "Didn't you want to make sure *I* was okay?"

"Ax, do you know how to knock?"

"Door was open, boss. Anyway. I'm ordering some grub. What do you two want?"

Ax handed Sam the menu. The suite offered twenty-four-seven butler service, but that was just another person spying on them. He and Bray could probably pull this off with someone listening, but not if they were watching as well.

"I'm glad you're okay too, Ax." Bray smiled.

Sam crumpled the menu when his hand fisted at his side. Ax patted Sam's shoulder and chuckled as he headed out of the room.

"I'll be ordering mine in about five minutes. Let me know if you want anything."

Sam handed Bray the menu.

"What do you want, Sam?"

Sam swallowed back a groan. How could his name on someone's lips be such a fucking turn-on? He watched Bray as he went over the menu.

"You know what I like."

Bray looked up at him with worried eyes. The kid was probably scared he'd order something Sam wouldn't like, but Sam wasn't picky. He'd eat pretty much anything.

Bray quietly walked over and stood next to Sam as he looked at the menu. Sam could smell him again, but it was a strange mix of the sweet odor of Bray mixed with the scent of Sam's own laundry detergent from his hoodie. The mixing of their scents shouldn't have distracted him so thoroughly, yet it did. Visions of them mixing other things flooded his brain.

Holding the menu between them, Bray pointed to a rib-eye steak. Sam was definitely a meat and potatoes kind of guy, so he nodded his approval.

"I'll go tell Ax what we want."

When Bray left the room, Sam found himself taking deep, cleansing breaths as he tried to rid his nostrils of the intoxicating smell that was Brayden Hart.

Chapter Thirteen

Brayden

"You want to add to the order, kid?"

"You guys act like I'm sixteen. I'm twenty-six."

"It's the baby face. I'm only a couple years older than you, but you remind me of my kid brother who's sixteen."

"I don't look that young."

"Maybe not, but there's an innocence about you."

"I'm definitely not innocent."

Bray had seen combat. He'd killed. He'd wounded, been wounded. He'd rescued people who'd been tortured. There was no way anyone could truly call him innocent.

"Maybe innocence is the wrong word. Naïveté, maybe? Then again, maybe it's your tenacity. What you did today was tenacious, kid, and don't let the boss tell you any different. Yet you still have this positive light about you—like no matter what you've seen, you think the world is a good place and people are ultimately good."

Bray didn't know what to say to that. It was probably one of the nicest compliments anyone had ever given him. He smiled and gave Ax a nod of thanks. The funny thing was that Bray didn't mind Ax calling him 'kid', but he sure minded when Sam did it.

"So what did you want to eat?"

"Sam'll have the rib-eye with mushrooms and mashed potatoes. I'll have a dragon roll, a tempura roll with eel and a strawberry tart."

"Okay, I'll add that on. It'll probably be here in thirty."

Bray thanked Ax, but when he turned around, he was surprised to see Sam standing in the doorway that led back to his bedroom. *Their* bedroom.

"Don't tell me you don't trust me to even get your dinner order right."

As soon as the words were out of his mouth, Bray's eyes widened in surprise. Not only was he not usually snarky, but that was a little bit of a break in character.

"I was actually coming to ask you to add mashed potatoes," Sam said.

"You were?"

Sam nodded and Bray let out a relieved sigh. They both headed back to the bedroom together and Bray's nerves began to make his movements a little stiff. He didn't want to ruin this for anyone, since he was the interloper.

"Calm down," Sam said. "I'm not mad, but don't flirt with Ax."

Bray had been unpacking his toiletries from his backpack, but he stopped and looked up at Sam. Was

Sam jealous? Of course he wasn't. He was just playing jealous.

"I wasn't flirting. Ax isn't interested in me. He thinks I'm a kid."

Bray gave Sam a sharp look. In return, Sam gave him a half smile. That little lift at the corner of Sam's mouth made a real smile break free on Bray's face.

"Ax is two years older than you. I can call you both kids if I want to. Now, take off your clothes."

Every muscle in Bray's body froze in fear and excitement.

"I want to check all your injuries."

Bray swallowed and nodded. He didn't examine his disappointment too closely at Sam tacking on that second statement. Wondering if this was an act or if Sam really wanted to check him, Bray raised his eyebrows in question. Sam nodded.

After putting his toiletry bag on the counter in the bathroom, Bray tried to will away the half chub that had plumped up as soon as Sam had told him to get naked. Bray slowly took off everything but his boxers.

Head down, Bray hurried out of the bathroom and plopped down on the bed. When Sam knelt in front of Bray's knees, his heart rate doubled. Images of other things Sam might do on his knees bombarded him. With his pants gone, Bray did everything he could to keep his body from reacting to the proximity of Sam's mouth to his dick.

His abdominal muscles tightened as Sam gently prodded and the pain took care of any problem he might have had with tenting his boxers.

"I don't imagine many people get to see you on your knees," Bray blurted.

He wanted to face-palm himself. Why did he get so tongue-tied around Sam?

"Only you," Sam replied with a smirk. "Unless of course you get yourself killed."

Bray rolled his eyes but then hissed out a breath when Sam continued to prod him. Sam covered up Bray's little blunder seamlessly. He wanted to apologize, but that would break character too.

"I think sex is off the table, for tonight at least."

Sam winked at Bray when he said it, like they should both be relieved for the reprieve. He could only nod and give a small smile to hide his…was it really disappointment? Bray was definitely curious about how they'd address the sex side of this. Would they moan and bounce on the bed?

"At least tell me a story to distract me from the pain you're inflicting."

"I'm almost done. I just want to check your head again. What kind of story do you want to hear?"

"You never talk about your family. Tell me about them."

"I never talk about them because I stopped existing to them when they found out I was gay."

"I know that part. Tell me about the part before that. Were you close to your siblings?"

Bray was taking full advantage of the situation, but he couldn't bring himself to feel guilty. He was very interested in Sam. He was pretty sure Sam wouldn't close up on him while they were playing lovers for their audience.

"I don't know why you find this interesting, but I was pretty close to my siblings. When there are a lot of you, the older ones start parenting the little ones. My sister is the oldest. She's a mother hen if there ever was one. She was a second mom to all the kids, but she could also be a horrible tattle-tale."

Sam huffed out a small laugh, probably at a memory. Bray stayed quiet.

"I was second oldest, so I helped with the younger ones too. Sometimes it just felt like my mom wanted us out of the house. She'd let us play outside for hours while she cooked or cleaned—or maybe she was inside watching TV—but she sure as hell expected us to keep track of each other."

"So you weren't close to your parents?"

"My dad was always at work. My mom was always doing something—cooking, canning, quilting, sewing, singing in the church choir. Her hobbies seemed endless."

"Sounds pretty old-fashioned."

"Total nuclear family, but we were always tight for money. I was lucky as the oldest boy. Most of my clothes were new or passed down from older cousins. By the time they got to my youngest brother, they were threadbare or patched or both."

"I always wanted more siblings, especially…" Bray stopped himself from talking about Mase. "Well, especially after I lost my oldest brother. I guess it's not always what you imagine it to be."

"I wouldn't say I was close to my siblings. I just didn't have many options when it came to playmates. But you were close to your brother before you…before you lost him?"

"He was my hero." Bray nodded. "I wanted to be just like him. I tried to copy everything he did. I guess that was what worried my dad. He didn't want me to be 'reckless with my future'. I didn't understand a lot of things when we lost him."

Bray heard a quiet buzzing as he'd made his last statement. Sam pulled his phone out of his pocket and unlocked it. He frowned at whatever he read but continued on with the conversation as if nothing had happened.

"I'm sorry you lost him," Sam said quietly.

Anyone listening would probably think his brother had died. In a way, he probably had. Bray couldn't imagine losing his whole family at seventeen. He'd lost part of his family when he was nine and another part when he'd been eighteen, but he'd always had his mom. She was steadfast and true.

"Thanks, Sam."

Bray was embarrassed at the soft emotion apparent in his voice. It might fit the character he was supposed to be playing, but he wasn't an actor.

"I need to find out what Ax did with the Epsom salt. I want you to take a nice long soak. It'll help with the soreness."

Sam stood and left the room. With the door open, Bray could hear the cadence of his voice while he talked with Ax, but he couldn't hear what they were saying. After a moment Sam was back.

"Ax left all the supplies in the car. I'm just going to run down and get them."

"Shouldn't Ax go with you?"

"Stop worrying about me." Sam was smiling when he said it. "I can take care of myself. Besides, no one wants me dead that I know of."

Sam also lifted each of his pant-legs to show Bray his back-up weapons. Bray had seen his main weapon in a holster at the small of his back as soon as Sam had taken his jacket off in the hotel room. Bray got the message. He was covered.

"Besides, I think I have more reason to be worried at this point in the game. You're the one who's been getting himself into trouble—mugging, stolen luggage, kidnapped and pistol whipped all in one day."

"All right. I get the picture. Just don't take too long or I'll send Ax after you."

Sam shook his head as he walked out of the room, but there was a smile on his face.

Chapter Fourteen

Sam

"What the fuck is my little brother doing in Kiev?"

Sam had been getting the plastic bag out of the front seat of the car, the bag they'd purposely left so he'd have a valid excuse to go downstairs when Mase called. He hadn't expected the text message he'd received while checking Bray's wounds. The text from Mase that had told him to get his ass downstairs so they could talk.

"He followed me. Is it safe to be meeting me here?"

"I have all the cameras in here blocked. No video or sound feed for up to ten minutes. You, on the other hand—you're losing your touch, Magnum. I thought you were an operator."

Mase punctuated his statement by shoving Sam back against the car. Sam would be just as pissed if he found out one of his brothers were in danger. Someone like Ax would already be punching him in the face if he were in Mase's place. So Sam didn't react, didn't defend himself physically. He tried to reason.

"He has a tech guy in his pocket. Some guy that goes by the code name Sin. Any idea who he might be?"

"I haven't seen or talked to Bray in seventeen years. You think I know his friends?"

"Mase, calm down."

That seemed to have the opposite effect, because Mase did punch Sam…right in the gut. Still, Sam didn't defend himself. And because he didn't, Mase didn't escalate. He simply stood there, breathing hard, hands fisted at his sides, hatred in his eyes.

"He's fucking in love with you," Mase ground out. "I didn't even know he was gay."

Sam couldn't help but laugh. Apparently, they even had Mase fooled. No way someone like Bray would ever fall in love with someone like him. He wasn't sure he'd be capable of loving someone, and Bray sure didn't deserve someone as hard and cynical as he was.

"You find this amusing?" Mase leaned forward an intimidating inch.

"It's you he loves, not me. Though he is gay, apparently."

"What?"

"I met him two days ago. He showed up at that apartment in Miami—the shit-hole we use for deals. Somehow his friend tied you to me and me to that apartment."

"Two days?"

"Yeah. If you're talking about the bug, he was talking about loving you."

"I saw how he looked at you." There was accusation in Mase's voice.

"Because he knew I was there to save his ass. Nothing more. Now we're stuck pretending until I can get him out of this. He came to me looking for you. I told him to go on home, that I couldn't help. Bro followed him to the airport to make sure he left. He had a flight to DC."

Mase's shoulders relaxed a little. Since he seemed to be calming down, Sam continued.

"Apparently he beat me to Kiev, thanks to his friend, and was waiting for me when we landed. We lost him at the airport but his friend pointed him to this hotel. He stumbled right into Sergiy and the rest of Kozak's welcome party."

"That's it?"

Sam nodded.

"That message about Nickel?"

"In Miami I wouldn't even let him into the apartment. He told me to tell you Nickel needs you and it looks like it could be life and death."

"Nick," Mase whispered. "Is he—?"

"I don't know. We didn't exactly talk about it, and the only chance we have to talk is in the car. We keep checking and it's not bugged so far."

"That's not their MO. They aren't that organized or that smart. They assume all deals and lies will go down in the hotel room."

Mase darted his eyes around the parking garage, but Sam knew he wasn't actually seeing anything. They were right on the verge of getting what they needed, but Mase's family might need him more.

"He's brave," Mase finally said.

"Tenacious too," Sam agreed with a chuckle. "Said he wanted to be like his big brother."

Mase snorted. "When he was nine."

"And yet he joined the army just like his brother."

"Nick's in the army too. They always did everything together."

Sam smiled. He wasn't surprised Mase knew exactly where his brothers were. Sam knew his siblings were safe too. They had followed in their parents' footsteps. All but Noah. Noah was the only one who wasn't married with kids, but Noah was the youngest. He'd been their parents' 'oops' baby. Sam had already been a teenager by the time Noah was born.

"Can you check to see if he was injured in combat?"

Shaking off thoughts of his own family, Sam nodded. He was able to check in with Jazz a lot more frequently than Mase was. He'd make sure to have the intel next time he saw Mase.

"I'd better get back," Mase said.

"Me too. I'm just grabbing something out of the car. Do you think—" Sam had to clear his throat before continuing on. "Any possibility you could be the one to listen to the recordings from our room? I don't want to resort to bouncing on the bed, but…"

Mase shook his head. "Kozak does that himself. He doesn't really trust anyone, not even Andreiko. Then again, I wouldn't trust Andreiko either."

"All right."

"Besides, even if I know it's you jumping on a bed, I couldn't handle listening to my brother."

Sam gave his friend a shoulder bump.

"We'll figure it out, okay? If you need a hiatus, we'll figure it out."

Mase nodded and gave Sam a quick, tight hug.

"Keep him safe," Mase whispered before he walked away.

Sam rubbed his forehead and watched until Mase was out of sight before quickly putting in a call to Jazz about Nick.

When he opened the door to his suite, Sam found Ax lounging on the sofa in the living room watching TV. Bray was pacing behind him, wearing only a pair of Sam's sweats. The pants were huge on him, but he'd pulled the drawstring tight. Sam was a few inches taller, so the cinched hem of the pants bunched at Bray's ankles. He wasn't wearing a shirt, but Sam guessed that was more because it would have hurt to put one back on.

"Food should be here any minute," Ax said without looking away from the TV.

"That took a long time," Bray said.

"Car's in valet, so it took a little longer than I thought it would."

Sam reached into the plastic bag he held and pulled out the Epsom salt.

"Are you hungry? Would you rather eat first then take a bath? We could save your food. You probably ordered sushi, so it's not like we have to worry about it getting cold."

Bray's eyes went wide with surprise. Sam had heard everything he'd told Ax. Sam winked. Bray opened and closed his mouth then shook his head. They didn't even know each other, yet Sam could almost hear him say 'good one'.

"Ugh. You two are too cutesy for me," Ax complained. "If you're going to start making out, at least take it to your bedroom."

Sam knew Ax was just playing along, but Bray's cheeks flushed pink and he looked away. After a few beats, he looked back at Sam, but it wasn't embarrassment in his gaze, just curiosity. Bray was wondering what it might be like. Sam was too.

"Sam said no sex tonight, so I guess we'll just keep you company."

Ax choked on the beer he'd been drinking. Bray rushed over and patted him on the back. When he could finally breathe again, Ax chuckled. His chuckle turned into a laugh that had Bray and Sam smiling as well.

"You're a good sport, kid, but you're sharp too," Ax said. "I'll have to remember that when I tease you. But be careful. I don't think Sam likes you talking about your sex life—or lack thereof, as it were."

Bray laughed but took a decorative pillow from the sofa and hit Ax on the head with it. The teasing continued through dinner. The more comfortable Bray got with Ax, the more uncomfortable Sam got.

Sam wasn't big on joking around. It had also never bothered him before, but watching Ax make Bray laugh or blush had Sam feeling hostile toward his friend. Even as he appreciated Ax putting Bray at ease, Sam still wished Ax would shut the fuck up.

After dinner, Ax excused himself to his room. As Sam walked with Bray to their room, he started to sweat. A bath was beginning to seem like a bad idea. He'd thought it would give him an excuse to leave the room and also help Bray feel better. As they stepped into the bedroom, he realized that, as Bray's boyfriend, he couldn't just hand him the box of bath salts, send him into the bathroom, shut the door and do his best not to picture him naked.

"I'll get your bath started," Sam said.

Bray nodded and trailed Sam into the bathroom. He watched as Sam tested the water temperature and added the Epsom salt. When Sam turned away from the tub, Bray was sitting on the closed toilet lid. He looked ready to fall over.

"You can't fall asleep in the bath, Bray. If you're too tired, we can just go to bed."

"I think a soak will help soothe my muscles before bed."

Bray stood and began to untie the drawstring of the sweatpants. Sam tried to swallow to get some moisture in his parched throat. Bray was beautiful. He was leanly muscled. There wasn't an ounce of fat on his young, fit body.

He wasn't skinny by any stretch, but he wasn't as heavily muscled as Sam. The lines of his biceps were deeply defined but not bulky. His small pecs narrowed down to a slender waist, but it was his ass that had Sam's cock filling and pressing against his zipper.

He didn't even know if Bray liked to bottom, but he couldn't stop himself from imagining what it would be like to watch that peach of an ass jiggle as Sam pounded into him. He tried to shake the thought out of his head. He wasn't going to fuck Mase's kid brother. Even the fantasy was a bad idea.

Bray was struggling to untie the knot in the drawstring of the sweats. Sam reached out to help him but then pulled his hands back to his sides.

"It's okay," Bray said.

Sam's gaze shot up to meet his.

"I mean, it's okay to touch me."

Bray's eyes widened at his own words when he realized his mistake. So the next words rushed out of his mouth.

"I'm not going to break. I'm not fragile. You don't have to back off, Sam."

Bray gave him a small nod of encouragement and Sam once again reached for the drawstring.

"I hate seeing those bruises," Sam admitted.

He quickly untied Bray's pants then turned his back so Bray could undress and get into the bath. When he heard the lapping of the water on the sides of the tub, he turned to make sure Bray was all right. But he wasn't seated in the tub. Bray was standing, turning this way and that, probably trying to figure out how to sit down without causing too much pain. Sam also noticed something else. Bray was half hard.

"Here," Sam said as he approached the tub.

He scooped Bray up in his arms. Bray sucked in a surprised breath when his feet left the ground. His skin was warm and soft where Sam held him at his back and behind his knees. Trying to keep his eyes off Bray's cock, Sam watched his face for signs of pain or distress, but Bray seemed too surprised to show any other emotion.

Slowly, Sam squatted down and placed Bray into the water. When Sam began to pull his arms from underneath Bray, his face was directly over Bray's hips. Bray quickly covered his erection with his hands.

Sam looked up at Bray. There was a tinge of embarrassment there, but not as much as Sam would have expected. When Sam watched his lips curve up in a self-deprecating smile, he knew he should leave the room.

"I'll let you relax," Sam said as he stood.

"Don't go. You said I couldn't sleep. I want to relax, but if you keep me talking, I won't fall asleep."

With a nod, Sam backed away and sat on the closed toilet. From there, he could only see Bray from the shoulders up. *Much less of a temptation.*

"This feels amazing. The warmth is seeping into my bones. Today definitely didn't turn out how I thought it would."

Sam snorted. "Ditto. I thought I was in for a fairly mundane business trip."

Bray reached for the little soap provided by the hotel but flinched. Sam jumped up to get it for him. He tried not to look at Bray's lower half, but his eyes caught on the bruises.

"Are they getting worse?" Sam asked.

"I'd only worry if it hurt to breathe. You're quite the mother hen, Sam Wheeler."

Sam looked up at the sound of his alias. The last name sounded so wrong coming from Bray's mouth, but the kid was smiling like he was proud of himself. Sam found himself smiling back until his gaze fell once again to the black-and-blue marks on Bray's abs.

"I feel responsible," he murmured as he returned to sit on the toilet lid.

"You couldn't have stopped me. I did my best to hide the fact I was following you."

"Next time I'll remember to have one of my men sit on you."

Bray's eyes went wide.

"Not like that. Don't get all offended. I meant trail you, make sure you don't leave the States."

"I want to apologize," Bray said. "I've caused you a lot of trouble today with your…associates and I didn't mean to. You don't know how relieved I was to see you walk into that room. I knew you'd come for me."

Sam wasn't sure how true that last sentence was, but he was sure the rest was true. The look in Bray's eyes made Sam uncomfortable.

"Don't look at me like I'm some hero, Bray."

"You're a good man, Sam Wheeler. I knew it right away, and today, you proved it."

"I didn't prove anything. My business is about as dark as you can get. I'm not a good man."

"You are to me. I might be naïve, but I think that counts for something."

"Don't see pixie dust where there is none. It wouldn't behoove me to have left you there at their mercy. I had selfish reasons for getting you out of there."

"I'm sure you did." Bray smiled.

Maybe he was getting too into his role, but that smile was one of both indulgent patience and dirty little nymph. It was a smile one boyfriend would give another and Sam hated how much he loved looking at it.

Chapter Fifteen

Brayden

They talked about nothing in particular for twenty minutes while Bray let the heat of the water leach some of the pain out of his muscles. When he said he was done, Sam was right there helping him slowly stand and wrapping him in a towel. At least the relaxing bath had allowed him to get control over his unruly body.

When Sam had untied his pants, Bray's mind had drifted off into a fantasyland where Sam was undressing him for an altogether different reason. Bray walked back over to Sam's sweats since he didn't have any clean underwear.

Before he could even attempt to get the pants on, Sam was there. He knelt down in front of Bray with a clean pair of boxer briefs. Worried about his wayward body's reaction, Bray twisted just enough to have a little pain shooting up his side. It was the best way to guarantee he didn't get a boner with Sam kneeling before him.

Bray stepped into the boxers and Sam pulled them up high enough that Bray could reach the waistband without bending. With a nod of thanks, Bray pushed them up under his towel as Sam left the bathroom.

By the time Bray stepped into the bedroom, the covers of the king-size bed had been pulled down. Sam had taken his suit jacket off but was still in his pants and button-down shirt. The sleeves had probably been crisp that morning, but now they were wrinkled, rolled up to his elbows and wet from lowering Bray into the bath. It was a sexy look. Sam's hair was also a bit disheveled. Bray's fingers itched to smooth it back into place.

As he moved toward the bed, Bray tried to thank Sam for being so accommodating, but the words stuck in his throat when he saw the bulge in Sam's slacks just before he turned away.

Was Sam as turned on as he was? Bray didn't picture himself as Sam's type. He imagined Sam would go for someone more like Ax, with his dark, tanned skin, light eyes and teasing sense of humor.

"Get settled in. I'll be right back after I take a quick shower and brush my teeth."

Bray nodded and took his time to slowly sit on the bed and slide under the covers. He was just starting to nod off when Sam walked back into the bedroom. Bray tried to soak in the sight of Sam's bare chest as he walked around the bed got in on the other side.

Sam had tattoos, a lot of them. There were a few on his chest and arms. Bray thought he even saw one on the inside of his bicep. He was curious as hell about the but couldn't exactly ask what they all were.

"I can hear the wheels turning over there. Go to sleep, Bray, or the jet lag's going to kick your ass."

"Yes, sir, Mr. Wheeler, sir."

Sam smiled and shook his head as he reached over and turned out the light.

"Get some sleep, Bray," he said in a gentler tone.

"Night, Sam."

Sam grunted in return as he settled into his side of the bed. Bray was sure it was going to take him hours to fall asleep, knowing Sam was barely dressed and inches away. But that was the last thought he remembered having.

* * * *

Bray's pillow was too hot. Was he back in the desert? Had the whole incident with his family been a dream? Had searching for Mase been a dream? Had Sam been a dream?

Sam. Talk about wet-dream material. Bray pressed his morning erection into the bed. He groaned at the feel of heat and pressure on his aching dick. He hadn't had a wet dream since high school.

Bray rubbed his face against the pillow. When he felt soft hair brush his cheek, his eyes popped open. Without moving a muscle, Bray took in his surroundings. All the events of the previous day came flooding back as he realized he was asleep in Sam's arms, on Sam's side of the bed.

Pulling in a deep breath, Bray smelled Sam's warm, musky scent. He wondered how Sam had been able to sleep with Bray's weight pressing down on his chest. Sam radiated heat, so Bray took a few moments to soak it up before he moved and woke the man beneath him.

"Morning," Sam said.

Bray gasped. He pulled back, turned his head and saw that Sam was fully awake. And boy, was Sam adorable in the morning. His hair was sticking up all over the place, his eyes were heavy-lidded from sleep and he was smiling.

"How did you know I was awake?"

"Your breathing changed."

Bray opened his mouth to apologize for climbing on top of Sam during the night. Sam stopped him with a finger to the lips and the shake of his head. Bray nodded as he remembered they were being monitored.

"I've been up for a little while, but I didn't want to move you off me and risk you jolting and causing yourself pain. But now that you're up, I really need to use the head. Can you scoot over a little? I guess it doesn't matter how big the bed is. You hog it."

Bray laughed and reluctantly rolled off Sam. He was pleasantly surprised there was only a dull pain in his movements. Sam rolled to the edge of the bed before standing. He stretched his arms overhead as he made his way to the bathroom. His sleep pants were all rumpled but still seemed to do an amazing job framing his perfect ass.

"At least I don't hog the covers," Bray said as he pushed up onto his elbows.

His abs were still sore, but nothing like they'd been the previous day. The bath and sleep had helped.

"No need to. When you're right on top of me, it's easy to share covers."

With a sigh, Bray fell back onto his pillow. It was going to be hell pretending to be with Sam when he wished there were a chance he could *really* be with Sam. Especially this teasing, sleepy, rumpled Sam.

After Sam came out of the bathroom, Bray rushed in to take care of his bladder. He also brushed his teeth. There was no chance of kissing, but he also didn't want to blow Sam away with morning dragon breath.

Since he didn't have a change of clothes and all he'd worn into the bathroom were the boxers Sam had lent him, that was all he walked out in. Sam was on the bed, his back pressed against the headboard and a laptop on his thighs. He didn't look up when Bray approached the bed and slid back under the covers.

Bray wasn't sure what he was supposed to do in his role of arm candy. Was he supposed to try to pull Sam away from his work? That was not something Bray would naturally do. He stared at the ceiling as he wondered if Sam would let him borrow more clothes.

"I can hear the gears clicking over there," Sam said still without looking away from his computer.

"I don't want to pull you away from your work."

"I'm just answering emails. What do you need, baby?"

Bray's gaze shot to Sam, who was smirking at him. Then Sam gave him a wink. Bray popped his knees up so his feet were flat on the mattress. No need for Sam to see what that wink had done to him.

It's just an act, Bray repeated to himself as he willed his dick to calm down.

When he looked up, Sam's eyebrows were raised in expectation. He had to think back to the last thing Sam had said and realized it was a question.

"I need some clothes. Yours are too big. Do you think Ax could run me to a store real quick while you work?"

"I have it all covered."

"What does that mean?"

Just then, there was a knock on the bedroom door.

"Come on in," Sam said.

The door opened and Ax peeked his head in.

"Just wanted to make sure the sex ban hadn't been lifted. Didn't want to interrupt anything."

"I bet the opposite is true," Sam grumbled.

Bray's cheeks heated as he pulled the duvet up to his chest. Ax was enjoying this act a little too much. Dragging the pillow from under his head, Bray flung it at Ax as he made his way toward the bed. His hands were full of bags, so even though his reflexes were fast, Ax was only able to slightly divert the projectile. It still ricocheted off his head and landed on the floor. Ax's mouth hung open as he stared at Bray for a second before he threw his head back and laughed.

"I so did not expect that from you, Bray. Teasing, yes. Physical violence, no."

"A pillow fight does not qualify as physical violence," Bray said.

His response just had Ax laughing harder.

"I don't think Sam would be okay with us having a pillow fight, but I sure can see why he's so tied up in knots over you." Ax winked.

"Stop flirting with my boyfriend." Sam closed his laptop with a snap. "Thanks for running out this morning."

As he reached them, Ax dropped the bags he was holding on the foot of the bed. With a smirk and a nod, he turned to leave. As he reached the door, he threw a comment over his shoulder.

"You two want me to add your breakfast to my order, or are you guys gonna get busy…I mean 'be' busy?"

"Ax, you're asking for an ass kicking. Don't embarrass Bray. Get me the egg white omelet I had yesterday after we checked in. Also, fruit and yogurt."

"Do they have pancakes?" Bray asked.

Both men looked at him.

"What? I like pancakes."

Ax shook his head and walked over to the desk along the wall opposite the bed. He picked up a folder and tossed it on the bed next to the bags he'd set there.

"You're gonna have to look for yourself, Hot Cakes. I haven't eaten pancakes since I was probably nine years old."

Bray opened the menu and found they did have pancakes, but decided he didn't want to be teased while he tried to enjoy them. So he searched for something else, something more grown-up. He liked bread at breakfast, so he found a compromise.

"I'll have a Croque Madame."

Ax snorted. He was shaking his head as he walked toward the door. Bray didn't know why that was funny too.

"And a fruit plate," he called as Ax rounded the corner.

Ax shot a thumbs up back into the doorway, then he was gone. Bray huffed out a breath and turned to see Sam watching him. There was something in his eyes that made Bray feel like he needed to apologize, but he kept his mouth shut.

Sam set his laptop on the nightstand and stood from the bed. He walked around the corner of the mattress, started digging through the bags Ax had dumped and pulled out some clothes.

"This should be fine for today," Sam said as he took out two pairs of jeans and two shirts, along with underwear and some socks.

"You didn't have to buy me clothes, Sam. I didn't get my money taken."

Bray reached for the money belt he'd set on his nightstand. He pulled out some cash and traveler's cheques before getting up and searching out his wallet in the pocket of his dirty jeans. Even if this was all an act, he wanted Sam to see that he didn't need his money.

Chapter Sixteen

Sam

Sam kept his eyes on the clothes in front of him and away from the sight of Bray in his underwear. Bray started throwing money on the bed. He needed clothes because he'd gotten roped into their op, so Sam would expense them. He'd tell Bray as much when they could talk freely.

"Were you going to wear the clothes from yesterday? The dirty, blood-spattered clothes?"

When Bray didn't answer, Sam looked up at him. Bray was twirling that large silver coin through his fingers as he stared at the money on the bed. Sam liked watching those slender fingers as the coin weaved in and out of them.

He'd felt those same fingers caressing his chest early this morning. Sam had still been awake and working on his laptop when Bray had started his migration across the bed. Part of it had been a nightmare. He was familiar with those same dreams, the ones that sucked him back into the heat of battle, that seemed so real he could feel the blood spatter.

Sam had thankfully been able to calm Bray with a few gentle words, since he'd been afraid the kid would hurt himself further as he tossed and turned.

When he'd set his computer aside and tried to go to sleep, Sam had ended up staring at the ceiling, listening to make sure Bray didn't have any more nightmares. He'd jolted awake at Bray's first touch. He probably hadn't been asleep more than a few minutes when Bray had snuggled up to him.

He told himself he'd remained still and quiet so he didn't jostle Bray's injuries. The truth was that it felt good—damn good—to have that tight little body pressed against his. He'd ignored the erection that had slowly grown as Bray had pressed more and more of his bare skin against Sam's.

The little groans that had escaped Bray's throat had nearly done him in. He'd given in a little when he'd rearranged his cock to be more comfortable, but he hadn't jacked himself. He wasn't that creepy guy who took advantage of someone's vulnerability.

When he'd woken up with Bray spread out on top of him, he'd smiled. Fucking smiled. He couldn't remember ever waking up in a better mood. That had ended up pissing him off. No way was he going all soft for his best friend's little brother—yet he hadn't moved one muscle.

In fact, he'd lain there for over an hour before Bray had finally woken up. He'd felt Bray's warm breath on his arm. He'd watched his hair catch the reflection of the slivers of light beaming in from the window. He'd berated himself for wanting to test the silky texture of those blond locks.

And finally, he'd felt Bray's morning wood pressing into his hip. That had been his undoing. He'd groaned as quietly as he could, but he'd still felt the exact moment Bray had woken up.

"No, but at least let me pay you back. I don't need a sugar daddy. I want to be equal partners in this relationship."

Sam had to think about what they were talking about. *The clothes. Paying for the clothes.* He respected Bray wanting to pay his own portion. He couldn't see himself dating someone looking to be supported financially.

If he were into relationships, Sam would want someone he could talk to about his job, someone he could trust with his life. There weren't many men who could qualify for that and the ones that did he thought of as brothers—all except his best friend's actual brother.

"Bray, I don't even know how much Ax spent. If you're so intent on paying, we'll work something out. But I will be paying for some of your clothes."

"But—"

"No buts. I want you to look a certain way when I take you to one of my business meetings, so I'll pay for that."

"All right." Bray nodded.

"Good. Now get dressed. We'll have breakfast then do some shopping. Once that's done, we can fit in a little sightseeing if you like. I'm expecting to hear back from Mr. Kozak, but I think we'll have a few days to ourselves before my next meeting."

"All right," he said again.

Bray looked at the clothes then back at Sam. It would probably seem weird for Sam to take his clothes into the bathroom to dress. As a compromise, Sam tried to give Bray a sign that he'd turn around to change.

It was apparent Bray hadn't caught on when he gasped as Sam dropped his sleep pants. A quick look over his shoulder confirmed it. Bray was looking right at his bare ass. He seemed to like what he saw, because he didn't look away, and Sam's dick was really happy about that.

Sam opened the drawer where he'd put his underwear, yanked out the first pair he touched and pulled them on. He still didn't want to turn around, so he talked over his shoulder to Bray.

"Are you okay? Was that pain from your ribs?"

When there was no answer, he chanced a look behind him. Bray's mouth silently opened and closed. His eyes pinged back and forth between Sam's eyes and his now-covered ass. Sam hadn't meant to shock him.

"Just a twinge," Bray finally said.

Sam nodded at him before going to the closet to pull out a pair of dark slacks and a charcoal sweater. He kept his back toward Bray, especially after he heard the quiet *thunk* of clothes, namely his boxers, hitting the floor. They'd have to figure out some sort of code for 'you can turn around now'.

When Sam finally did turn, Bray was pulling the blue Henley Ax had purchased over his head.

All through breakfast, Ax teased Bray about eating pancakes for the first meal of the day. Bray teased right back and Sam found himself annoyed by the banter.

Ax only teased the guys he was close to, guys on the team. Sam had never seen Ax date someone, but he imagined this was exactly how he flirted, and it was happening right in front of his face. With a shake of his head, Sam once again had to remind himself that Bray wasn't really his in the first place.

Ax gave them the all-clear when they got into the car. Sam explained to Bray that the only place they knew for sure was safe to talk was the car, because Ax checked it multiple times a day for listening or tracking devices.

Shopping was much easier and much harder than Sam had expected. Easier because Bray hadn't balked when Sam paid for his clothes. But it had been hard to watch Bray dress up in all those outfits.

Bray looked good in every single thing he tried on. If it was his size, he looked good in it. His ass was flawless as it filled out the back of his pants. Sam knew the front was filled with just as much perfection.

They spent most of the day out of the hotel room, seeing the sights, finding good places to eat, strolling around the city. Sam found himself enjoying Bray's company. He had an optimistic outlook on virtually everything and it forced Sam to look at things from a different perspective.

Whenever Bray was nervous or embarrassed for blurting something he tried to take back, he would fidget. Mostly he'd take that same coin out of his pocket and twist it through his fingers. If they were working together, Sam would point out all Bray's tells, but they weren't really working together.

Bray's nerves were understandable. What normal person got sucked into a world of drugs and trafficking and had no second thoughts? It also made him appear more authentic to the men Ax and Sam knew were following them.

That night, Sam was able to continue the no-sex rule, since Bray's bruises were still an angry color. Bray was able to undress and bathe himself with no assistance. Sam was both relieved and disappointed.

The next day was much the same, except more sightseeing than shopping. When they stopped for dinner, they ended up at the same high-end restaurant as Kozak. Sam didn't know if it was a coincidence or not, but they drank the local delicacies Kozak sent over to their table. Drinking both had probably been a mistake, especially for Bray, who seemed to be a bit of a lightweight.

"Looks like you two had fun," Ax said as he opened the rear door for them.

"Did you see Kozak's men?" Sam asked.

"Yep. Made sure they came nowhere near our car and also tested it just now to be sure," Ax said quietly.

Bray started singing some pop song as he struggled to get his seatbelt on.

"Too much champagne for the kid?"

"Try too much Spotykach."

Ax laughed as he closed the door behind Sam. He was still chuckling when he slid into the driver's seat. Bray was still singing, though more quietly.

"Why'd you let him order Spotykach?"

"I didn't." Sam rolled his eyes. "Kozak sent over Horilka and Spotykach. I couldn't exactly remind him in the restaurant that he needed his wits about him, so we could pretend to be boyfriends when we got back to the hotel."

"I can still pretend to be your boyfriend," Bray said with only the tiniest slur in his voice.

Why did Sam find it adorable? He should be pissed as hell that Bray had drunk too much. He took a deep breath as he assessed the kid.

"Maybe a quick stop for coffee might be a good idea."

"You want coffee? Now?" Bray asked.

"Not for me. For you."

"*Pfft*. I don't like coffee."

"You drank coffee this morning," Sam reminded him.

"Of course I did. Ax called me a child for wanting pancakes. I love pancakes. Grown men can love pancakes. I mean, millions of men eat chicken and waffles. They even eat them for dinner. Why can't I have pancakes for breakfast, the meal they were actually made for?"

"Nothing you just said related in any way to coffee." Ax shook his head.

"Sure it did. I said I didn't want to be called a child for not liking coffee."

"That's not—"

"Ax. He's not firing on all cylinders."

With a shrug, Ax let it drop. Sam and Ax remained quiet for the rest of the drive back to the hotel. Bray continued to sing softly as he looked out of the window. Sam shook his head as he caught himself smiling once again.

Bray pulled the silver coin out of his pocket and began sliding it in and out of his fingers. His coordination wasn't at its best, so he struggled for a moment until the coin flew through the air and landed on the floor at Sam's feet. Sam reached down and picked it up.

"Can't lose that. It's for luck," Bray said.

He reached for the coin but apparently forgot he was buckled into his seat. Bray lunged forward only to be jerked back by his seatbelt. He sucked in a breath at the jolt.

"Relax. I was going to give it back."

Sam didn't think it could be that lucky, since Bray's luck had been nothing but bad since they'd crossed paths. The phrasing he'd used also piqued Sam's interest. He hadn't said it was his lucky coin, only that it was for luck—like someone had given it to him for luck, but who?

Even though it was none of his business, Sam wondered about it anyway. He ran his fingertips over the smooth metal. He also didn't give it back to Bray immediately.

In the passing streetlights, Sam looked at the coin. It wasn't US currency. It was about the same size and weight as one of those old, large silver dollars.

By the time they reached the hotel, Bray was practically asleep. Sam pocketed the coin and got out. He had to go around the car and help Bray up out of his seat.

When they reached their room, rather than passing out as Sam had hoped, Bray seemed to get his second wind. Ax arrived a few moments later with one of the bellmen in tow, along with bags and boxes of items they'd purchased the day before that had needed to be altered.

While Sam tried to put things away, Bray would take them back out as he explained to Sam what he liked about each one.

"Bray, we need to put your clothes away."

"I want to try some of them on again."

"Why?"

"I liked how you looked at me in these pants," Bray said.

Sam stood in shock as Bray dropped the pants he was currently wearing and kicked them aside. Sam remembered those particular pants. They'd looked like they were made specifically for Bray, except they'd been a touch too long.

Bray wanted Sam to look at him like that? Like he wanted to slip off every shred of clothing he was wearing and lick his body from head to toe?

Beads of sweat popped out on Sam's forehead when Bray kicked off his boxers as well. A naked Bray was apparently a dangerous Bray.

It wasn't an option to tell Bray to get his fucking clothes back on. A guy would only say that if he caught his boyfriend with another man. Before Sam could get another word out, Bray pulled on the slacks they'd been discussing.

Sam had liked the pants before, but knowing Bray was going commando underneath had him loving them. How the hell was he going to stop Bray from making a horrible, drunken mistake without blowing their cover? Boyfriends in a committed relationship had drunk sex all the time, didn't they? It wouldn't ring true if he used that as an excuse.

"Fuck," Sam groaned.

Bray must have zeroed in on Sam's obsession with his ass, because he was showing it off by bending, stretching and dancing. With the fluid way Bray was moving, Sam had a sinking feeling that using Bray's injury wouldn't work either.

"B, your ribs," Sam said but it was only half-hearted.

"Mm-m, I like it when you call me that."

Sam was already justifying to himself that they wouldn't actually have sex. He just wanted to see Bray naked and turned on. He wanted the chance to touch all that skin. He'd find a way to get them off without using the condoms and lube that were in his toiletry bag.

Trying to reel himself in, Sam shook his head. He'd use a different tactic on Bray, one that would probably have the kid hiding under the covers. He'd show Bray what he really liked in bed.

He'd make the kid back off before they both did something they'd regret. It was the only scenario he saw working in both their favors. He'd push Bray too far and piss him off. It would sound like a lover's quarrel. Now if Sam could just keep his hands and his dick to himself...

"B, you'd better not be getting pre-cum all over those new slacks I bought you."

Bray turned around at that. His eyes were glazed with alcohol and lust. His pupils were blown. And the smile he gave Sam was sex and sin.

"What if I am?"

"Take them off and hang them up," Sam ordered.

Bray rushed to do just that and almost tripped over his own feet. When he turned to hang the pants, Sam ran a hand over his ass cheek before smacking it. Bray gasped but didn't move. In fact, Sam could have sworn he stuck his ass out a little farther. He was well and truly fucked if Bray liked a little power play.

The pants dropped from Bray's hands, and when he bent over to pick them up, Sam smacked the other cheek, much harder. This time, Bray didn't gasp. He took a deep breath in and out like he was settling in for more.

"Hang them up and do it right. I don't want any wrinkles when you accompany me."

"Yes, Sam," Bray whispered and hung the pants perfectly.

When he was done, Sam inspected his work. With a nod of approval, he commanded Bray to go lie on the bed.

Chapter Seventeen

Brayden

Bray wasn't drunk. Well, he wasn't *that* drunk. He was aware of everything. The alcohol had just given him a boost of confidence and a little freedom to be reckless.

He'd been sure Sam was going to put a stop to what was happening, but he hadn't…yet. Was this the result when Sam was pushed past his limits? Bray sure hoped so. Pushing the man when his hands were tied might not be the brightest idea, but Bray would at least be able to see if there was a spark.

He'd been shocked when Sam had spanked him, but he hadn't hated it. In fact, he'd liked it. He had never played any kind of sex games, but now he had to wonder if he'd been missing out on something.

As he crawled onto the bed, he wondered what position he was supposed to be in. Didn't people normally kneel while waiting in sex games?

"Fuck," he grumbled.

He'd never thought S&M shit would have him panting. Maybe it was the way Sam looked at his ass, or maybe it was just that he wanted Sam badly enough that what turned Sam on would turn him on.

When he got a few moments to himself, he'd have to think about how deep into this he might be willing to go. Was this something Bray was truly interested in? Was this something Sam wanted or was this Sam's way of getting Bray to back out before they did anything physical?

That made his position on the bed even more important. Should he lie on his stomach and display his ass? Not wanting Sam to think he'd passed out, Bray decided to stay on his back. Sam wouldn't be able to miss how turned on his body was. The idea that Sam would walk out and see his hard dick was should have made Bray shy, but he was tingling with anticipation.

Sam came out a moment later. He stopped mid-stride when he saw Bray on the bed. Bray tightened his ass cheeks and squeezed his thighs together to try to alleviate some of the tension throbbing through his body. Sam's broad chest was bare and he only wore his sleep pants.

His heavily muscled arms and chest bulged as he clenched his fists around what he held in his hands. His erection was trying to point north as the head peeked from the waistband of his pants.

Sam strode forward again. He threw lube and a couple of rubbers onto the bed, but he didn't climb on. Rather than cover himself, Bray was surprised at his desire to arch up and make sure Sam's attention stayed on his cock. Sam paced around the bed. When he got to the other side, he slowly walked back, but he didn't say a word.

Normally Bray would think he'd done something wrong. He suspected Sam was still trying to make him retreat first. Rather than cover himself, Bray reached for his aching dick.

"Did I say you could touch yourself?"

The harshness of Sam's tone had Bray's gaze clashing with his.

"That's mine to do with as I will. Keep your hands at your side, B."

Bray smiled at his use of the nickname. The idea of Sam calling him something no one else did made his chest ache a little. Bray did as he was told.

"It's all yours," Bray said. "Hop on."

He sent Sam what he hoped was a cheeky grin. Sam didn't smile back. Something flashed over Sam's face, but Bray didn't know what emotion it was. He would have called it pain, but that couldn't be right. Sam looked a little haunted for a moment before giving his head a slight shake and meeting Bray's eyes once again.

"If anyone's ass is getting fucked, it's yours."

"I'll take it any way I can get it."

Sam looked at him for a long time. Bray didn't know what he was searching for until it dawned on him that Sam might think he was lying about being vers. Bray gave him a nod of confirmation. Sam seemed to relax as he walked around to the end of the bed. He licked his lips as he assessed Bray's body.

"Show me," Sam said.

For a full minute, Bray just lay there, not knowing what Sam meant.

"Show me," he said again.

Bray swallowed when he realized what Sam was asking. He avoided being watched, avoided making himself so vulnerable. But he wanted Sam and he loved the way Sam looked at him. He slowly bent his knees and pulled them up toward his chest, exposing himself to Sam's gaze.

"You know exactly how gorgeous you are, don't you?"

Bray shook his head.

"Yes, you do. You've been teasing me with this ass all day. I've never seen such perfection."

Bray didn't demur like he might have with anyone else. He simply kept his eyes on Sam's face. But Sam's gaze was glued to Bray's opening. His hole quivered and Sam groaned in response.

Sam leaned forward for a closer look. When Bray felt a rough fingertip graze over his puckered flesh, he fluttered his eyes at the sensation. He struggled to keep them open so he could watch. Sam's nostrils flared. His eyes never left that spot between Bray's legs, even as he spoke.

"Pink and sweet. That's you, isn't it, B?"

"Not so sweet," he replied as he tried to spread his ass cheeks farther apart.

"Bullshit. You're sweeter than honey. Probably deserve someone better, someone who isn't as twisted as me, but here you are spreading yourself out for me. Red means stop, yellow means slow down, green means go." There was a pause before Sam added, "Unless you want to pick a specific safeword this time we play."

"Green," Bray whispered.

Sam flicked his finger back and forth, back and forth over the sensitized flesh. Bray tried to push himself harder against Sam's finger, but his position didn't give him much leverage.

After plucking up the bottle of lube, Sam fell to his knees between Bray's feet. The move had Bray struggling not to close his legs. This position was more intimate than Bray had ever been with another man. No one had ever…

Bray moaned as he felt the heat of Sam's breath caressing the skin of his ass. A lubed finger began rubbing circles around the small opening, loosening him up. Bray tried to relax, but Sam's face was right there.

He didn't know if Sam intended to use his mouth. Bray found himself both hoping for and dreading the feel of Sam's tongue on him. It was such a personal experience, something one did with a lover they were extremely familiar with. Yet here they were, pretend lovers, and Sam had his face in Bray's crack.

"I can hear your brain whirring from here," Sam said. "Relax."

Bray stiffened. If Sam had told him how pretty he was again, he probably could have relaxed, but calling attention to his nerves only made him more anxious.

"We've never done this before," Bray said.

It was true, and yet it worked with the roles they were playing for their audience. Bray waited for a response, but nothing came. He wasn't going to be the one to call a stop to this, so he continued to wait.

Finally he received his answer in the form of a wet tongue gliding all the way up his crease. When it rasped over his opening, Bray cried out. He knew some guys liked this, but he'd never imagined it would be that good.

"Holy fucking shit."

Bray arched his back, his dick beginning to throb. He wanted so badly to let go of one leg so he could jerk himself off. Why did the wet rasp feel a million times better than the pad of a finger?

As Sam's tongue circled him, poked at him, Bray heard a needy whimper. It took him a moment to realize that the sounds were coming from him.

When Sam's stiffened tongue finally breached him, Bray had to reach farther under his leg and tug at his balls to stop himself from coming. Before he could even take a breath, Sam was on him. They were nose to nose as Sam scolded him.

"I said that dick was mine."

"I didn't touch my dick. I touched my balls."

"Your whole body is mine. Isn't that right, B?"

Bray couldn't get his mouth to work in order to respond.

"I decide how to use this body," Sam said.

Bray was writhing around, trying to get some relief. The move brought their cocks together. The little bit of friction and pressure had them both groaning. Bray watched as Sam's eyelids fluttered. There could be no doubt that he was as turned on as Bray. He could feel the evidence not only pressing against him but leaking on the underside of his erection.

"What color, B?" Sam asked as he reached for a rubber.

Bray had to give his head a shake to get his brain to kick in enough for him to process what Sam was saying.

"What color?" He asked again.

"Green. Green. Fuck me, Sam."

Bray felt a surge of humiliation at the whine in his voice, but he didn't change his color. In fact, he tried to pull his legs wider apart to give Sam more room to maneuver. They hadn't even really kissed, and here he was, spread-eagle and begging.

The tear of foil echoed in the room. Sam rolled the rubber down his length—his large and very girthy length. He was easily bigger than anyone Bray had ever had inside him, not that there had been that many.

Sam covered the condom in lube and suddenly Bray felt a pressure against his opening. He tried to relax and bear down, but Sam was big, really big.

When the head finally breached him, they both paused and panted. Bray appreciated the reprieve as his body adjusted to the invasion. The initial stinging sensation eased, so he experimented a little. As he released and tightened the muscles of his ass, Sam groaned and punched his hips forward another inch.

"So fucking tight, B? If I didn't already know better, I'd think you were a virgin."

"It's your fucking big-ass cock. It stretches my ass to the breaking point."

Sam chuckled then groaned.

"I wasn't going to touch you," Sam said. "I was going to let you heal from that beating."

Bray knew he was saying that he'd meant not to have sex. It gave him a little surge of confidence that maybe—just maybe—Sam had tried and failed to resist his attraction.

Arching up, Bray let go of his knees and gripped the back of Sam's head. He pulled him down and slammed their mouths together. Sam growled as his tongue fought with Bray's.

Yet he was still gentle as he inched his way deeper and deeper inside Bray's body. Every inch forward brought a new sting, a new burn before easing into a familiar pressure.

They were both sweating by the time Sam finally bottomed out. Sam swiveled his hips and Bray gasped when it caused a momentary pressure on his prostate. Sam pulled back and looked deep into his eyes.

Bray wasn't sure what it was Sam was looking for, but he must have found it, because he thrust forward. The ridge under the head of Sam's cock caught on Bray's hot spot. Bray's muscles locked up.

"Fuck," Sam ground out through clenched teeth.

"Harder," Bray breathed.

That one word seemed to be permission for Sam to stop holding back, because his hips began a frantic pounding as they both raced toward the finish line.

Bray didn't dare reach for his dick. In truth, he didn't need to. The ridges along Sam's stomach offered just the right pressure and resistance against the sensitive underside of his erection. His balls began to draw up as Sam snapped his hips back and forth.

The headboard beat against the wall. The weight of Sam's balls smacked Bray's ass with each forward thrust. The sound of flesh slapping flesh rang out. Bray closed his eyes to take in all the sensations. His spine began to tingle even as Sam's pace became more frantic.

"Open your eyes," Sam demanded.

It took a moment for Bray to comply. When he did, what he saw threw him right up to the edge. Sam's nostrils were flared. The veins and muscles in his arms bulged and twitched as he held himself up. Sweat dripped down his temples. There was something in his eyes that pulled at Bray. It looked like need. It sent Bray over the edge.

The orgasm was so powerful that he couldn't keep his eyes open any longer. He arched his neck back and all the muscles in his body contracted. Pleasure so powerful that it was almost too sharp zapped out from his core to his fingers and toes as the warmth of his release pulsed out onto his chest and stomach.

Everything went black and hazy for a moment. He worried he was going to pass out. Almost from a distance, he heard Sam curse and felt him surge forward one last time. Bray felt that huge cock throbbing inside him. Sam jabbed his hips forward in a few tiny thrusts as he emptied himself into the condom.

It was an experience beyond anything Bray had ever imagined. Even though he was grateful it had happened, he had to regret that it was over.

Bray kept his eyes closed. He didn't want to see the regret or even accusation that would be in Sam's eyes. He had taken advantage of the situation. He'd backed Sam into a corner. Though Bray would never regret the act itself, regret at manipulating Sam into having sex washed over him.

When Sam collapsed on top of him, his panting breaths skittering across Bray's sweat-slicked skin, Bray still kept his eyes closed. He used the lack of vision to take in everything else about the moment.

He could smell Sam's sweat and he liked it. The weight of Sam on top of him was comforting, almost familiar. Because he was concentrating on physical sensations, Bray felt a few aftershocks tighten the ridges of Sam's ab muscles. At least the orgasm had been good for both of them.

Hopefully Sam wouldn't regret it too much. He felt the weight of Sam's body lift away. Bray told himself to open his eyes, but it must have taken too long.

"Bray?"

Sam pulled out slowly. Bray groaned a little…but not from pain. It was more that he missed the full feeling of Sam stuffed inside him, and it was definitely from the fear that he'd never feel that again. The bed shifted as Sam stood.

"Guess I can't be too old if I can wear out a kid like you," Sam said.

It was too late to let Sam know that he was awake, so he just continued to play possum. The water in the bathroom turned on. He'd have to get up at some point and wash the drying cum off his stomach, but he could wait until Sam fell asleep if he had to.

The water in the bathroom shut off, so Bray got comfortable and kept his eyes closed. The mattress dipped again. Bray's eyes shot open when he felt a warm wet cloth rasping over his abdomen.

Sam was smirking at him as he rubbed the washcloth down Bray's stomach again, cleaning off all the drying jizz.

"Guess we can talk tomorrow," Sam said, as if to himself.

He was giving a reprieve and Bray grabbed at it with both hands as he nodded. Humiliation curled in Bray's belly as he rolled onto his stomach. He thought it would take a while to get to sleep, but the day seemed to catch up with him. His eyelids got heavy as he heard Sam *tip-tap* on his laptop.

Chapter Eighteen

Sam

He hadn't meant to touch Bray. He'd tossed the condoms onto the bed to scare some sense into both of them. He definitely hadn't meant to eat the kid out, let alone fuck him into the mattress. When he'd seen how hard it was for Bray to expose himself, Sam had half-hoped Bray would stop everything.

But he'd been brave and Sam had been strangely proud. Bray had opened himself up, and Sam hadn't been lying when he'd called Bray perfection. He was all peachy skin and pink pucker. He'd only meant to give it a few licks as a reward—a reward to Bray for being so brave.

He'd just wanted a little taste—just little bit of something he knew he'd never have and would never be worthy of. Rimming wasn't something he did often. In fact, he'd only done it with one other person, and that had been over twenty years ago.

He sure as fuck didn't deserve the gift Bray had handed to him. Bray would regret everything as soon as he opened his eyes in the morning. Hell, he probably already regretted it. That was why he'd pretended to be asleep before Sam's orgasm had even faded.

He'd allowed Bray to play possum because it was easier on both of them than trying to talk things out in code because of the listening devices.

Bray's breathing finally settled into sleep. And just like the night before, there was a nightmare. And just like the night before, after Sam calmed him with some gentle words, Bray inched his way closer.

Tonight it was even more dangerous for him to allow Bray to cuddle close. He liked the feel of their skin pressing together a little too much. When Bray nestled his head into Sam's armpit, Sam closed his laptop and plunged the room into darkness. Maybe if he didn't have to see what was happening, he could pretend it wasn't wrong for him to allow it.

Bray moaned a little as he snuggled in for the night. Before he could talk himself out of it, Sam wrapped his arm around Bray's back and let his hand settle on his naked ass—the ass he'd just been balls-deep inside, the ass that even now tempted him to do it all over again.

But there was one thing that kept repeating in his head. Bray was vers. It was yet another way Sam was sure he was the worst person the kid could develop any kind of feelings for. He hadn't even attempted to bottom in over fifteen years. Even the idea of it had the past bombarding him.

Sam squeezed his eyes shut and clenched his ass cheeks so tight that he could probably make a diamond. His mind was spiraling to a bad place, so he took a few deep, cleansing breaths. Then something happened.

"Sam." Bray sighed the name like a prayer.

All the muscles in Sam's entire body relaxed as Bray slid his warm hand over Sam's chest. The calluses on his fingers had goosebumps popping up in their wake. It took Sam a moment to realize that the relieved sigh that floated up from the bed had come from him.

He turned toward Bray. Bray curled his legs up and entangled them with his. The kid was a definitely a cuddler. If anyone had asked him seventy-two hours ago if he enjoyed snuggling, Sam would have laughed. Yet he couldn't seem to get enough of Brayden Hart wrapping himself around his body.

Sam ignored his growing erection as he slowly caressed miles of smooth skin. Soon Bray would be out of his life and it would be business as usual. *The sooner the better,* he told himself.

The last thing he needed was someone to care about. It was a liability in his line of work. He was in deep enough just caring about the ragtag team of dorks Mase had put together—a team he didn't really consider himself a part of.

The best thing he could do for Bray would be to send him home in one piece and forget he ever existed except in the fond memories of his big brother. He would do just that as soon as he could. And he wouldn't touch the kid again, at least not beyond the late-night embraces Bray seemed to need.

* * * *

Best. Dream. Ever.

Bray's hot, wet mouth was taking him deep. Sam arched his back and thrust his hips toward the sensation. It should have been some nameless, faceless guy's mouth, but it wasn't anymore. It was Bray's.

The perfect amount of suction, just the right glide of the tongue along his underside. Sam slid his hand down and gripped Bray's hair. He guided Bray to show him the best rhythm to get him off. His balls were drawing up, and there was a tingle at the base of his spine.

Then he felt the tip of a finger along the crease of his ass. That wasn't a dream. It was a nightmare. Sam sat up straight and willed his eyes to open. What he saw surprised him.

It hadn't been a dream. Bray was choking himself on Sam's cock. His erection had flagged a little, but the sight before him had his dick once again at full mast.

He'd been sure Bray would regret what happened. The kid would either beat him out of bed or play possum again. Bray kept surprising Sam with his bravery.

When Bray's free hand began to sneak up between Sam's legs again, Sam grabbed his wrist and shook his head. Even if no one were listening, he wouldn't be explaining to Bray why his ass was off limits.

"You want my cock, B?" Sam practically groaned the words.

Bray nodded.

Even though Bray had passed last night with flying rainbow colors, Sam wanted to test him again. The sight of that plump, pink mouth spread wide around his cock was one of the hottest things he'd ever seen.

"On your back," Sam said.

A visible shudder ran through Bray. He sucked a moment longer before pulling off Sam's dick with a wet pop. Bray rolled onto his back. He must have assumed

Sam was going to fuck him, because he began to pull his legs up to his chest.

The sight was tempting, but the feel of his mouth was more tempting. Sam hopped up and grabbed Bray's shoulders. He situated Bray so his head was hanging off the edge of the bed but the rest of his body was spread across the mattress.

"You're going to swallow everything I give you, aren't you, B?"

Bray licked his lips and nodded. Sam looked down and saw Bray's cock bob against his stomach. He wanted to spend hours just tasting the body laid out before him. The desire was frightening because it was so powerful.

He pressed his thumb to Bray's chin and opened his mouth. Sam slid forward faster than he'd meant to and Bray gagged a little. Sam groaned at how good the vibrations felt against the head of his cock.

Bray pressed his thighs together. His slender hips jerked around on the bed as his dick continued to bob. Sam reached down and felt along Bray's neck. The position he was in arched his head back so Sam could fuck right down his throat.

"You like this, don't you?"

Bray groaned in response.

"And you'll swallow every fucking drop, won't you?"

Another groan. Bray may not have been using words, but his erection was nodding even when his head couldn't. Then Bray wrapped his hands around the backs of Sam's thighs and slid toward his ass. Sam froze and grabbed Bray's hands.

"Hands on my thighs. If I block your air for too long, tap me and I'll pull back."

Bray rubbed up and down Sam's thighs but didn't slip his hands around back, so Sam relaxed. He bent over Bray's body as he fed himself a little deeper down the kid's throat. It was so fucking hot and wet. Sam wouldn't last long.

He reached down, encircled the base of Bray's dick with his hand and gave it a squeeze. Even though Bray's mouth was stuffed full, Sam knew he'd groaned the word 'fuck'. His bottom teeth scraped the base of Sam's cock and he had to pull back a little, or he'd blow too soon.

Since Bray had a way to communicate that didn't require Sam watching his reactions, Sam leaned down and sucked on the head of Bray's cock.

Bray arched off the bed and yelled something. The vibrations along Sam's length had him groaning as well. Bray writhed against the bed as he tried to get more of himself into Sam's mouth, but Sam held himself a little too high. He wasn't giving away any control.

When Bray spread his legs, bent his knees and put his feet flat on the bed, it afforded Sam a peek of his opening. Bray used the move to try to push himself into Sam's mouth, so Sam pulled back even more. Bray pinched Sam's thigh. Sam laughed, even as he pulled back to make sure Bray had enough air.

He wasn't being fair. He knew it, and what he was about to do was even more unfair. He was a total hypocrite, but it didn't stop him from wetting his finger in his mouth then reaching down to press it against Bray's gorgeous little pucker.

Bray spread his legs farther. He tried to pull his legs up to his chest, but Sam was partially in the way. Sam was envious of how open Bray was, of how needy he allowed himself to be. He wished things could be different.

Sam scooped his hands behind Bray's knees. He spread Bray's legs and pulled them up. He gave himself total access to do to Bray what he himself wouldn't, couldn't allow.

This time, though, Bray didn't balk like he had the previous night. This time, he pressed his ass against Sam's tongue. He opened himself up as he swallowed Sam down.

When his tongue had Bray whimpering and writhing and humping, Sam pulled back. He felt the distinct bite of teeth around the base of his cock as he pressed in to the root for a moment before pulling back to allow Bray room to breathe. It wasn't a hard bite, but Bray was definitely topping from the bottom, so Sam gave his balls a small slap.

Cold air was pulled in around Sam's hot flesh as Bray gasped. When he smacked Bray's balls a second time, Bray groaned and sucked him in so deep that his nose was pressed against Sam's pubic bone. The gasp-groan combination told him that even Bray hadn't realized how much he liked power play.

With Bray's opening relaxed from his tongue, Sam slid his middle finger in to the root and put a tiny bit of pressure on Bray's prostate. Bray pulled back for air before sliding Sam all the way to the back of his throat again. He was swallowing around the head of his cock and it was pushing Sam toward the precipice.

Sam was barely even thrusting his hips. He was allowing Bray to set the pace, and it was quickly becoming frantic. In return for the amazing head Bray was giving, Sam swallowed the hard length before him all the way down. The vibration of Bray's groan on the tail end of the undulations of his throat muscles tightening had Sam's balls drawing up.

There was no way he was going to come first, so he bobbed his head up and down as he pressed harder against Bray's little button. Bray started thrusting up off the bed but Sam held close, allowing Bray to fuck his mouth. He wasn't at the perfect angle like Bray was, but Sam was still able to deep-throat him.

When he pressed a second finger inside Bray's tight hole, Bray squeezed him so fucking tight that he couldn't have scissored him open farther if he'd tried. One more pass over Bray's prostate and he blew like a geyser. Sam swallowed every drop.

Sam continued to suck until he heard Bray whimper. He wasn't sure why he was reluctant to let Bray slip from his lips, yet he was. He gentled the suction but didn't release Bray's softening cock. He also continued to gently pump his fingers in and out of Bray's tight little ass.

Just as Sam was slowing down, Bray was ramping things up. He slid one hand up and caressed Sam's aching balls. Usually, even that was too close to his ass for him to allow, but then Bray pressed directly behind Sam's balls and traced circles with his fingertips.

It was a hot button Sam hadn't even realized was there. The sensation had him thrusting harder than he should have, considering he was fucking a mouth and not an ass. But the sharp pleasure of it, along with the panic of fingers so close to his ass, had him frantic.

A few more thrusts and he was shooting down Bray's throat. He tried to pull back, to give Bray some air, but Bray grabbed the backs of his thighs. It didn't even occur to him to be afraid of those hands straying upward. He was too far gone. His abs seized with aftershocks.

When he finally did pull back, Bray gulped in air. Not one drip had escaped. Bray had hoovered him better than anyone ever had. Sam managed to roll himself off to the side as he collapsed onto the bed.

Their labored breathing sounded hollow in the large bedroom. As his libido cooled, shame seeped into all Sam's pores. He'd fucked his best friend's brother again, his best friend's *vulnerable* little brother.

Even if Sam had had the freedom to say anything that came to mind, he would have remained as silent as he was at that moment. He hadn't been able to resist.

He'd realized it wasn't a wet dream, and he'd still done it. Once he'd realized Bray had instigated the encounter, he hadn't been able to stop himself.

They could easily have gotten away with only having sex last night, and yet Bray had woken him up in the best manner he could have ever imagined.

He'd let Bray's hands wander dangerously close to his ass, a place no one touched. Sam only touched his ass to clean it. He'd once considered himself somewhat vers, though he'd always preferred to top. But then… Sam shook his head. He didn't want to dwell on the past. It would just suck him into a vortex of shame.

That was probably the hardest thing about this whole situation with Bray. The kid was sweet and gentle and sexy as hell. He was someone Sam could probably trust, someone his body seemed to trust already, considering his erection hadn't wilted as soon as Bray's fingers had inched so close to his asshole.

What a fucked-up mess. They'd have to talk. Sam would have to set Bray straight. They didn't need to act out any more sex scenes for their friends listening in.

Chapter Nineteen

Brayden

It was probably the best blow job Bray had ever had. Definitely the best sixty-nine of his life. Then again, he'd only just discovered last night that he loved being rimmed. He could probably come just from having Sam sink his hot tongue into him, sucking at Bray's opening with thick lips.

Even though his breath hadn't evened out from what they'd just done, Bray's dick twitched with interest. He'd have to keep finding ways to tempt Sam.

He didn't fool himself into believing he'd ever see Sam again after he stepped onto a plane back to the States. He might not ever see his brother again, either. So he'd take the risks he needed to ensure he'd done everything possible to bring his family back together.

If there was one thing Bray had learned, it was to take what he could while he had the chance. People made choices. Sometimes they were forced to make the decisions that pulled them out of your life. Sometimes, they did the forcing. Other times, people just left.

Bray had experienced them all. The only person who had never once let him down in his entire life was his mom. He'd taken this risk as much for her as he had for Nick and his father. His mom deserved her family back.

She was a victim in all this, and yet she'd found forgiveness in her heart. She'd done what she could and had made peace with the rest. Bray wanted to emulate that.

His mom constantly sent invitations to all her sons to every celebration and holiday. And if Bray had been the only consistent attendee for a few years, she never showed any disappointment. She'd been happy to at least have one son there, even though her heart obviously bled with missing the other two.

So Bray had taken this risk to find Mase. And though he was in the middle of a huge mess as he tried to get a moment alone with his brother, he'd selfishly grab a little happiness for himself as well—even if it was fleeting, even if that happiness wasn't real.

Because Bray simply couldn't act like what had just happened was an everyday occurrence, he got out of the bed and headed straight for the shower. His silence would probably do enough to make it seem like this was normal to anyone listening in, but what had happened the night before—had simply rocked his world.

He wasn't sure if sex with Sam was always that good, but in Bray's experience, sex was never that good. That was all-the-more reason to have as much of it as they could fit in.

Sam was on the bed working on his laptop when Bray got out of the bathroom. In the mirror, Bray saw

Sam lift his eyes to watch him get dressed, but they both remained silent. When Bray was fully dressed, Sam shut his laptop with a snap and dropped it on the bed.

"I haven't heard back from Mr. Kozak. What do you say we go sightseeing again today?"

"Sure," Bray said. "I've heard they have a bar here that's laid out like a morgue."

"That's what you want to see?" Sam shook his head and laughed.

"Not necessarily, but obviously their culture is different here if they find that humorous."

"I'm sure we can find a lot of quirky things to see. We just want to keep PDA to a minimum. Don't get testy if I don't hold your hand. This is hostile territory for queer people. A lot of people here think along the same lines as Sergiy."

"All right."

With a final nod, Sam stood and walked into the bathroom, so Bray headed into the living room.

"Well, don't you look nicely fucked," Ax said as he pushed a cart on wheels into the dining room. "Got your man wrapped back around your finger, I see."

"Not sure I'd say that, but he lifted the no-sex rule."

"So I heard. He must have missed you. I've never known him to be so…vocal."

Ax chuckled as Bray blushed. They quietly set breakfast out. After the past night, Bray was more nervous about spending the day out of the hotel room.

Once they were in the car, Sam asked Ax to jump out and get them some coffee. Bray knew what was coming. As soon as the car door clicked shut behind Ax, Bray decided he'd try to control where this conversation went.

"We don't have to have a private discussion. Apparently Ax heard everything."

"I have no doubt. It's his job to watch my back. He probably gave us some space last night, but I'm sure he wasn't expecting a reenactment this morning."

"I don't know why not. Last night was great. This morning was even better."

Sam huffed out a laugh but shook his head.

"Look, Sam. You don't have to let me down easy. Just because I'm younger doesn't mean I don't know the score. I'm not over here scribbling my first name and your last name in my notebook, okay?"

That seemed to take the wind out of Sam's sails. He didn't reply, but he nodded.

"You had a pretty good time, right?"

Sam snorted. A smile twitched at the corners of Bray's lips, but he pulled it in. He didn't want to seem cocky.

"I wouldn't go off like a rocket if I didn't like what we were doing," Sam said.

"That's a rocket? I'd really like to see what you consider having staying power."

"Bray—"

"I bet you don't get a lot of ass while you're undercover."

Sam's only response was a tolerant sigh.

"I don't get a lot while I'm deployed. I'm on leave trying to fix my broken, fucked-up family. You're in a situation where you're surrounded by homophobes. We're attracted to each other. Really, what's stopping us from enjoying ourselves?"

"You're my best friend's kid brother."

"That excuse went out of the window as soon as your dick breached my ass."

"I wasn't exactly planning on fucking you. Things got a little out of hand."

This time Bray couldn't stop the smile that stretched his lips. Sam found him irresistible? He'd take that.

"I disagree. We're both consenting adults, regardless of who my brother is. Besides, I'm sure he doesn't give two fucks who I have sex with."

"I beg to differ, and I have tender ribs to prove it."

"What does that mean?"

"The bath salts. We left them in the car on purpose so I could take the call from Mase that I knew was coming. Instead of calling, he was waiting for me in the garage with a nice love tap to the gut for getting you involved in all this."

"It really didn't seem like he recognized me." Bray shook his head. "I didn't expect a hug, but a light of recognition in his eyes, or at least…something."

"It would put you in danger. There's a reason he's deep undercover. He's good at what he does."

Bray's heart stuttered and his eyes stung. He'd worried Mase had forgotten he even had brothers—or that maybe he just didn't care. Sam's words gave Bray hope. If his brother cared…

"I can guarantee Mase is the reason you only got a few kicks to the ribs. Well, that and you getting a few shots off."

"Even though he was speaking Ukrainian, I recognized his voice. I thought I was saved when I heard him, but then…his eyes were so cold when they looked at me."

"Well, that was probably real. It was probably anger at me for allowing you to get tangled up in this."

That gave Bray a funny feeling in his stomach. He'd always felt cheated out of having a big brother look out for him the way Mase had before he left. They'd been so close, then Mase had just been gone. But he hadn't forgotten. Mase had recognized him.

"I'm not sure how your big brother will feel about us fucking like rabbits, especially if he happens to hear something through bugs in our hotel room."

"If he was the one listening, you wouldn't have let anything happen between us at all."

"True. But that doesn't mean he might not hear bits and pieces."

"And he'll either think we're fucking or faking it, but he lost the right to tell me what to do when he walked away. I've lived longer without a big brother than I ever lived with one."

"He never forgot about you."

Bray hated the part of him that sat up like a little puppy looking for love—the part that felt all warm at the thought that Mase was out there thinking about him, maybe even worrying about him. Then again, he could have replied to any of the emails Bray had sent.

"Did he ever talk about us? Me and Nick?"

"Mase and I don't talk about the past. We've both done enough things we're not proud of that we decided to just let the past go."

Bray nodded and looked out of the window. He was Mase's past.

"I didn't mean it like that. He told me he had younger brothers, but obviously he didn't tell me you guys were twins. He did talk about you a little—just in generic terms, like he never thought he'd miss the lack of privacy you guys gave him. I think he preferred you two digging through his things to our CO."

Bray smiled at the memory of Mase catching Nick and him after they'd eaten all the Halloween candy

Mase had taken as a 'tax' from their trick or treat bags. They'd tried to deny it, but they'd still had chocolate on their faces and fingers. Bray had never liked his commanding officer's, or CO's, ability to go through his footlocker.

"He probably still sees you as a kid, though you never really want to know about a sibling's sex life," Sam said.

"I didn't realize how much I'd enjoy someone's tongue inside me."

A surprised laugh burst out of Sam like a gunshot.

Bray had almost said 'your tongue' but had stopped himself in time. It was only Sam's tongue he imagined. Because this encounter was destined to be brief, Bray was determined to fit in as much as he could while they had the chance.

"You sure don't pull any punches, do you, kid?"

"Why should I? We're in a situation where we need to be able to trust each other. You saved my life back at that compound."

"I told you before, I'm no hero."

Bray shrugged. "It would have made you look tough if you hadn't cared if I lived or died."

"You're hopeless," Sam huffed.

"Hopeful, Sam. I'm hopeful. I believe in giving the benefit of the doubt whenever possible."

"You're a better man than I am, B."

Bray smiled at the nickname.

"I also think you should take happiness wherever you can get it. Having sex with you definitely makes me happy, so while we're here, we should try to give each other as much happiness as possible."

"You make me sound like the fucking Dalai Lama because I want to ream your ass."

"Sex can definitely be spiritual." Bray nodded solemnly.

Sam burst out laughing. Bray didn't know if that was a yes or a no to his proposal. Then Sam yanked him forward and kissed him until they were both panting. When they pulled apart to get a breath, Sam pressed their foreheads together.

"Your brother's going to kill me."

Bray smiled and dove for Sam's mouth.

Chapter Twenty

Sam

All day, Bray had teased him with small touches and looks as they'd toured the city with Ax. He watched Bray with more interest than he should have. When he was relaxed, Bray smiled easily. When he was embarrassed, he withdrew. When he was nervous or anxious, he took that coin out of his pocket and threaded it through his fingers over and over.

In the afternoon, Sam got a call from Kozak, setting up a meeting for the next day. Disappointment tightened his gut. Things were going to go his way—he felt it in his bones. He had them just where he wanted them, but all Sam wanted was more time with Bray. With tomorrow looming over them, they'd have the make the best of their last night together.

When the meeting was over, he'd figure out a way to get Bray home safe. Then Sam would be off to Thailand for a meeting that would hopefully be much less eventful.

After dinner out in one of the most expensive restaurants in the city, Ax drove Sam and Bray back to the hotel. The mood since his call with Kozak had been much more subdued. That spark was still burning low, but the expiration date on whatever this was between them had just popped up and it was in twenty-four hours.

"Today was really fun," Bray said as they entered the hotel room.

Sam knew part of it was for show, but he found himself hoping it was also true. Ax bumped shoulders with Sam and tilted his head toward his side of the suite. Sam nodded.

"Night, kid," Ax said. "Remember the no-clothes rule is restricted to your bedroom."

"I might deserve pancakes as a reward for putting up him," Bray muttered once Ax was out of the room.

Sam laughed.

Even though tomorrow would be stressful with the unknown of taking Bray along, tonight Sam felt lighter than he could have imagined. He'd probably smiled and laughed more today than he had in the past year.

What that said about his life he wasn't sure, but it told him that someone like Bray wouldn't be single for long. It was hard to be a gay man in the military. He didn't picture Bray being a life-er. Once he was out, he'd probably find some nice guy, settle down and do whatever it was he dreamed of doing.

Why that had dinner souring in Sam's gut, he couldn't say. Sam had never dreamed of a white picket fence. His parents had enough of that. As far as he was concerned, that same fence just seemed like jail bars.

"Bedtime," Bray breathed as he grabbed Sam's hand.

He smirked as Bray walked backward toward their bedroom, pulling Sam along with him.

"And you call me 'old'. You're heading to bed at eight p.m."

"First of all, I don't call you 'old'. You call me 'kid' and I hate it."

Bray poked Sam in the chest for emphasis. It only made Sam's smile grow a little wider. He wasn't sure why the term 'kid' bothered him. He was a kid.

"Second, who knows what time it is back home? Time here doesn't matter because…jet lag. And finally, I didn't say 'go to sleep'. I said 'go to bed'. I might not let you get any sleep at all tonight."

Sam chuckled. Only a kid would think to give up an entire night of sleep before an important meeting. Sam was willing to try, but only because there was something about Bray. That and the sex had been off-the-charts fantastic.

"Tell me where you want me, Sam," Bray whispered as they crossed the threshold to their room.

Sam swallowed then blew out a breath. There was so much he would love to do with Bray. The kid was willing to try so many things and he was an open book. For someone like Sam, who needed to be in control in order to let go and get off, that was a total fucking turn-on.

When they reached the bed, Bray fell to his knees and unbuckled Sam's belt. Sam stopped him by laying his hand over Bray's. When Bray looked up at him, he shook his head. Bray's eyes lingered on the bulge behind Sam's zipper, but he finally released the slacks.

"Undress yourself then get back on your knees."

Bray was naked and back on the floor in less than ten seconds. Sam smiled at his enthusiasm. Reaching down, he gave in to the urge to run his fingers through Bray's hair.

"You want to suck my cock?"

Bray licked his lips. Sam groaned. When Bray hesitated, Sam knew there was something more he wanted.

"What is it, B? Tell me what you want. I just might give it to you."

"I want...I want to taste you. I want to taste you the way you tasted me."

Bray's eyes were hungry and fully dilated. His lids were heavy with lust as he practically begged on his knees for what he wanted. He was trusting Sam with his desire, but Sam didn't think he could give him that.

Sam's ass cheeks reflexively clenched together, but something else happened—something that hadn't happened in well over a decade. His hole twitched. Along with the fear was a longing for things to be different. That had not happened once since those teenage days when his life and part of his sexuality had changed.

"Is everything all right, Sam?"

He erection was completely deflated as the past tried to overtake on him. Closing his eyes for just a moment, he took a deep breath. When he opened his eyes, he looked down at the desire in Bray's.

His dick started to fill as he saw that Bray was still fully erect. He liked being naked on his knees while Sam was still fully clothed. They could be a very good match sexually, if not for his hang ups.

"Tonight is about you, B. It's about me pampering you. What do you want me to do to you?"

"Everything," he breathed without reservation.

"Take my cock out. Get me ready to fuck you."

Bray groaned even as he unzipped Sam's pants with deft fingers. He pulled Sam's erection out of his underwear and swallowed it down without undressing Sam any further.

Sam instinctively snapped his hips forward at the feel of the wet warmth of Bray's mouth. Bray choked a little. Before Sam could back off, Bray reached around and pulled him forward.

Sam reached back to dislodge Bray's hands from his ass cheeks before he lost his erection again. The kid gagged himself until Sam had to pull him off, or he was going to blow way too soon.

"Get on the bed and show me what's mine," Sam said.

Bray scrambled up to his feet. He crawled onto the mattress and rolled onto his back. With no hesitation or shame, he pulled his knees up to his chest and spread his thighs wide. He learned so fast and was so eager to please that he had Sam's cock throbbing and leaking like a faucet.

Sam didn't have any sex toys with him. Bray had been correct that he didn't get to play often, especially while on an assignment. But he could improvise.

"Don't move," Sam said as he strode into the bathroom.

He quickly dug through his toiletry bag and found what he was looking for. Next he entered the walk-in closet and took a few things from there as well. When he stepped back into the bedroom, he paused.

Bray hadn't moved a muscle. From his vantage point, Sam could see that sweet pink hole twitching and calling to him. Sam licked his lips as he remembered the salty, bitter, forbidden taste.

"Can I trust you to stay still, or do I need to bind you?"

Bray arched up to look at Sam. When he saw the silk ties dangling from Sam's fingers, his nostrils flared and his cock danced just beneath his belly button.

"Looks like I'll be tying you to the headboard," Sam smiled.

Bray didn't respond, except to let his head fall back on to the mattress. Sam made quick work of tying each of his wrists to one of the sturdy bedposts. He would have loved to have used a spreader bar on Bray. Instead, he tied each of Bray's ankles loosely to his thighs, ensuring he would keep his legs bent and open.

"Sam," Bray whispered.

Sam pulled back to look at his work. "What color, B?"

When Bray looked confused, Sam gave him the same options he had the previous night.

"Green, yellow or red, B? If you can't answer, I'll assume it's red and we'll stop."

The demand in Sam's voice had Bray arching his head up. Sam gave him a wink he hoped would convey the sternness had been for the listening device.

"So fucking green," Bray sighed.

The last tie was used to cover Bray's eyes. When he was sure Bray couldn't see him, Sam looked his fill. He didn't school his reactions at all as he ran his hands up from Bray's ankles to his thighs to his sweet little pink pucker.

The blindfold was mostly for Bray, to allow him to concentrate on the physical sensations. It was also for Sam. It allowed him freedom, just as Bray's bindings allowed him freedom to let go.

Sam didn't typically have any type of sexual encounter without bindings in place. Last night and even this morning had been such a rarity, and yet he'd come harder than he had in years. If they had time, if Sam's job allowed, if Bray were anyone else, Sam would have wanted to explore the why of that. None of that was possible, so he would take what was offered and walk away grateful that Bray had trusted him with this.

Chapter Twenty-One

Brayden

Bray couldn't see anything. He could only hear his own heavy breathing. He could feel Sam's callused hands caressing him and his balls were already drawing up.

What kind of pathetic mess was he, that he was so hot for someone who didn't really like him at all? He had to wonder if these were 'daddy' issues…or even 'brother' issues.

Mase had been the one to say "fuck you," and walk away. Nick had been lucky enough to get their father's affection. Bray? Well, Bray had always been the one striving for love. He'd been the one worried he was going to lose his father's affection just as he had Mase's.

Then he had. His father had turned him away as well. And here he was, panting after a man who might care if he lived or died, but not much beyond that.

Every thought that had been running circles in Bray's mind evaporated when he felt something smooth and hard slap his balls. He gasped. There was both pleasure and pain in the hard tap. His mind cleared. He focused solely on the present.

"The blindfold is so that you'll concentrate on the sensations, not get lost in your own head," Sam said.

There was another slap, this time on his ass. Bray groaned. He wasn't sure why this did it for him, but it really, really did. The next smack was harder. Bray arched but he couldn't go anywhere. He had no traction.

When the next taps came in quick succession but in a random pattern across both ass cheeks, Bray humped the air. He was desperate for any sort of friction on his dick. The next slap came directly on his pucker.

"Oh fuck. I'm gonna—"

"No," Sam said.

Sam clamped down on the base of Bray's cock and his other hand tugged a little on Bray's balls, just barely staving off the orgasm.

"Your sweet little hole is so sensitive. I wish we had a vibrator with us."

Bray groaned. He'd used a dildo before, but it hadn't vibrated. He hadn't known how sensitive he was. Guys usually fingered him and fucked him, or Bray fucked them. Either way, sex was good, but not blow-his-head-off amazing.

When Bray calmed down, Sam started again, this time with his thighs. As Sam moved closer and closer to his hole, Bray tensed. He tried to squeeze his thighs together, but Sam's shoulders filled the space between them. The flashes of pain got harder and harder as Sam moved whatever he was using all over Bray's ass.

The prickle was there at the base of his spine. Even as the orgasm built, the tingling spread to Bray's fingers and toes. At first he thought it was from being bound, but his hands had a lot of freedom. The bindings weren't tight at all. It was some crazy sort of pre-orgasm. Sam wouldn't be able to stop it from barreling into him this time.

Sam started caressing Bray's skin after each barrage of smacks. The contrast between the sharp swats and the soft caresses was making his balls tingle with the need to come. Sam's sweet words of encouragement just pushed him further toward the edge.

Bray shook his head from side to side in frustration and anticipation. When Sam gave him five hard slaps directly on his entrance, Bray's hole spasmed as his dick spurted wildly. Hot jizz landed on his chest, on his chin, on his stomach.

Just when he thought the orgasm was calming down, Sam's hot, wet tongue circled his opening. Sam flexed his tongue and poked at Bray's pucker. Bray shot off a second time at the contrast of soft, wet and warm to the hard, cold slaps that had come before.

The orgasm had been intense, especially in that it had been a sort of double orgasm. Bray's dick seemed satisfied, but his ass? His ass felt empty. He'd wanted more for their last time together.

"We're just getting started, baby," Sam whispered in his ear as he removed the blindfold.

Bray hadn't even realized that Sam had moved, his ankles were no longer bound to his thighs. Sam quickly released his arms as well. When he was completely unbound, Bray stretched out like a starfish on the bed.

He looked over and noticed that Sam was still hard as a rock. Bray licked his lips but Sam shook his head. He did, however, start unbuttoning his shirt.

"I'll be coming in that ass of yours. Watching you like that was…" Sam shook his head. "If you swallow me down that tight throat, I'll shoot my load way too soon."

Bray preened at the compliments Sam tossed out so easily in the bedroom. He wished Sam were like this all the time. Bray froze as he remembered they were being listened to. Sam was playing a role and he was apparently really good at what he did. He might even deserve an Academy Award for his performance in this very bedroom.

Bray's heart sank as he remembered that it was he who had backed Sam into a corner. Then again, it wasn't as if Sam hadn't been hard. He was currently stiff as a spike, his eyes hot with lust as he they darted all over Bray's body.

"On your hands and knees," Sam said as he unzipped his pants.

Bray did his best to look tempting. He slowly rolled to his stomach and stuck his ass high. The cool air of the room made his skin tingle. His flesh was still warm and stinging slightly from the beating Sam had so expertly given. He was beginning to feel that he was in way over his head, both with the sex games they were playing and with Sam himself.

"This ass could tempt a saint," Sam growled as he pressed his palms to Bray's cheeks and slightly spread them.

The click of the lube bottle opening had Bray on edge. His ass was sore already and that final spank had been directly on his hole. How would that affect the burn when Sam stretched him?

Bray sucked in a breath when Sam breached him with a fingertip. The sting was sharp but not unbearable. Sam didn't go gently either. He pressed his entire finger in to the webbing, and if Bray had to guess, it was his longest digit, his middle one.

The zap of pain intensified until the pad of Sam's finger grazed Bray's prostate. The pleasure was also strong. Up until that moment, Bray had been pretty much flaccid. That one bump to his hot spot had him thickening, hardening. When Sam pulled his finger out, Bray whimpered at the loss.

Sam leaned over him and pressed his chest to Bray's back. He bent and bit gently at Bray's earlobe. His hard, bare cock was gliding up and down Bray's crease. Bray arched his back just an inch more and the bare head of Sam's dick caught on the raised flesh of his opening. They both gasped.

"I'm not going to prep you any more than that," Sam whispered in his ear. "The stretch will hurt so good."

Bray groaned as his cock filled to full hardness and began to bob in anticipation. He had to stop himself from stuttering out a request to fuck bare. The crinkle and tear of the condom wrapper were almost jarring and painful to his ears.

Then he felt the bulb of Sam's cockhead press against him. Sam placed a hand on each of Bray's shoulders. He didn't stop to let Bray adjust once he passed the tight ring of muscle. He just continued to slowly press forward.

"Color," Sam demanded.

"Green. Please. Fucking *green*."

Sam snapped his hips forward until he was fully seated. Bray sucked in a breath at all the sensations bombarding him. Yes, there was pain, but there was also pleasure, and both were strong. Sam pulled back until only his tip remained lodged inside. Again Bray begged. Again Sam thrust forward.

Sam began an unforgiving pace, one that didn't allow Bray to adjust to being so full or so empty. On every pass, the ridge of Sam's dick plucked Bray's prostate.

It had been less than thirty minutes since the most intense orgasm of his life. Bray should have been embarrassed at how close he was to blowing his load. But between the tight grip Sam had on his shoulders and the groans wrenching from Sam's throat, Bray couldn't bring himself to care.

His ass was burning, but his cock was leaking like a sieve. He wasn't sure he'd be able to sit down for days. Hell, he'd probably have to sleep on his stomach all night, but the sweet fire spread from his ass out to his entire body.

Sam released one of his shoulders and reached down to wrap his hand around Bray's neglected dick. One stroke from Sam's tight fist and Bray threw out a warning.

"I'm close."

"Thank fuck," Sam said, "because I'm there."

Those words were what threw Bray over the edge. He bit his arm to keep from screaming at the flames that licked through him, followed by the most intense pleasure he'd ever felt. Even as his body floated with elation, his mind sank in despair.

He'd never known he needed this. The pain wasn't bad. Bray had been shot and stabbed. His body had been battered. The pain Sam offered was nothing in comparison, and yet it was the perfect balance to the pleasure he made Bray feel.

The praise Sam gave in the bedroom was something he needed as well, something he craved. And he couldn't just pop anyone into the role Sam was filling. It was Sam he wanted and that was exactly what he couldn't have.

Bray soaked in the pleasure he felt when Sam fell on top of him. The weight was warm and comforting.

"How do you know?" Bray asked.

"Know?"

He wanted to ask how Sam could look at someone and know that they needed to be dominated. That question was unfortunately not conducive to their act as lovers.

"How do you know when I need pleasure and when I need pain?"

"I try to read your body."

Bray nodded, though he wasn't fully satisfied with the answer. Exhaustion began to pull him under so quickly that he could only moan a protest at the cold air assaulting him when Sam's weight lifted from his back.

Chapter Twenty-Two

Sam

Sam wanted to punch the smirk right off Ax's face. Bray had been loud the night before. He'd been loud when Sam had woken him before dawn and he'd been loud a third time this morning in the shower.

It wasn't Ax who Sam was pissed at and they both knew it. He'd wanted to make last night good for Bray. He'd selfishly wanted to make it so good that the kid would feel him for days and remember him for years. That, and after Sam had realized what a good fit they were, he couldn't keep his hands or his dick to himself.

"Shut up," Sam grumbled.

Ax snorted in response. Bray, who had been staring out of the window of the car, turned to look between the two of them.

"You two are like an old married couple," Bray said.

"The fuck you say," Ax growled.

"No, seriously. It's like you're constantly bickering, but you know each other so well you don't even have to open your mouths. Nick and I used to be like that."

"So we're more like twins. I can get behind that. Sam's too…top-y for me."

It was Bray's turn to snort, but it turned into a laugh. Sam found himself smiling as well.

"Well, now we all know what position Ax prefers," Bray said.

"I like variety. Besides, I figured it's only fair, since I know exactly where you guys stand," Ax quipped.

When the smile fell from Bray's face and his cheeks pinked, Sam reached over and lightly punched the back of Ax's seat. The jolt did nothing to curb Ax's laughter.

"Look at him defending your honor," Ax said. "It's so cute. I've never seen Sam so protective."

"You haven't known me that long, asshole."

"How long have you two worked together?" Bray asked.

"'Bout a year," Ax responded. "Before that I was working on my own."

"On your own? You mean without…" Bray left the sentence hanging.

"Government assistance?" Ax threw it out as a joke, but it was probably what Bray meant.

"But why?"

Sam and Ax both stiffened at the question.

"Sorry," Bray said. "I didn't mean to pry."

"It's all right, kid. I'm looking for something. And I realized I have a much better chance at finding it with government assistance."

As they got closer to the compound, Bray pulled that silver coin out of his pocket. Sam watched as he tested the weight of it, then he began flipping it over and under each of his fingers. Sam liked watching the smooth way, he moved the coin but he didn't like what it signified.

"For luck?" Sam nodded to Brays hands.

"Sort of. I have two of them. I was… Here. I wanted to give one to you."

After handing one to Sam, Bray took out the matching piece of silver and began threading it through his fingers.

Like Bray had done, Sam tested the weight of it in his hand. He tossed it up and caught it before turning it over and over to look more closely at it. He had no idea what kind of currency it was.

On the front was a woman's likeness. Sam wasn't aware of many nations who put a woman on their currency. The woman wasn't the Queen of England. There was no denomination on the coin. Wondering if it was some type of collector's item, Sam flipped it over. On the back was an embossed image of a honeybee. Circling the bee were words that looked to be Latin, but he had no idea what they said.

Sam used his fingers to press the now-warm metal to his palm. Knowing Bray had two intrigued him. Was this something he shared with his twin? Even knowing it wasn't one of a kind, the coin had to be rare, and he was touched that Bray would let him keep one, even though they both knew there was no future for them.

When Ax pulled through the gates of Kozak and Andreiko's compound, Sam pocketed the coin. He'd received a text from Mase that there had been some fighting, but things were going his way.

Usually mafia had a hierarchy, much like the military, but Kozak's group and Andreiko's group coming together had been a merger of sorts. Jazz had received intel that the groups had been combined at the request of their US partners. Why have two isolated operations that were sometimes duplicating effort? Drugs and human trafficking went hand-in-hand.

One of Kozak's men walked alongside their car, directing them as Ax drove between the buildings at a snail's pace.

"They're going to separate us," Sam told Bray. "Do me a favor and keep your mouth shut. The guy watching you will likely be a total homophobe. He might try to insult you to get you to talk, to instigate a fight."

"I won't talk."

"Other option is, they'll try to seem friendly. Still just keep your mouth shut," Sam said.

"Go for stoic. Got it." Bray smirked.

"This isn't a joke, Bray."

"Sam, I'm not being flip, but I'm scared. I *was* scared when they were bringing me here alone and I wasn't sure you were still here. Now, I know you and Ax have my six, so I feel a little more confident."

"We're still outnumbered at least ten to one."

"I won't talk," Bray said.

He touched Sam's knee when he said it. The gesture had Sam relaxing a fraction, but as soon as Bray was out of view, Sam felt a pinch of stress between his shoulder blades. He had to make an effort not to hurry his stride and try to get this meeting over with.

When he sat at the table across from Andreiko and Kozak, Sam nodded a hello at each of them. Mase stood in the corner of the room, his mouth kicking up for just a second, and Sam felt relieved.

Mase thrived on the adrenaline of close encounters like this. Sam preferred the end of an op and the satisfaction of putting scum like the two men in front of him in jail. He wouldn't cry if a few died either.

Usually Sam enjoyed backing someone into a corner, like he had with Andreiko and Kozak. This time, though, he couldn't enjoy it. He was distracted. He was worried and that pissed him off.

He gave the correct responses and was easily able to drum up some anger when appropriate, but his mind kept drifting to the room a few doors down. Bray had promised not to talk, so why was Sam's gut twisting?

When they finally agreed on a deal, Sam was relieved. And the relief wasn't because he'd negotiated well within the budget. It was because he needed to lay eyes on Bray.

When he opened the door to the room where he'd left Bray and found it empty, his lungs seized. Bray's backpack was sitting on the table but the man himself was nowhere to be seen.

"He's probably just in the john," Ax said from behind him.

Sam turned to see Kozak and Mase sauntering up behind them.

"Where's Bray?"

Mase's eyebrows snapped together in confusion and probably concern as he turned to Kozak and shook his head. Kozak told the guy standing behind Mase to find Fedir.

"You let that homophobe watch him?"

Sam's voice was louder than he'd expected, but the anger burning in his gut had him fisting his hands.

"Sam," Kozak said quietly, "all my men have…reservations."

"Reservations? He told me to my face that I was disgusting. I understand I have to make allowances for your country being in the dark ages, but if one hair on my boyfriend's head has been mussed, I'm going to burn this fucking place to the ground."

Kozak's eyes widened slightly before he schooled his expression. Sam expected a reply about a piece of ass not being worth ruining a deal, but Kozak simply turned to Mase and asked him in Ukrainian to get Andreiko.

When Mase suggested checking the security cameras, Kozak nodded. Sam paced the hallway as they waited. Finally, the guy who'd been sent to find Fedir came back empty-handed. Sam made a noise of disgust as Kozak told him to get others to help him find Fedir and essentially what translated to 'Mr. Wheeler's little pedophile'.

"Let's go to the security room. Mr. Mason will have the videos queued up." Kozak turned and started walking down the hallway.

Ax lagged behind as he leaned over to tie his shoe. When they stopped at a security door, Kozak entered a code. While they waited, Ax sidled up to Sam and gently slid his backup weapon into the waistband of Sam's slacks.

Sam turned and nodded his thanks. Just as Kozak slowed in front of a door, it flew open. Mase hurried out and—ignoring Sam—turned to his 'boss'. He told Kozak that Fedir had carried an unconscious Bray through the compound.

"Where would he take him?" Sam demanded.

Kozak shrugged and shook his head. Mase whispered something about Sergiy and Sam's spine stiffened. *Were Sergiy and Fedir in cahoots?*

"I'm going to find my boyfriend myself." Sam turned and lengthened his stride down the hallway.

"Is this really worth ruining a long-term business relationship?"

Sam turned and looked at Kozak. The lie flowed off his tongue a little too easily.

"He's it for me. You may go through women like people go through tissue, but when I find something special, I hold on to it. Bray's special. He's unique. He's a sweet-hearted optimist. He's smart and loyal, resourceful and tenacious. That's not something you find every day."

Kozak's Adam's apple bobbed. He was probably realizing he was going to lose everything because he'd been stupid enough to trust a bunch of ignorant assholes.

"If he's alive, there might still be hope for our business relationship, especially if you use your resources to find out where the fuck he is."

Kozak nodded. That was all the response Sam had time for as he hurried out of the building. As soon as Ax shut the car door behind him, Sam was dialing for a secure line. When Jazz wasn't available, Sam almost threw his phone across the car until an idea hit him. He pulled up the number that had called him a few days ago.

"Is he in trouble?"

Sam pulled the phone away from his ear and looked at it for a moment.

"Hello? Is this Sin?"

"Let's not waste time on pleasantries if Bray's in trouble. I can't imagine any other reason you'd be calling me."

"Someone named Fedir took him from Kozak's compound while we were in a meeting he couldn't sit in on."

"Does he still have the coin?"

"Coin?" Sam asked as he pulled out the coin Bray had given him.

"Yeah. Was he able to give one to Mase? The other one was either to keep track of you or to keep for himself, depending on what was needed."

"He still has one. He gave one to me. He hasn't had the opportunity to give one to Mase."

"Give me your coordinates so I know which is you and which is Bray?"

Sam had Ax pull over as he gave Sin the address. He heard the click of computer keys being tapped. Within thirty seconds, Sin was spouting off a location.

"But they're on the move," Sin said. "Any idea where they might be headed?"

"No. He might be double-crossing his bosses or he might be working under his boss' orders. I tend to think the former, because Mase should have had a heads-up if it were sanctioned."

"But what if it's Andreiko who's double-crossing?" Ax asked.

The sun was moving toward the western horizon and there was no way Sam was letting Bray spend a night with the likes of Sergiy.

"They're still moving, but I'm going to text you coordinates to move toward. I'm also sending you a link. Download the app. It'll allow you to track Bray's signal for up to seventy-two hours. I'll extend that if needed."

Sam's phone pinged with a message just as Sin stopped talking. It pinged again a moment later.

"When they stop moving, I'll tap into any cameras nearby. Someone needs to call me as soon as you have eyes on him. Bray's going through a hell of a lot of trouble for family who've turned their backs on him."

Sam opened his mouth to demand to know what Sin was talking about, but the line went dead. It didn't take a genius to figure out what he was saying, but he wanted to know how old Bray had been when his family had abandoned him for being gay. Had he been reaching out to Mase for support?

Sam rubbed at the ache between his eyebrows. He did not want to be the one to tell Mase his family was still a bunch of assholes. He also wanted to punch his friend in the face for not returning any of his brother's emails. Bray could have used a big brother.

When the app had finished downloading, Sam opened it. It was a map of Kiev. A blinking 'B' was moving through the city and a solid 'S' was sitting at his coordinates.

Sam quickly got out and looked around before opening the trunk. He pulled out the small bag containing his weapons before jumping into the passenger seat and directing Ax.

Thirty minutes later, they slowly approached a club that was owned by Vladyslav Bagan, Andreiko and Kozak's biggest rival.

"Looks like Sergiy and Fedir went to the darker side," Ax said as he put the car in park.

Sam pulled a ski mask out of his bag of tricks and handed it to Ax. Just as he was getting ready to put it on, his phone pinged. It was a text from Mase.

Right behind you.

A moment later, Mase slipped into the back seat of their car. He had a dark hoodie on that hid his face.

"Mase—"

"Don't fucking say it, Sam. He's my brother."

"We can handle it."

"Kozak sent me to follow you anyway. Andreiko went M-I-A. It seems he's been hiding things from Kozak that I hadn't even picked up on."

"Shit," Sam said.

"What makes you think Bray's in there?" Mase asked.

"His ace in the hole is now helping us track him." Sam showed Mase the app.

Sam's phone pinged again and again and again. Sin sent him the architectural layout of the building. He sent him stills from the video cameras showing Bray was inside…and alive. He flagged the room he thought they'd tucked Bray into. Sam showed the texts to Ax and Mase.

"Who is this fucker and how do we pull him onto the team?" Mase asked.

Sam had been wondering the same thing.

"We need to wait until the club opens," Mase said. "All his men will be distracted by the strippers and there'll be fewer men downstairs."

Sam's muscles twitched to jump out of the car and bust his way in, but Mase was right. After a moment of silence, Sam felt a fist to the back of his shoulder.

"What was all that about Bray being 'it' for you?"

"Did you know your family turned on him for being gay too?"

Sam turned to look at his friend. He expected Mase to be surprised, but there was raw rage in his eyes. "My dad wouldn't make the same mistake again."

"Maybe you should have answered one of his fucking emails."

Mase's jaw ticked, but he didn't say anything for a moment.

"I promised my dad I wouldn't—"

"Fuck your dad. I'm talking about your brother."

"I was stubborn, okay? I took it too far, but I didn't know how to turn back. I told Bray to leave me alone when he first reached out. He did. He left me alone until I got kicked out. Then he started again, but I was too raw, too—"

"I get it. Fuck. But that first time he was probably reaching out because he needed support," Sam said.

"And the second time he was reaching out in case I needed support. I get it, okay? I'm an asshole. I never said I wasn't."

"No one's going to dispute that," Ax said.

All three men huffed out a laugh. For once, Sam was happy that Ax was there to break the tension. The streetlights flicked on and they looked at the clock in the dashboard.

"It's time," Mase said.

Chapter Twenty-Three

Brayden

Bray's head felt like it weighed three hundred pounds. He tried to open his eyes, but they were glued shut. Then the rank odor hit him and his stomach revolted. It smelled like an outhouse.

The last thing he remembered was waiting for Sam, trying to keep his mouth shut. The guy in the room with him had paced like a caged animal. It had made Bray uneasy, but he hadn't asked him to stop.

The guy had paced closer and closer. Bray had just gotten uncomfortable enough to say something. He'd opened his mouth and…nothing. He didn't remember anything after that.

His hands and legs were bound tight with what felt like zip ties. Spreading his ankles, he tested the restraints. Whoever had bound him had been smart enough to put the zip ties directly onto his skin. They'd hurt like a motherfucker, but he could break them if he needed to.

He'd wait to see what they had in store for him first. He didn't want to lacerate his skin in a place that smelled like sewage.

With effort, Bray finally got his eyes to open. He had been tossed onto what was probably the world's most disgusting mattress in the middle of a dark, tiny room. There was a table and chair in the far corner and a lone lightbulb hung from the ceiling with a pull-string dangling from it.

He could feel the pulse of dance music beating through the floor. Was he underneath some dance club? He had no idea where he was or what these people wanted from him.

The door rattled open. Bray closed his eyes and hoped they wouldn't try to beat him awake. If it was Kozak's men who'd taken him, they'd know he had no intel on Sam's dealings.

When the men in the room began speaking English, Bray almost opened his eyes in relief. A man with a French accent thought the plan was ridiculous. Another man assured him the plan would work. A third man confirmed that having Bray would at least get them a meeting with Sam.

"I was promised bait that would have Wheeler on his knees."

"Believe me. Wheeler will grovel over broken glass for this piece of shit. It's his lover."

"Wheeler is gay?" asked the man with the French accent.

"It's disgusting."

"It's interesting. All the women who come through… It's genius. He's completely immune to their wiles."

"Men come through too."

"Mostly boys. And contrary to what you believe, being gay and being a pedophile are not synonymous. He wouldn't touch the women or the boys. So often the inventory gets manhandled before they reach their destination."

"You thinking of trying to hire Sam away from his employer?"

There was a laugh.

"As you've said, Wheeler is a loyal man. We're counting on that by holding his boyfriend. If he's that devoted, I doubt he'll walk away from Bernard for a few extra dollars."

The men moved around the room. They were probably coming around to look at Bray since he was facing away from the door. He tried to even out his breathing and kept his eyes lightly closed.

One of the men mumbled in Ukrainian. Someone else chuckled but said something back that sounded like reluctant chiding. The Frenchman remained quiet for a moment. Bray heard shoes shuffle closer and he had to concentrate all his effort on not tensing his body.

"No one touches him. If Wheeler doesn't want him, I don't care what you do. For now, he's a commodity."

"He deserves—"

"Bagan, if you can't keep your men under control..."

There were harsh Ukrainian words spoken and someone left the room, closing the door with a bang.

"I control my men, Clement. I am completely in charge of my operation, unlike Andreiko."

"I had no plans of pitting you against each other. You can work together, much like Andreiko and Kozak."

"I can handle both sides. I can handle everything."

"And yet Andreiko is the reason we have this opportunity to get information from Wheeler."

"I'll be the one to get the information from him."

"We'll see if your methods are successful."

Bray's breathing kicked up, but it was muffled under the grumbled Ukrainian and the *clip-clap* of feet moving across the concrete floor.

When the door clicked shut, Bray cracked one eye open and listened to see if he had a guard in the room. Hearing nothing but his own breathing, he opened his eyes and looked all around. He even took the chance to twist around and search for anything he might be able to use as a weapon

They were going to torture Sam and they were using him as bait. His arms were bound in front of him, so he tried to pat his pants. He felt coins jingle in his pocket. The sound both relieved him and sent fear coursing through his veins. Sam was sure to find him, and if he didn't, Max would.

His phone wasn't in his pocket and was probably turned off somewhere or ground to bits. This whole thing had turned into a huge mess, and if Sam got hurt, if Mase got hurt, even if Ax got hurt, it would be his fault.

Bray closed his eyes as soon as he heard the door handle a few minutes later. The footsteps he heard sounded a little like the Frenchman's, but the stride was different.

Hands gripped Bray's bound wrists and wrenched him up. He cracked his eyes open as he flew through the air. He landed with a thump onto a wide shoulder. In the distance, he heard someone speaking in Ukrainian.

Were they moving him to try to bait Sam? As relieved as he was to be out of that room, Bray feared the destination he was headed for would be much worse.

If they were taking him to a meeting with Sam, then Max was their only hope. If Max couldn't get a hold of them... Max would think of something—he had to.

Bray kept his eyes slitted open, but the hallway was too dark to see anything. The man carrying him moved sideways. Bray realized he was stepping around something lying on the floor. The beat of the music got louder as he was carried up a flight of stairs. The screech of a heavy door opening on a rusted hinge had cool, fresh air blowing over him. He took a breath and tried to assess the situation.

Everything was dark, but he could make out a car. The streetlights were too far away to help him see anything. The headlights of the car shed light on everything far away, but Bray couldn't make out much up close.

A few long strides over gravel in the back-alley parking lot and Bray was unceremoniously plopped down in the back seat of the car. Everything clicked into place at once. This was his only chance.

Curling up, Bray got all the momentum he could. Spreading his legs, he sucked in a breath at the pain of breaking the zip tie, but he was able to kick out harder with both feet. It was a direct hit to the chest. The guy stumbled back but didn't fall. Bray slammed the door shut and locked himself in as he threw his body over the console and into the driver's seat.

His hands were still bound, but with his legs free, he could easily drive. Bray struggled to get the car in drive. He crouched low in case they shot out the windows. Just as he changed the gear, he heard someone yelling.

The car lurched forward, because with the pain in his ankles, he hadn't had enough pressure on the brake.

Nothing would stop him now. As he lifted his foot, someone stepped in front of the car.

He was just getting ready to run the guy over when he pulled back his hood enough for the headlights to illuminate his face. It was Mase. Bray slammed his foot on the brake and moved his bound hands back to the gear shift. He fumbled as he tried to get the car back in park.

Mase walked around and tapped on the window. With shaking fingers, Bray pressed the unlock button. He was confused and scared about what exactly was happening, but he was trusting his brother.

"Scoot over," Mase ordered as soon as the door was open.

Bray scrambled into the passenger seat. Before he was fully over, Mase was in the driver's seat with the door shut and his foot pressing on the gas.

"What's going on?"

His voice sounded hoarse and rusty. He hadn't actually spoken with his brother since he was nine years old. So many emotions and questions bubbled up now that they were actually alone together. In person.

"All hell's breaking loose. Ruslan Andreiko's nowhere to be found, which is a surprise to me, and I was his second-in-command. Then you end up in the hands of their competition, Vladyslav Bagan. Kozak's going insane because he doesn't know who he can trust. I'm waiting on orders as to who I'm supposed to remain loyal to. So, yeah. Total shit-storm."

Before Bray could respond, Mase pulled over to the side of the road.

"Get out," Mase ordered. "We're changing cars."

Bray got out and as soon as he stood up, Ax was there with a knife. He cut the binding off Bray's wrists and patted him on the shoulder a few times before turning him toward a different car…Sam's car.

"Was that your car?" Bray asked Mase.

"No. I stole it. Didn't want Bagan to know who rolled up and took his prize, just in case I end up having to work with him."

Mase got into the front seat with Ax and started giving him directions. Bray slipped into the back. Sam cast a glance in his direction, but his whole body was stiff as a board.

"I'm sorry I kicked you, Mase. I didn't know it was you. I thought—"

"It wasn't Mase you kicked, kiddo. It was Sam," Ax said.

Bray turned his horrified face to Sam, who gave him a side eye with a dash of raised eyebrow.

"Don't sweat it, kid," Sam said. "You might have gotten away if they'd been short on men and had left the motor running and the driver's seat empty."

"I could've gotten the car started. Might have been able to kick the driver out too," Bray said.

He wasn't sure any of it was true, but he wanted to impress his brother. Ax snorted as he turned the car around another corner. At the next stoplight, he looked over his shoulder at Bray.

"You got balls, kid. I like that about you."

Bray smiled. He was a little dizzy and nauseated. His ankles hurt like hell, but he felt good—like he was one of the guys, like he'd accomplished a goal. Technically, he had. He was going to get the chance to talk to Mase.

Chapter Twenty-Four

Sam

Sam's thoughts were an absolute mess and this was exactly when they needed to be crystal clear. He was livid. He was elated. He was scared and yet relieved. The jumble of emotions lay at exactly one person's feet.

And yet Bray sat there oblivious to the turmoil as he joked with Ax about what had just gone down. If that had been any of Bagan or Andreiko's men, they would have sent a few bullets through the window as soon as Bray had slammed that door shut.

Sam's phone buzzed in his hand and he finally felt a little bit of calm move through him. With a quick shush to the car at large, he answered the phone. He heard the clicking and entered his code.

"Sam, what the fuck is going on?" Jazz asked.

"We need a safe house in Kiev and we need it *now*."

"Give me an hour."

"What's going down is bigger than us—or me, rather. I think it has a lot to do with you. I think

Andreiko and Kozak have had a falling out over my ultimatum."

"That's not necessarily a bad thing," Jazz said.

"Ax saw Andreiko in a club owned by Vladyslav Bagan. Clement's here as well."

"Clement's in Kiev?"

"I saw him myself."

"Sam, he never handles anything himself. He's getting nervous."

"They were going to use me," Bray said.

Sam turned to him. He looked at him full-on for the first time since he'd picked him up off that filthy, stained mattress. He'd wanted to fall to his knees in relief and he'd also wanted to beat Bray's ass for putting himself at risk with his crazy plan in the first place. Neither had been an option, so he'd thrown the kid over his shoulder and lit out of there.

"Use you for what?" Mase asked.

"To get Sam to talk. Three men came into the room. I was pretending be out. One of them said he was going to get information out of you. They didn't think you'd betray your employer for more money, so they were going to use me to try to get intel."

"Who do you want Mase to declare loyalty to?" Sam asked.

"Can you take out Andreiko?" Jazz asked.

Sam licked his lips. He wanted to torture that motherfucker for taking Bray.

"Of course."

"You, Sam. I can't risk Mase, and with your cover, you have reason for retribution if he was planning on using Bray to get to you."

"It'll be me," Sam said. "So Mase sticks with Kozak?"

"If this is the way it splits, we stick with Kozak. Get Andreiko out of the way. He was probably going to roll over on Kozak somehow and either run the whole operation himself or pass the narcotics side to Bagan."

"What about Bagan?" Sam asked.

"I have no orders for Bagan. That's at your discretion. I'll contact you with an address for a safe house within the hour."

The line went dead. Killing Andreiko and Bagan would ease his conscience. Two fewer people in the world who might go after Bray to get to him. It was the exact reason that relationships were a liability.

"You stick with Kozak," Sam told Mase.

"Ten-four. Figured that would be it if Andreiko's in cahoots with Clement."

"How are we on gas?" Sam asked Ax. "We'll drive around for an hour until we get an address."

"I have someplace safe for an hour," Mase said. "Then I'll get rid of this car for you."

"Where do you have that's safe?"

"I know someone."

After ten minutes of driving, Mase directed Ax to pull into an underground parking garage. He led them to an elevator and finally to a door, where he knocked.

A small, attractive woman opened the door. She seemed glad to see Mase, but her face pinched with worry when she saw the rest of them. She shook her head at Mase.

"Yulia," Mase said as he placed his hand on the door to keep it open when she tried to close it.

He whispered in Ukrainian that his friends needed help, that they were in trouble, that they were like her brother. He promised it would just be for an hour until they could find a safer place.

When Mase said the word 'brother', Yulia's gaze had flicked over his shoulder to look at the three of them. They all waited in limbo while she made up her mind.

After what seemed like an eternity, Yulia nodded and pulled the door open enough for them to enter. The apartment was small and utilitarian. There were two doors down a short hallway that presumably led to a bedroom and a bathroom.

Mase excused himself and Yulia down the hallway. Sam was sure they were trying to be quiet, but he could hear every whisper-yelled word.

"What's going on?" Bray whispered it to Ax as they sat on the small sofa.

"She's pissed he brought us here. No one's supposed to know they know each other. He thinks that's the reason we'll be safe here."

"Is she…an informant?"

"No," Sam answered.

"Mase knew her brother. He's gay, so he had a rough time of it," Ax said.

They all remained quiet after that, but the argument didn't last much longer. Yulia said she didn't have much choice after what he'd done for her brother. Mase told her that the men in the living room were like brothers to him.

Sam knew Mase couldn't exactly claim Bray as his real brother. Even though they'd smuggled Yulia's brother Kyrylo out of Ukraine, that didn't mean they could fully trust her. There was also the fact that Bray didn't understand Ukrainian and had no idea what was being said.

And still, Sam felt anger surge on Bray's behalf. The kid had jumped in with both feet. He'd risked everything, including his own life, to find his brother, a brother who wouldn't claim him.

Bray was rubbing at his ankles through his pants. With a resigned sigh, Sam gave in to the urge to make sure he was all right.

He walked fully into the living room and sat on the coffee table in front of Bray. Reaching down, Sam pulled Bray's feet up onto his knees and lifted the cuffs of his slacks. Each of Bray's ankles had an angry red strip of flesh along the outside. The zip tie that had been binding his legs had cut into his skin and left it welted and bleeding.

He knew better. He should have cut the zip ties before he picked him up, but he'd been in such a rush to get Bray off that filthy mattress. He hadn't wanted anyone to stop him or to risk having to use Bray's body as a shield for any gunfire.

When Mase and Yulia came back into the living room, Sam asked if she had a first-aid kit. Yulia's eyes widened in horror when she saw Bray's ankles and she hurried down the hall.

"I have to get back," Mase said.

"Do you have to leave right now?" Bray pulled his ankles from Sam's lap and stood.

"I can't be gone too long."

"But we just... I need to talk to you." Bray looked over his shoulder at Sam and Ax.

Sam would be willing to give the brothers the moment of privacy Bray seemed to need, but there was no place for him and Ax to go.

"If I don't go back now, they won't believe anything I say. I have to get back before they find out what went down at Bagan's club."

Bray nodded. He hesitated before throwing himself into his brother's arms. Mase stood there stiff for a moment, his arms outstretched like he wasn't quite sure what to do with them. He blinked a few times before finally closing his arms around Bray's back. The two brothers squeezed each other closer before finally letting go.

"I'll tell Kozak I lost you," Mase said as he headed for the door. "If Andreiko's taking his walking papers, Kozak will be even more desperate for your business."

Sam nodded.

Yulia came back into the living room with a first-aid kit just as Mase was closing the front door. Bray stood there for a moment, watching the door as if he was worried Mase had been a figment of his imagination.

"Bray," Sam said after a moment, "come sit down. I need to look at your ankles."

Sam thought maybe Bray hadn't heard him, because he didn't move right away. Finally, he turned and walked back to the sofa. He plopped down next to Ax and laid his head back on the cushion.

Sam reached his hand out to Yulia, who stepped forward and handed him the little box she'd been holding to her chest. Giving her a quiet 'thank you', he popped open the large plastic container and dug through the contents for what he needed.

"It's not that I didn't want to help," she said as Sam cleaned Bray's wounds.

"We get it," Sam assured her. "And we do appreciate the respite."

Yulia opened her mouth to respond, but Sam's phone rang, cutting her off. He picked up and entered his code when he heard the clicking.

"Go," Sam said as he signaled to Ax. Ax handed Sam a small notepad and pen from the interior pocket of his jacket.

Jazz gave him an address. Sam scribbled it down and handed it to Ax before updating Jazz on their situation. Things were tenuous, but Jazz didn't seem too concerned.

"We should have a secure flight out for Brayden within twenty-four hours. Will you be good to go to Thailand or do we need to delay?"

"I'll be good to go," Sam said.

The line disconnected. If he were smart, he would be at the safe house just long enough to drop off Bray and Ax and change his clothes. But Sam wasn't smart.

He set his phone on the table and returned his attention to Bray's torn skin. Even as the need for retribution bubbled up inside him, Sam knew he'd remain with Bray. He would delay his mission to have a few more moments. That made him very, very stupid.

Chapter Twenty-Five

Brayden

The safe house wasn't actually a house. Technically, it was a warehouse, but it was secure. Walls of thick concrete brick, all-metal doors and a top-of-the-line security system definitely made it safe. There was an apartment in a corner of the upper floor that seemed to hang from the ceiling three stories high.

The space had at one point been the office of some type of manufacturing plant, allowing management to have a view of the entire operation. It was like being in a bird's nest. There was a wall of windows that gave a view of the empty space below.

A silver car, the car Ax had boosted, sat alone in the center of the concrete floor. The only downside to the place was all the stairs. Bray's ankles were sore, and climbing all those steps had felt like someone was trying to saw off his feet.

The apartment was unadorned but spacious. There were two bedrooms and a security room that housed multiple monitors showing feeds from cameras around the perimeter.

Yulia, relieved they would be leaving sooner rather than later, had agreed to do a little shopping for them. By the time she'd returned from the store, Ax had come back with the silver car.

Bray was tasked with keeping his feet elevated as Ax set up the security room and Sam put away the groceries. His mind was running in circles. Had Mase been giving him the brush off? He'd hesitated to hug Bray back, but then he'd squeezed so tight that Bray couldn't breathe.

"Can I borrow your phone?" Bray asked.

Sam shot him a look over his shoulder as he put a carton of milk in the fridge.

"I just want to call Sin."

"Fuck," Sam said and swung around. "I promised him you'd call. He's the reason we found you so fast. He tracked your coin. Hang on." Sam went into the security room.

Bray took in a shuttered breath. He wasn't sure how he felt about Sam knowing the coins were tracking devices, especially since he'd given one to Sam.

After a moment, Sam came back out of the security room with a phone. He turned it on and pressed a few buttons before handing it to Bray.

"It's a burner. Keep it until we get everything sorted out."

Sam returned to the kitchen and resumed putting the groceries away. When Bray looked at the phone, he saw that both Sam's and Ax's phone numbers were now programmed in. He dialed Max's number.

"Sin City," Max answered.

"That's the worst one yet," Bray said but couldn't hold back a smile.

"Bray. Oh thank fuck. Are you okay?"

"Yeah. Sam found me. Thanks."

"It wasn't a big deal," Max said.

"It was to me. It was a huge deal. I don't know what I'd do if you didn't have my back."

"You've always had mine too. Anytime you need help…"

"I still do."

"Still do what? Need help?"

"Exactly," Bray said. "This will be my number until we figure out what happened to my phone."

"Got it. What do you need help with? Want me to track your phone?"

"I'll talk to you later, okay? I just wanted you to know I'm safe."

"Aah, you don't want your new bodyguard to know what you're up to. I get it."

"You always do, Sin. You always do. Talk to you later."

"Text me what you need if you can't get any privacy," Max suggested.

"Okay. Bye."

Bray leaned back on the sofa and put his feet up on the box he'd been using as an ottoman. Now that everything was put away, Sam took out a few pots and started boiling some water.

"What do you still do with Sin?"

Bray turned to find Sam looking at him over the kitchen island. The kitchen, living room and dining room were essentially just different corners of the same great room. There was one bedroom on the east side of the great room and one on the west side. Since they didn't have bags to unpack, they hadn't discussed sleeping arrangements.

"What?"

"You told him you still do."

"Oh, have his back."

"Does he need someone to watch his six?" Sam asked.

"Don't we all?"

Sam grunted and turned back to the stove. Bray considered texting Max now, but didn't want to risk Sam asking him what he was doing or, worse, walking up and seeing what he was doing.

"Seems like a smart kid," Sam said.

"He's a genius. He tends to overstep boundaries, but sometimes I'm glad when he does, like when he pressed those coins into my hand before I got on the flight here."

"Where did he find those?"

"He made them."

Sam took the coin out of his pocket and looked at it. He flipped it up in the air and caught it. Then, he laid it on his fingertip as if he were weighing it.

"It's pretty amazing. Has the weight of a coin, the metal feel of a coin. It's perfectly balanced like a coin. He can just…make more?"

Bray nodded.

"Nice to have someone like that in your corner."

"Obviously. I wish I could say this is the first time he's literally saved my life, but it's not. Doubt it'll be the last either."

Sam lowered his eyebrows in a severe scowl. He stepped out from behind the kitchen counter and made his way over to the sofa.

"What other crazy shit are you planning?" Sam demanded

"Nothing. But being in the army isn't exactly a walk in the park."

"Sin's in the army with you?"

"Not technically. But he always has the best intel."

Sam shook his head and made a disapproving hum as he turned back to the kitchen. Bray got up and told Sam he was heading to the bathroom. With the door closed and locked, Bray pulled the phone out of his pocket.

I got the tracker in Mase's pocket.

You talked to him?

I saw him, but there was no time to talk. I'm hoping you'll be able to help me find him when I'm able to.

Good thing you told me. I gave Sam ability to track that signal for seventy-two hours. I'll change his access now.

Has he opened the app?

Not since his location first matched up to yours.

Bray let out a breath of relief. The last thing he needed was for Sam to plop him onto a plane home, which was exactly what he'd do if he found out that Bray still had every intention of talking to his brother.

Keep an eye on him. Make sure he's safe.

After a moment Bray added one last request.

Make sure they're both safe.

Max's only response was a thumbs-up emoji. It still gave Bray some relief. He wasn't sure how long the coins would send a signal before their power source died, but he liked knowing that both Mase and Sam had someone looking out for them.

Bray deleted all the messages to and from Max. The phone was a burner—no way was Sam aware of what he'd just done. Still, his adrenaline spiked when there was knock on the door.

"Dinner'll be ready in ten," Sam said.

Bray let out a slow breath and closed his eyes. He was shaky and little lightheaded. He needed food and sleep. He hoped he wouldn't be getting much of the second, though, even if he needed it.

Dinner was a much more low-key event than it had been the past few nights. Sam had made a simple pasta with chicken and a cream sauce.

"Mm-m. I love it when you're on KP, Magnum," Ax said as he helped himself to seconds.

"It's really good. Thank you," Bray added.

Sam smirked at how much Ax was loading onto his plate before giving Bray a nod of acknowledgment. Things seemed a little awkward between them.

Bray imagined it was because they no longer needed to play the role of boyfriends. He missed their banter. Even if it hadn't been easy, it had felt more real than this stilted silence between them.

"Well, since you had KP, I have night watch. Thanks for the grub." Ax lifted his full plate in thanks as he stood from the table.

The silence when Ax left the room seemed to grow. Bray shoveled a few more bites into his mouth, but his appetite quickly disappeared. If Ax was going to be watching the security cameras all night, that left both bedrooms open.

Chapter Twenty-Six

Sam

Sam knew what he had to do in the morning. Hell, not even morning…in a few short hours. It was a little past midnight—not the best time to eat, but none of them had been able to have dinner since Bray had been taken.

As soon as Ax left the room, Bray had gone silent. He'd stopped eating and just used his fork to make strange designs with the noodles on his plate.

He seemed so relaxed and easy with Ax, yet so tense with Sam. Did he want to be told what do to? Did he need that? He shouldn't.

They didn't need to pretend to be lovers anymore. If he was going to explain himself to Mase, he could almost excuse what had happened in the hotel, but if anything happened tonight, there was no hiding behind the op. This was simply him not being able to resist having a little more time wrapped up in Bray's body.

Sam's dick twitched under the table at the thought of one more night of play. They'd thought last night would be it. He planned on taking advantage of the few extra hours as long as Bray was willing.

"Tell me," Sam said.

Bray looked up at him. He lifted his eyebrows as if Sam was going to tack more onto that sentence.

"Tell you what?"

"Tell me which bed you want to sleep in tonight. Tell me if you still want me to take charge. Tell me what you want."

"Please, take charge." Bray sighed.

Sam had to lift his hips a little to adjust as any extra room in his slacks disappeared. Raw images of all the things he wanted to do to Bray flashed through his mind. He knew he'd have to narrow in on one, but it would be a tough choice.

"We'll continue to use the color scale—green, yellow, red."

Bray nodded.

"If you're finished, clean off your plate and put it in the dishwasher. Then I want you to pick a bedroom. I don't care which one. Strip down, lie on the bed and wait for me."

Bray stood so quickly from the table that his chair tipped back and fell on the floor. That comforted Sam a little. Maybe Bray wanted him almost as much as he wanted Bray. *One last time.* And it would be one. He had one rubber in his wallet, and it wasn't like he could have added condoms to the list he'd given to Yulia.

After righting his chair, Bray emptied his plate into the trash, rinsed his dish and put it in the dishwasher. He chose the room on the east side of the apartment, the one farthest from the security room. Sam smiled as he stood to clean the kitchen. That also happened to be the room with the en suite bathroom.

Sam took his time cleaning the kitchen. The anticipation would turn Bray's crank, but he didn't want to make him wait long enough that he started to doubt his appeal. Bray was irresistible, and the fact that Sam was giving up precious hours of sleep to spend a few last moments with him just proved that.

"Fuck."

The word burst from Sam unwittingly when he entered the bedroom to find that Bray had pulled his knees to his chest and spread himself as Sam had asked him to the first night. The position was so vulnerable and so fucking sexy that Sam stumbled over himself to get naked.

"I only have one rubber," Sam said as he dug it out of his wallet, along with a packet of lube.

Bray nodded.

They were both hard and leaking. Sam wasn't usually this excited after he'd already taken someone.

Maybe it was because Bray was forbidden, the brother of his best friend. Maybe it was that they had been on borrowed time since the beginning. Maybe it was because Sam hadn't expected a softhearted kid like Bray to get off on being dominated. Maybe it was simply because Bray was sweeter than chocolate and Sam had always had a sweet tooth.

"I don't think anyone could resist such a sexy temptation."

Sam ran the pad of his thumb over Bray's pucker. Bray groaned and writhed on the bed.

"If we had more time, I'd take you to the edge so many times you'd beg me for relief. When I finally let you come, you'd fly."

"Please," Bray begged.

"We don't have time for that right now." *Or ever.* Sam shook that thought from his mind, because it was simply too depressing to think of Bray exploring this new side of himself with someone else.

"Because we're short on time," Sam continued, "I'm going to let you choose. What will send you flying? Do you want my tongue inside you? Do you want me to spank you? Do you want something new?"

"I want it all."

"Something new then," Sam decided. "I'll be right back."

Sam took a fresh pillowcase from the cabinet near the bathroom and blindfolded Bray. He went to the bathroom and the kitchen to find things he needed.

Bray was exactly as Sam had left him. The sight not only turned Sam on but released something in his chest. Bray wanted this. A part of him had worried Bray was just putting on a show for the listening devices in the hotel room. But here he was begging for more. It made him wish this night could last forever.

Sam took the new toothbrush he'd pulled out of the cabinet in the bathroom and opened it. Bray's head tilted to the side as he listened.

"Hold still. Don't move. I won't hurt you, but I want you to pay attention to the sensations."

Bray gave a nod and relaxed his head back onto the pillow. Sam laid the toothbrush on the mattress by Bray's hip. He wished he had his own things to use. In truth, even if they'd been in Sam's apartment, he'd be scrounging a little. He'd barely had time to find a hook-up here or there to scratch his itch and his collection of toys was pitifully small.

He hadn't played like this in years and he didn't remember it being quite this exciting. He'd taken some training, done some scenes in D/s clubs, but he'd never had his own partner to play with, to explore with.

Pulling the wrapping off a new feather duster, Sam tossed it on the bed as well. And finally, a metal dental pick. More than anything, he'd love to add a vibrating dildo to his array, but they didn't provide those in a safe house.

Sam used the toothbrush first. He tried not to put any weight on the bed so Bray wouldn't know what was coming. He knelt on the floor between Bray's spread legs, reached up and gently brushed over Bray's balls.

Bray's gasp echoed in the empty room. His erection bobbed up and down and his hips twitched.

"No moving," Sam said as he swatted Bray's ass.

Bray groaned but tried to remain still. His erection bobbed again, but Bray couldn't control that if he wanted to. Sam pulled back then leaned forward and brushed over Bray's hole.

"Holy fuck. What *is* that?"

"Shh-h," Sam chided.

The door was locked, but he didn't want to bring Ax out of the security room. This place did not have the sound blocking that the high-end hotel had boasted.

Bray's muscles were tight as he awaited the next touch. Sam gently laid the toothbrush down and picked up the duster. Plucking out one feather, he gently ran it up the underside of Bray's cock.

"Oh God," Bray groaned.

His dick bounced up and down in excitement and he clenched his ass cheeks, his hips lifting slightly up off the bed. Sam knew he was close, but he spanked him anyway. He gave him three on each ass cheek for the disobedience.

Bray growled and shot all over his chest on the fifth slap. Sam smiled and still continued on with the sixth. Bray's abs spasmed and more semen shot from his cock. Sam was elated that he'd made Bray come without so much as a finger on his dick. He was also disappointed he hadn't gotten to the third sensation of the cold, hard metal.

Bray's spent cock deflated a little and lay gently along his belly. Sam leaned forward and licked it from base to tip. He felt it jitter under his tongue and Bray spouted some unintelligible gibberish before ripping away his blindfold and watching Sam clean him off.

Sam licked the jizz off Bray's abs and worked his way up to his chest. Bray started to harden again.

Oh, to be young and horny, he thought.

When he licked Bray's nipple, it beaded up and Bray's breaths began to come out in pants. Sam gently bit down and pulled. Bray puffed out a breath and Sam felt Bray's cock pulse against his ribs.

"Please," Bray begged.

"Do you think I can make you come just from nipple play?" Sam asked.

"I…I want to play too. This is the last… Please."

Sam knew what he'd cut himself off from saying, and he wanted to give Bray something, something neither of them would ever forget.

"What do you want? Tell me?"

"I want to taste you like you tasted me."

Sam's first instinct was to roar a big fat 'no'. But his mouth didn't open and he found himself contemplating something he had promised he would never allow again—his own vulnerability. Bray was so gentle, so sweet. Could he trust him enough to open up like that?

"Never mind. Just please fuck me. I don't—"

Sam placed a finger over Bray's lips to quiet him while he tried to make sense of the chaos in his brain. When he thought about Bray's face in his ass, his hole twitched—but not in fear, in excitement. Sam swallowed thickly and pulled back to look at Bray.

"I didn't mean to ruin this," Bray said when Sam lifted his hand.

"You didn't ruin anything. I told you to ask for what you wanted and you did. That's exactly what I expect of you."

Bray nodded but looked pointedly at Sam's flaccid dick.

"I'll be right back," Sam said before escaping to the bathroom.

After turning on the hot water, he leaned forward over the sink. Sam took a good, long look at himself. *Am I really ready to do this?*

Sam wet his hand and reached back to touch his own pucker. He hadn't even done that in all these years, except for a cursory scrub in the shower. He was surprised when his first thought was to wonder how Bray's tongue would feel there. The dark memories were there under the surface, but they weren't choking him.

He found himself wanting to give Bray this first as well. The first time Bray had both received and given a rim job. *You never forget your first.* And though Bray technically wasn't Sam's first, he was Sam's first…well, his first everything anal since he'd figured out he had to be in control in the bedroom in order to have any kind of sex.

He used the water to clean himself up as best he could without a shower. Then he washed his hands and stepped back into the bedroom.

Bray lay back on the bed, worry causing his lips to pinch into a frown. When Sam sat on the bed and smiled, Bray smiled back.

"It—" Sam's voice cracked and he had to clear his throat before he could continue. "It's been a long time since I've bottomed in any sense of the word. If we do this, I'll be the one using the color scale and we'll be starting on yellow."

Chapter Twenty-Seven

Brayden

Bray felt a weight drop onto his shoulders when Sam said 'yellow'. He had a feeling Sam was giving him something very private, very special as a goodbye present.

Bray's chest puffed up a little with pride that Sam would trust him with something that was so obviously hard for him. He was also scared to death he'd fuck it up, since he'd never done it before.

He considered backing out and coming up with an alternative, but then he looked at Sam. His eyes were clear, but there was apprehension there. He guessed that was what 'yellow' meant.

Bray would do his best to try to make it good. Sam needed control and Bray thought of a way to give it to him.

"I'll lie down," Bray said. "You can kneel over my—"

"B, you've never done this before. Having someone sit on your face is a little intimidating."

"I like when you control things. It…it does it for me. I don't want this to be any different."

Something inside him surged at the look of relief in Sam's eyes as he nodded. It took Sam a minute to situate himself facing the foot of the bed. Bray lay back and enjoyed the view. He liked looking at asses—he was gay, after all—but he'd never been so close to someone's hole before. Sam's pucker was more of a raspberry color and Bray's mouth watered to find out what it tasted like.

Sam knelt back, placing himself inches from Bray's face. He felt Sam's hands on his hips as he steadied himself. Gently, Bray began to caress Sam's cheeks and slowly pull them apart just to get a better look.

"God, I can't wait to see what you taste like." Bray groaned.

It gave him hope when Sam didn't say 'red'. His cock throbbed a little when he saw that his words actually had Sam's hole twitching. When he leaned up, Bray felt Sam's fingers dig into his hips, but he couldn't bring himself to stop.

Wanting to take it slowly, he leaned forward and just touched the tip of his tongue to the very center of Sam's opening. Sam gasped but didn't warn him off, so he licked again, this time more firmly. Sam flexed his ass muscles and shot back his hips a little, seeking more.

Bray smiled as much as he could with his tongue all the way out. The taste was foreign. It was more tangy and bitter than semen, but he didn't mind it at all, especially if he could make Sam lose control.

Flattening his tongue, Bray laved at Sam's pucker. Sam controlled the pressure but Bray wiggled his tongue randomly, causing Sam to groan. Eventually, the muscled ring began to loosen. Bray felt it flutter open a little, so he pointed his tongue when Sam rocked forward. On his backward thrust, Bray's tongue breached him.

Bray's balls drew up tight as he heard a noise he hadn't even been sure Sam was capable of making, a whimper. For a second, Bray worried it might be a sound of distress, but on the next pass, Sam pushed back even harder. Bray's tongue pressed inside and he chanced a little flick of his tip.

Sam gasped and pushed back again. Bray pulled Sam's cheeks even farther apart and pressed himself forward. He'd meant to let Sam take charge, but he also wanted Sam to lose that tightly held control.

Sam's thrusts became fast and erratic. Bray wondered if he could make Sam come by pressing his prostate. On the next press back, Bray pushed his fingertip in along with his tongue.

"Red," Sam said and pulled away.

Bray scrambled up and grabbed Sam's wrist. Sam pulled himself free and rushed back to the bathroom. Bray sank back onto the bed and put his head in his hands. This was not how he wanted his time with Sam to end.

When the bathroom door clicked open a moment later, Bray's head shot up. Sam stood there. The light was at his back, so Bray couldn't see his expression.

"I'm sorry. I just wanted—"

"It's not you," Sam interrupted.

Bray knew this had to do with something in Sam's past, but he couldn't help but berate himself for pushing too hard. He really didn't want Sam's last memory of him to be wrapped up with fear and regret.

"I pushed too far," Bray said.

"I pushed your limits and you pushed mine. It's only fair. That's what a safe word is for. You stopped right away. That's perfect. I just… I needed a moment. I shouldn't have left without telling you what was going on. That wasn't fair."

"I understand," Bray said.

"Do you? Because I don't always understand myself."

He was surprised by Sam's honesty. The last thing he wanted was to overstep and make Sam close off again. Bray licked his lips.

"I don't always understand myself either. I mean, I've never done the things I've done with you." Bray circled his hands helplessly between the two of them.

He couldn't bring himself to put a name to it. Maybe if they were building a relationship, he'd be able to find the words, but he just couldn't seem to spit them out.

"So I gathered," Sam said with a small smirk.

"I'm sorry I made you uncomfortable. I knew you didn't like your ass touched."

"It's not… I don't… It's something I thought I'd worked through."

Bray nodded but didn't call Sam out. It seemed like Sam's way of working through his issue was making sure his lovers couldn't really reach his ass. Mentioning that would ruin the little time they had left together.

"Still, I'm sorry I broke the mood."

"B, you're naked in my bed. If you're still up for it, just spread yourself out and I can get it up."

Bray's ears went hot at the compliment. He had to keep in shape because, well, it was literally part of his job, but the husky way Sam had said that made him feel so fucking sexy.

Spreading out on the bed, Bray arched his back and stretched. He was still naked, though his erection had waned. They'd only known each other a few days, yet Bray had never felt as free and as safe as he did in Sam's bed, in Sam's arms. It was a heady feeling and something he would really mourn the loss of.

"Besides," Sam said as he ran his hand from Bray's chest to his growing erection, "I'm the one who broke the mood."

Sam gave Bray's dick a tight squeeze that had him humping up into his hand. When Bray opened his eyes, he found Sam watching his face rather than his cock, and for some reason, that made him even harder.

"I wish we had time so I could edge you. You're so responsive, and your face is like an open book. It's fucking gorgeous to watch as everything plays out."

Bray had to bite down on his bottom lip to keep from offering Sam more time—or his bed whenever Sam was Stateside. It would never work, especially if Bray re-upped for another tour.

Sam squeezed him again then did some sort of twist thing with his hand that had a shout leaving Bray's lungs before he even realized it. Bray watched in fascination as Sam's erection stiffened and grew.

"What do you want?" Bray asked.

"A few more hours. But since that's not possible, I want to lose myself in your sweet ass one more time."

Bray nodded and pulled his legs up. He was pretty sure Sam would have preferred doggy style, but Bray wanted to watch any play of emotions across Sam's face and he definitely wanted to see Sam let go.

Luckily, Sam didn't complain. He simply tore open the packet of lube. Sam rubbed it between his fingers to try to warm it before smoothing it over Bray's opening.

Having Sam slowly and patiently stretch him was its own sweet torture. By the time Sam had two fingers scissoring inside him, Bray was already on edge.

"Not yet," Sam said when Bray reached for himself. "That cock is *mine*."

Those last four words pushed Bray even further toward the edge. How could Sam be so distant then so gentle and thorough— caring even—when they were naked together?

It wasn't until he heard the tearing of foil and opened his eyes to watch Sam roll the condom on that Bray realized he'd closed his eyes. Sam hadn't scolded him, but then Sam's gaze was locked on Bray's ass.

When the tip of Sam's cock touched his opening, Bray made an effort to keep his eyes open and on Sam's face. His nostrils flared. His lids fluttered and his eyes rolled back a little when he breached Bray's ring of muscle. Sam had prepped him so well that there was barely any sting.

The muscles of Sam's pecs danced as he slowly inched forward. When his balls finally pressed against Bray's ass, they both took a breath. Sam looked down to watch where they were joined as he pulled quickly back out then pressed slowly back in.

He used his hands to hold Bray's legs open. When his thumbs began gently caressing Bray's inner thighs, Bray lifted his gaze from Sam's chest to his face. The sweetness in the move had Bray's heart thumping even harder.

"What are you thinking?" Bray blurted.

Sam looked up at Bray's face. There was tenderness in his gaze, but he didn't speak. Sam's Adam's apple bobbed then the tenderness was gone.

"You're so fucking tight," Sam finally said.

It almost sounded like Sam said, "You're so fucking *right*," but Bray shook that idea out of his head. Bray wouldn't fool himself into thinking this was more than it was.

Then Sam pulled back and slammed home, scattering all Bray's maudlin thoughts like a firecracker exploding. All that was left was the feeling of Sam gliding in and out of him at the perfect tempo.

Sam explored Bray's body, from flicking his nipples to pressing two fingers into that spot just behind his balls. All of it had Bray gritting his teeth to make it last, even as Sam hurtled him toward the edge of ecstasy.

"I'm close," Sam said between gritted teeth.

Was he trying to make it last as well? That thought had Bray watching him more closely. Sam's gaze met Bray's and they both hung there for a moment, watching each other. Without breaking eye contact, Sam reached down and started stroking Bray's cock in time with his thrusts.

That was all it took…a few hard tugs. Bray did his damndest to keep his eyes open, even as the edges of his vision went dark. His muscles seized and his back arched. The pleasure was so powerful that electricity flowed through his body.

Bray's vision cleared just in time to watch Sam thrust in to the hilt and growl out his release. He wished in that moment that there weren't the barrier of the condom between them. He knew his ass would be sore, but he also wished Sam could have left something of himself, something deep inside.

Bray closed his eyes against the thought. It had been four days. No way was he letting himself fall for the surly, loyal man—the man who'd saved him when he could have walked away, twice, the man who even now was closing off from him.

Chapter Twenty-Eight

Sam

By the time Sam had Bray cleaned up, he was snuggling into the blankets like a milk-drunk kitten. The kid was so fucking cute and sweet that it should have made Sam's teeth ache. All it did was make his balls ache.

Being inside Bray was something he'd remember for years, maybe even for the rest of his life. The kid was so open to experimenting. So many people were afraid to try something new, even if it intrigued them. Bray jumped in with both feet. It was a quality Sam found pretty damn irresistible.

Sam stood with his back against the wall. After a moment, he looked at his watch. He'd been watching Bray sleep for a good thirty minutes. He'd allow himself five more minutes before he had to walk away for good.

He scrubbed his hands over his face. Telling Bray he'd dealt with his past wasn't an outright lie. He'd talked to a therapist for a few years. She'd specialized in shit like that. She'd been gentle at first, then frank and honest. She'd even offered to refer him to some type of sex surrogate.

For years, Sam had been determined to get every fucking inch of himself back. He'd pushed through college in three years so he could start the next Chapter of his life as quickly as possible.

But it wasn't like he could be open about his sexuality. Being in the army was worse than ROTC. Don't Ask Don't Tell hadn't ended until 2011, and by then, Sam had already been in the military, keeping his mouth shut, for years.

After boot camp, he hadn't bothered to find another therapist. He'd thought he'd made peace with the past, even if he couldn't stand the thought of bottoming anymore.

He'd thought the part of him that had loved ass play had shriveled up and died—until Bray had asked to tongue his hole. Sam's cock pulsed to life at the memory.

When the surprising and foreign sensation of Bray's finger had been added to the mix, it had been too much. There had just been a flash of muscle memory, but Sam hadn't wanted to associate any of that into his memories of this short time with Bray. So he'd run—just for a minute, but he'd run.

Sam made a disgusted noise and looked at his watch again. It had been eight minutes. He'd already stayed too long. He reached out to run his fingers through Bray's soft hair one more time but curled his hand into a fist and pulled back at the last moment. He didn't want to risk waking him.

Silently, Sam made his way through the great room to the security post. Ax was working on a laptop. His eyes flicking up to the monitors as he typed.

"I'm heading out," Sam said.

"I don't like you doing this alone."

"I'll be fine. Bray's the one who keeps getting kidnapped."

Ax's jaw ticked, but he nodded. Sam didn't like this scenario either, but they couldn't leave Bray alone, even if he was asleep.

"I'll text you when it's done."

Ax sighed but gave another nod before turning back to his laptop.

Sam turned to go but heard Ax mutter something about Sam needing two 'bodyguards' after this shit-fest. If they could spare anyone else, he agreed.

* * * *

Sam saw his breath puff out into the darkness. The clothes available in the safe house that had fit him hadn't really been made for such cold weather. Then again, it was March not December, so the supplies were meant for spring. Sam had on black tactical pants and a black hoodie. He blended in with the predawn darkness and that was all that mattered.

The sky was just beginning to lighten when he hit pay dirt. Clement was angry as a hissing cat and Sam took plenty of pictures of him interacting with Bagan and all his men. It was clear that Clement was the one in charge there.

The crowning glory was the photo of Clement holding a gun to Fedir's head before saying something that had the man scurrying like a rat from the building.

Sam figured his job was to find Bray or even him. Another few men were dispatched as well, so Sam sent Ax a text letting him know what was happening.

Then, at about five-fifty in the morning, Andreiko showed up with his entourage. The man was clearly pissed, his movements quick and jerky as he got out of the car and barked orders at his men.

Sam kept the camera zoomed in on the space at the back of Bagan's mansion. He had a perfect vantage point. He could see anyone arriving and also see into the window on the side of the house where all the men were pacing and arguing.

The best part was that Sam was almost impossible to spot. He'd perched up in a tree about twenty-five feet from Bagan's property line. He'd been watching men patrol the perimeter for over an hour. Every fifteen minutes, like clockwork, an armed guard would pass right below him.

He didn't know when his moment would come, so he'd put a suppressor along with the scope on his Sig and had it ready to roll. Sam calculated that he was about sixty feet from the window he was aiming at. He was no sniper, but he had always been an excellent marksman.

There was a flurry of activity through the house as Andreiko arrived. Sam kept his gun aimed directly at the room but pulled back to look around. The guard was just passing in front of him. Sam looked down at his watch before leaning into the scope and letting the small camera hang from his neck as soon as he uploaded the photos to the cloud.

Andreiko marched into the room like a king and laid something that looked like a small glass statue on the desk in front of Clement. Clement crouched down to look at it. Sam leaned into his scope. *Why would a trinket like that be of any importance?* He quickly snapped a picture before moving his eye back to the scope.

The sculpture seemed very valuable to Clement and that gave Sam an idea. His mission was Andreiko and only Andreiko. Now he knew where the man was, but he needed to cull him from the herd. His plan had only one hitch. He'd need to get out of there fast and he had no getaway driver.

With a mental shrug, Sam took aim at the small statue. Slowly, he squeezed the trigger. One small square pane of the window was quietly shattered. There was a faint scream in the distance as Sam silently jumped down from his perch and ran to the car he'd boosted.

He had parked far back from the house but close enough that he could see the front door. The sun was just beginning to light the sky, which gave him the advantage. He wouldn't need his headlights. Lifting his scope like a telescope, Sam watched the front of the house.

As he expected, everyone burst from the front door. Bagan had his hand wrapped and hugged to his chest. One of Clement's men was guiding him to one of the cars in the driveway, a white cloth held to the side of his face and soaked with blood. Sam had done a lot more damage than he'd expected, but he couldn't drum up any regret.

Clement's driver was already in his car, so he was the first to leave. Andreiko was next. Sam wasn't sure if Bagan would even leave, considering it was his house. He let Andreiko's driver round a corner before he followed.

Sam was surprised and wary when Andreiko's driver drove through the gates of the compound he shared with Kozak. The place looked fairly deserted, though it wasn't even seven in the morning. When the gate remained open after Andreiko turned a corner, Sam took a chance and pulled in behind him.

There was no guard at the gate and no men around to stop him or question him. Sam was worried he'd driven right into a trap until he heard a gunshot ring out. Not sure what he was running into, Sam surged forward anyway. Mase might be the one in trouble.

Andreiko's driver was standing guard next to his car. Sam snuck around the side of the building and pistol-whipped him before he even knew there was someone there. Sam zip-tied his hands behind his back and stuffed him into his own trunk for good measure before sneaking into the building.

Yelling rang through the halls, but he couldn't make out who it was or what was being said. Andreiko's second man was standing guard outside the door where all the noise was coming from. There was no way for Sam to sneak up on him, so he took aim as he rounded the corner.

The bodyguard reached for his weapon, but Sam shot him in the shoulder before he could get a grip on the butt of his gun. Knowing he had to appear merciless, Sam shot him in the chest then the head, Mozambique-Drill style.

The shouting continued. It was in Ukrainian, and now that he was closer, he knew it was Andreiko and Kozak. Kozak was blazing Andreiko for his betrayal and claiming he had closer ties with 'the wraith' than Andreiko ever would. There was a shot. Sam busted through the door, gun drawn.

"Wheeler," Andreiko said, his eyebrows pulled down in confusion.

"You took him," Sam said as he shot him in the knee.

Andreiko collapsed to the floor, putting his hand over his leg as he groaned in pain. Sam held his gun and swung it back and forth between Andreiko and Kozak, who was on the floor in the corner. Kozak was in a similar position, but he was holding his hands to his diaphragm as he tried to stop the flow of his own blood.

There was a body in the corner that must have been the first shot he'd heard. Andreiko had killed Kozak's bodyguard first before drawing out Kozak's death.

"You took him back," Andreiko growled.

"That's right, you fuck. And you'll never lay a hand on him again."

Sam quickly squeezed the trigger three more times in another Mozambique, two to the chest and one to the head for good measure. Sam swung around and pointed the gun at Kozak. The man didn't whimper or beg, but he did set the record straight.

"I didn't know he had your lover," Kozak said quietly.

"Looks like we've both been betrayed here," Sam said.

"No honor among thieves," Kozak said.

"Where are all your men?"

"He knew when to come. Barely anyone is here at night, and those who were disappeared, so they must claim allegiance to him." Kozak nodded at Andreiko's body.

"And now that he's dead?"

"I'm dead too."

"Don't you have a doctor on the payroll?"

"Aren't you…?"

"Going to kill you? Not today. The fact that he shot you tells me that not only were you not in on it, but that he wanted you to die a slow and agonizing death. Maybe we shouldn't give him that satisfaction. He can watch from Hell as you live on."

Kozak smiled, but it turned to a grimace.

"There is someone," Kozak said.

"Tell me where to take you."

Chapter Twenty-Nine

Brayden

Bray felt like the lowest of the low. He liked Ax, he really did. Guilt overwhelmed him as he dashed out of the door of the warehouse. He'd been pretending to sleep for over an hour as he'd discreetly been texting back and forth with Max.

At five in the morning, Max had texted to let him know that Sam was long gone but Mase had been stationary for over four hours at an apartment building. Apartment 16F was leased to a Drew Mason.

Bray had asked Max what he thought was the safest way to be able to actually talk to Mase. They'd agreed this was his chance. It was practically the middle of the night. The sky was still pitch black.

Max was sending a car to pick him up and deliver him to Mase's address. He hadn't known how he was going to get out of the warehouse, but luck had been on his side. Just as Bray was sneaking out of his room, he'd spotted Ax on his way to the bathroom.

Bray had no idea what kind of alarm would go off when he opened the outer door, but Ax's pants around his ankles had to slow him down enough to allow Bray to make a break for it. As soon as he'd turned the knob, Bray had thrown the door open and run as if his life depended on it.

He hustled down the stairs. His ankles were stiff, but he ignored the throbbing pain as he took the stairs two at a time. When he reached the outer door, he heard Ax's voice behind him. Bray swallowed all the guilt and flew out of the door, letting it slam behind him.

The car was exactly where Max had said it would be. His friend was tracking his cell signal, sending him periodic thumbs-up emojis letting him know that the driver hadn't veered off course.

Once he spoke with Mase, they'd order another car to take him back to the warehouse to face the music. Bray would gladly head to the airport with his tail tucked between his legs, but he didn't have a passport.

Bray had the gun Sam had given him tucked at the small of his back, but he had no wallet and no ID, just a gun and a phone. As he got out of the car, he sent up a prayer to the universe that he wouldn't die like that, in a place where his mom wouldn't even know where and how his life had ended.

Shaking off his morbid thoughts, Bray pressed the buzzer for apartment 16F. When there was no answer, he called Max to see if he could somehow get him inside the building.

"Target's on the move," Max said when he picked up the phone.

"Where's he going?"

"He ran to a coffee shop around the corner. He's on his way back to you."

"Thanks, Sin. I owe you about a million after this adventure."

"Just get home safe and we'll call it even."

"Not even close," Bray said before disconnecting the call.

Bray had the hood of his sweatshirt pulled low over his head. He wasn't sure if any of Mase's associates also lived in the building, so he wanted to stay under the radar. His brother rounded the corner, a cup of coffee in one hand and a bag in the other. Bray pulled back his hood just enough that Mase saw his face.

Mase's eyebrows shot up in surprise, but before he could do or say anything else, Bray's gaze slid over his shoulder to the familiar man trailing behind him, the man who was reaching under his jacket. Bray had distracted Mase or he probably would have been more aware.

Without a word, Bray crouched low as he ran forward. He pushed Mase out of the way just as the quiet *pfft* of the suppressed round broke the silence of the early morning. Bray's left shoulder exploded in pain and he tumbled to the ground.

He scooted himself until his back pressed against apartment building and looked up to see the man, Fed-something, aim his gun at Mase. Groaning and pretending to writhe in pain, Bray reached around his back and wrapped his hand around the butt of his gun.

"Why am I not surprised, Fedir?" Mase said.

"Wait until I tell Andreiko who helped steal back Wheeler's little fag."

Bray didn't know how high he was going to be able to raise his right arm, because the pain from his left shoulder radiated across his chest, but he lifted it as much as he could and squeezed the trigger.

As soon as Fedir crumbled to the ground, Mase threw his coffee and breakfast into the street and pulled his weapon. He took Fedir's weapon, shot three more suppressed rounds and Fedir was dead.

"Bray. What the actual fuck?"

Bray opened his mouth. There was so much he wanted to say, so much he'd planned to say once he had Mase's undivided attention. All that came out was a groan.

"Fuck, fuck, fuck," Mase chanted as he pulled Bray up and wrapped his good arm around his neck. "You were pre-med, right? Was anything valuable hit?"

Bray's head was swimming, his vision a little blurry, but somehow he realized that Mase shouldn't know what his major had been in college. He wouldn't know unless…

"Mase," was all Bray was able to get out before emotion clogged his throat.

Mase must have taken emotion for pain, because he lifted Bray completely off the ground and started running. He set Bray in the back of a car. Bray groaned at every turned corner. The ride seemed to last forever and yet he couldn't pull up the words he wanted to say. The pain was too sharp.

* * * *

When he woke up, he was alone in a hospital bed. Everything came flooding back and Bray reached up to touch his shoulder. His left arm was in a sling. The pain wasn't bad, but they probably had him shot up with all kinds of painkillers. He slid off the bed. When his legs supported his weight, he walked slowly to the only other piece of furniture in the room, a wardrobe.

His pants were there and a shirt that he didn't recognize but would probably fit him. A plastic bag was hanging from a hook. Bray pulled it down and looked inside. His gun was gone but the burner phone was there, along with his socks and shoes. Only having one usable arm, Bray set the bag on a tray near the bed and dug out the phone.

First, he checked the time, ten-fourteen a.m. Next, he texted Max that he was alive. Of course, Max texted back that he knew it and he wasn't happy Bray had been careless enough to get shot. Bray snorted at his friend's response as he settled back in the bed.

When the door to his room opened, Bray tucked his phone under his pillow. He didn't know who he could trust. A nurse walked in and tutted that he was sitting up in bed. At least that was what he thought she was upset about, since she was speaking Ukrainian, and gently but firmly pushed him back until he was lying on the pillow. Bray tried to explain that he didn't speak Ukrainian.

"Doctor come," she said with a thick accent. "He speak."

Bray hoped she meant the doctor spoke English. He didn't have much time to worry about it, because the door opened again. In walked a man in scrubs. He was wearing a surgical cap and mask, but as soon as Bray saw his eyes, he gripped the nurse's arm.

Chapter Thirty

Sam

Sam was driving like a bat out of hell when he got an alert on his phone. The vibration caused his pulse to quicken. Even as he sped through the streets at Kozak's direction, he pulled his phone out of his pocket.

His heart seized in his chest when he saw the notification. There had been a security breach at the safe house. His first thought should have been for Ax's safety. Ax was his teammate.

His wayward mind went directly to the man he'd known less than a week. He could tell himself that it was because if anyone were in danger, it was Bray, but it would be a lie. He cared about the kid. He cared a lot more than he was comfortable with.

"Here," Kozak said.

Sam made a quick right to where Kozak was pointing. He pulled in, parked and looked up at the sign over the door.

"A veterinarian?"

"She's saved my life more than once," Kozak said as he struggled to open the door.

"I'll come help you."

Sam jumped out of the car and dialed Ax as he ran around the hood. Every ring that went unanswered had Sam wanting to dump Kozak on the doorstep and get back to the safe house. Finally, when the young veterinarian rushed Kozak into some back room, Sam had a chance to call again.

"He ran," Ax panted when he answered.

"Bray? Bray ran?"

"Fucking kid. I thought he was asleep, but apparently he was just biding his time. I literally went to take a piss and came out to the alarm going off."

"Did you catch him?"

"No. There was a car waiting on him. He jumped in and they took off. I don't exactly have a car to give chase."

"Fuck. I'll…" Sam had his hand on the door when he remembered Kozak.

The man was severely injured and unprotected. Bray, on the other hand, had made his own mess. Not that Kozak hadn't as well, but Kozak was actually Sam's job. Bray was just… Bray was a huge distraction.

"I'm not exactly in a position to go chasing after him either. A lot's going down right now," Sam said. "I have a pretty good idea where he's going."

"We both do, but it's not like we can just call Mase up and warn him."

"Let me see if his friend can find him."

"Find him? His friend probably made all the arrangements."

Sam snorted his agreement and disconnected the call. He had never felt so torn in his life. They'd invested years in getting to this place with Kozak's organization. He'd saved Kozak, but others who were loyal to Andreiko and even Bagan's men might know exactly where Kozak would go if he was hurt.

Soon, more men would show up at that compound. They'd find Andreiko and his men's bodies. They'd see evidence of other people coming and going. They might come looking for Kozak to protect him or to kill him while he was vulnerable.

Bray was being reckless, and this time Sam couldn't afford to drop everything and save him. As much as he wanted to protect the little shit, he also had to stop chasing him down. There was someone who might be able to give him a little peace of mind.

"It wasn't my idea," Sin said as soon as he picked up.

"So you did order the car?"

The only answer was a faint clicking sound of the keys on a keyboard.

"Tell me he's all right."

"He made it to Mase's apartment building. I assume they're talking about now or Bray would have called me to order another car."

"Where would he have gone if Mase had turned him away?"

"The airport?"

"With no passport?"

"I might be able to help him work around that."

"Of course."

"Look, Sam. The burden's off your shoulders, okay? He's a big boy. He's made it through a few tours. He's seen combat. He's not as helpless as you seem to think."

"I don't think he's helpless, but he's sure as fuck not prepared for what he's facing here. It's much more subtle than in-your-face combat, but just as dangerous. He doesn't speak the language. He has no money, no ID, no clothes, nothing."

"And yet he's made it this far."

"With help," Sam yelled, then took a deep breath.

"We all have help. I'm sure somewhere you have some guy just like me keeping track of you. You have backup, you have someone to call if things go to shit and you need a safe place. I'm that for Bray."

Sam couldn't argue any of those points except one.

"I don't have anyone on my team who can do the things you do. I'd feel a lot more confident with you watching my six. Maybe that's why Bray's overconfident."

"I'll take that as the compliment it was meant to be."

Sam didn't know what else to say. He wanted to tell him to call if Bray needed help, but that was the worst idea in the world. He wished Sin could imbed some sort of tracker under Bray's skin so he could always be found.

"Look, Sam. I appreciate you protecting him. He's always protected me. If you... If you ever need anything, keep this number."

"Thanks, Sin. Just watch out for him, all right?"

"Sure."

Sam disconnected the call and stuffed his phone into the pocket of his tactical pants. His clothes would probably invite some questions. He hadn't planned on confronting anyone but Andreiko.

After pacing the halls outside the surgery room in the vet's office for over an hour, Sam's phone rang. Normally, he would have let it go unanswered, but when he saw it was Mase, he rushed outside, pressed the green button and hoped the conversation wouldn't be overheard.

"Is he with you?" Sam asked.

"Yes and no. We're at the hospital."

"What happened?"

"He fucking saved my life. I mean, I wouldn't have been so distracted if I hadn't seen a hooded guy loitering by my building. When he pulled his hood back and I saw who it was, I froze. Someone was behind me."

"Who?"

"Fedir. Bray shoved me out of the way and took one to the shoulder."

Sam felt all the muscles that had been strung tight release and he almost fell to the ground. No wound was a walk in the park, but a shoulder wound was one a soldier could pull through easily.

He was dizzy with relief. The strength of his reaction made him uneasy. He'd be happy any of his teammates were alive. But the sheer terror he'd felt for that moment and the joy he'd felt when Mase had named the wound was too much. It was all too much and he had no idea what to do with that.

"What happened?" Sam demanded.

"I had a crushed coffee cup in one hand and a smushed bagel in the other, so it wasn't like I could reach for my gun without being obvious. He would have gotten a shot off before my cup hit the ground. Luckily, Fedir chose that moment to gloat instead of shoot. Bray got him in the knee and I took care of the rest."

"The knee? What is it with him and shooting people below the waist?"

"He was on the ground. He just lifted his hand enough to squeeze off a round and distract him."

"What's the damage?" Sam asked.

"It looked like a clean wound. They're stitching him up now. I was... I can't stay here watching over him forever. Can you take over or send Ax?"

"Yeah. Yeah, Of course. It'll have to be Ax, though. Andreiko shot Kozak, so I'm standing guard over his surgery room. Andreiko's dead."

"Fuck. I should... Just let me have a few minutes with Bray once he wakes up and then I'll be wherever you need me. It's my job to watch Kozak."

"We're gonna talk," Sam said.

"Dude, we are talking."

"No. I mean we're gonna talk about how you never answered any of your brother's emails and so he got so desperate to talk to you that he followed *me*."

"Way to pile on the guilt, Magnum. I'm not happy about what happened either, but there's no one else I'd rather have at his back, y'know? I didn't know... God, I had no idea he still cared so much."

"We'll talk," Sam said again.

There were things Mase needed to face. Some of those things had been out of his control, some not. He needed to take a look at the truth either way.

"I have to get back. I need to make sure no one gets to him," Mase said.

"I'll send Ax. Text me the hospital and room number. He'll be there in less than thirty minutes. I'll make arrangements to get Bray home as well."

"Thanks."

As soon as he pushed the button to end the call, Sam was dialing another number and planning a way to get Bray safely out of the country.

Chapter Thirty-One

Brayden

Mase didn't pull down his surgical mask, but he said something to the nurse. She nodded and went about taking Bray's vitals.

"The bullet went clean through, so there are just some stitches, four in front, six in back." Mase spoke with a fake Ukrainian accent.

"So am I free to go?"

"No. You will be released soon. You have family to come get you?"

"No. No, I came here alone. I was looking for—" Bray almost said 'you' but stopped himself at the last moment, his eyes darting to the nurse.

"I came looking for my brother," Bray said instead. "My family situation is complicated. Technically I'm not sure you can call us a family anymore. I mean, I've barely spoken to my father in years until recently. My brother Nick and I… I think we're finally good again. My mom… She's the reason I'm here."

"Here in Ukraine?"

"No. I meant she's my rock, the only person who's never let me down."

Bray saw something flicker in his brother's eyes. Guilt, maybe shame, he wasn't sure—but that wasn't what he'd been aiming for. This was all going wrong. The words started to flood out unchecked since he didn't know how much time he'd have with Mase.

"My dad gave me my walking papers when I came out. I was almost eighteen. He'd done the same to my brother. I guess he hadn't really learned his lesson yet. He did finally learn since he went easier on Nick, but it was too late for me by then. Nick couldn't understand why I wouldn't talk to my father, so…we drifted apart."

"And your mother?"

"She's a saint. She tried to pull everyone back together. When my dad wouldn't budge, she left. They've been divorced a long time now. She met someone else a while back. He's really great. I don't know how she forgave Dad for tearing the family apart, but she did. He just became a bitter old man, even though he's not that old."

"And Nick… He's ill?"

"No. No, that was a, well, a little manipulation on my part. I made two statements that separately are true but can be misconstrued when strung together."

Mase's eyes darted around the room as he thought about what Bray had said, what Sam had passed along—probably verbatim. He shook his head.

The nurse said something to Mase then patted Bray's hand and left the room.

"So the old bastard's dying, huh?" Mase said as he paced the room.

"It looks that way."

"And you came all this way, risked your life so he could have a deathbed moment with the prodigal son?"

"I'm here just as much for myself and Mom. She doesn't understand why you won't even give us a chance. I don't really, either. I tried to contact you eight years ago, then again four years ago when I was officially in the army—and almost three years ago when we found out you'd been discharged. Mom will never forgive herself for not sitting behind you in that courtroom."

"I guess I'm as bitter as the old man." Mase turned and walked to the small window in the room.

"I don't understand."

"I wasn't quite eighteen when I came out to Dad. Technically, I didn't come out. He heard a rumor about me kissing a guy. But when he confronted me, I didn't deny it. He threw down an ultimatum and I walked away, but I kept waiting for him or Mom to reach out and say it had been some terrible mistake, some gross overreaction."

Bray snorted. "I knew damn well that wasn't coming after I figured out that was why you left too."

Mase turned back to face him. He put his hands on the windowsill at his hips and leaned back. His shoulders sagged like he was tired or overburdened, maybe both.

"I was sure it was coming. Then, on my eighteenth birthday, he had me served with papers disinheriting me. I was shocked and gutted. I didn't know that he knew where I was staying, and believe me when I say it was not a nice place."

Bray automatically pictured the apartment building where he'd first met Sam. The stained carpet in the hallway, the sour smell of rotting food, the paper-thin walls that didn't insulate any noise. How long had Mase had to live like that?

"He had no problem finding me to twist the knife, even as I hoped for an olive branch. So I joined up. I was looking for a place to belong. The paperwork he sent said I wasn't to contact any of you. Mom…"

Mase took in a deep breath. When the air came out, there was a shaky quality to it. Bray tensed. It caused a twinge in his shoulder, but he couldn't relax until he heard what Mase was going to say about their mom.

"Her name was on the papers. I wasn't to contact her either."

"Did she sign them?" Bray demanded.

"I was a kid, a sheltered, spoiled kid. I didn't know to look for anything like that. You were all named in the document. I didn't even read completely through them. When I realized what they said, I burned them. I fucking burned them until they were ash. Then I left for boot camp. I met Sam and Kota, then Jazz and Mitch and finally Wade. I formed my own little family and I never looked back."

Bray nodded, because he didn't know what else there was to say. They both knew that wasn't one hundred percent true, since Mase knew about Bray's major in college and probably some other information about him and Nick.

Mase laughed, but there was no humor in it. "I also had no idea about the trust that Dad couldn't revoke. Imagine my surprise when after my twenty-fifth birthday I got a letter from the law firm who oversaw my trust. Suddenly I was a multi-millionaire."

"That was from Grandpa Hart. It had nothing to do with Dad."

"Yeah, well, I didn't know about it."

"That was Mom's doing," Bray said. "She wanted us to live as if we'd have to make it on our own. She never realized it might be a lifeline."

"Looking back on it now," Mase said after a moment of tense, awkward silence, "I realize I was punishing all of you for Dad's actions. But if Nick's okay, don't expect me to trip over myself or try to sneak off to pay my last respects to a man who not only told me to go to hell but who gave me a map to get there."

Bray nodded. He wasn't all that surprised by that response. But it didn't answer the real question, the one he'd come to ask.

"But Mom?"

Bray would have to ask her about the documents, but he was sure his mom would never have signed anything like that. Dad kicking Mase out was the main reason they'd split up.

"I'll give it a chance, okay?"

Bray hadn't realized he was holding his breath until it exploded out of his lungs in relief.

"I'll listen to what she has to say. I'll give her a chance to tell her side."

"She deserves it."

"And what about you?" Mase asked.

"Me?"

"You came all the way out here for Mom? Threw me out of the way and took a bullet for Mom?"

"I came because I finally had the time, the resources and a good excuse to find you. I don't really have a side to tell. I heard you arguing with Dad when he threw you out, but I was angry at you. I didn't hear the whole conversation, just the end. I heard the part where he asked you to shape up to be a good example to us. I thought he was talking about the friends you hung out with."

"He was in a way," Mase said. "That was part of what he was demanding I give up—anything with a whiff that I wasn't totally straight."

Bray's stomach tightened as he remembered the fight he'd had with his father after he'd come out to him. Their dad had blamed Mase, like it was contagious, even though he'd been gone for years.

"Even half a world away, Mase is cursing this family."

The words hit Bray like a slap. The puzzle pieces clicked into place as Bray realized the implications of what his father had said. That was why Mase had left? That was why he'd turned away from his family? Because of their father? It wasn't selfishness or recklessness as Bray had believed.

He'd hated Mase for not being willing to be a little less wild so he could still hang out with his little brothers. All the time it had been their father, and for the same reason, Bray had come to their father that day, to come out.

He didn't have the heart to tell their dad that Nick was gay as well. It wasn't his right to out his brother, but the thought of what he would say to Nick when the time came made Bray's gut burn with rage.

"I can't believe you would ask Mase to do that. No wonder he left."

"He's 'bisexual'," his dad said, using air quotes, "not gay. He could have just dated women."

"I don't know what it's like to be bisexual but I can imagine how it would tear my heart out for my father to ask me to cut half of myself off for…for—"

"For the good of the family," Russ finished for him.

"Not for the good of the family but for your comfort. It tore our family apart. I blamed him but it was all you. *For all you know, he could have decided to come out to you*

because he was in love with a guy. So then you might have been asking him to cast aside someone that he loved because it wasn't convenient for you."

"Not my convenience. It was for your protection."

"From what, being open-minded? What a horrible example you'd be setting by loving your first-born son unconditionally."

"It's not that simple, Bray. I – "

"Oh no? Well, now you're down by two kids. You only have one left. On all the holidays and birthdays, I hope your prejudices keep you nice and warm."

"I did what I thought was best for this family."

"And I bet you'd fucking do it again. I hated him for leaving. I hated Mase for choosing his stupid friends over us. If I'd known you threw him away like trash because he wasn't straight enough for you, then believe me, I wouldn't have come out to you at all. Now I can just say 'fuck you' and be done with it."

"Brayden – "

Bray had run like the hounds of hell had been nipping at his heels. He'd tucked his tail between his legs and told his mother what had happened. She hadn't said a word when he'd cut his father off. The only time she'd stepped in was when his relationship with Nick had crumbled. But even she hadn't been able to mend that rift.

Bray pushed the dark thoughts back. His forgiveness for his father was tenuous at best. Dwelling on the past wouldn't do anyone any favors. He'd allow his father to die knowing he'd made amends with at least two of his sons.

"I didn't know," Mase said.

Bray shook the memories away. When he looked at his brother, there was sympathy in his eyes and maybe even a little shame.

"Didn't know what?"

"Any of this." Mase made a big circle with his arms. "I didn't know you were gay. I didn't know dad did the same thing to you. I didn't know you might need me. I thought—or at least I was worried—it was just morbid curiosity that had you reaching out."

"Even though Dad didn't serve me papers formally removing me from the family, we didn't speak for almost six years. Nick and I didn't really speak for four. It would have been nice to have had you to talk to, but my aim was never to make you feel guilty."

"I know. I can do that all on my own."

Bray gave a half-hearted smile.

"Listen, Bray. I have to go. I'm still…working. I don't know when this will be over. Until it is, I can't exactly pick up the phone and call, but when I get home—"

"I'll be around. I gave my four years. I'm not going to re-up. I don't know what I'll be doing exactly, but I'll be there, so let me know when you're home."

Bray couldn't bring himself to feel too bad for their father. He was just selfish enough to be happy that Mase might step back into his life, that he couldn't bring himself to plead their dad's case.

"Jazz is gonna get you home safe."

"Jazz?" Bray had heard Sam say that name as well.

"He's our chain of command. He's also a friend. I've known him almost as long as I've known Sam and Kota. Maybe you'll meet Kota someday too."

Bray nodded. He hoped to spend enough time with Mase that he'd meet all his friends, though seeing Sam again would be rough.

"Ax is here. He'll stay until they release you. Then he'll make sure you get safely on the plane."

"Is Sam—?" Bray cleared his throat. "Tell Sam I'm sorry I took off this morning. Tell him I'm sorry for everything. I didn't mean to blow this thing to hell."

Mase walked up to the bed. He still had on his surgical cap and mask, but Bray could tell by his crinkled eyes that he was smiling. He leaned in and squeezed Bray's good arm.

"Thanks. I can't say I'm glad you ended up in Kiev, but since you did, I'm glad we got a chance to talk."

"Me too," Bray said.

"Stay safe," Mase said, then he turned and left the room.

* * * *

When the hospital released him, Ax took Bray to a small airfield. He tried to relax in the cabin of the private plane where he was the sole passenger. He even managed to doze off, since the painkillers made him tired and groggy.

When he woke up, he didn't know where they'd landed or how long the flight had been. The thought made him anxious after what he'd just been through. He no longer had a weapon or a GPS tracking device.

The pilot came out of the cockpit and Bray stood from his seat. He was a little woozy and not sure how much fight he had in him, but he'd fight if he had to. The pilot smiled and went to open the cabin door.

Bray didn't have any luggage, so he made it to the doorway and almost fell to his knees when he saw Nick and his mother waiting behind a chain-link fence. Both their fingers curled around the metal as they watched Bray slowly and carefully descend the stairs. *Am I in California?*

"Mr. Hart?"

A man stepped up to the stairs as Bray made his way down. He didn't look military, with his long hair and beard scruff, but his countenance was military, one hundred percent.

"Yes," Bray said as he stepped onto the tarmac.

"I'm Mitch. I'm here to escort you to your debrief."

"But my family."

"They can follow us. Your brother's aware a debrief is needed, but he and your mother just wanted to see you step off the plane."

Bray knew Mitch could have prevented them from coming. In fact, he was surprised he hadn't. Then he remembered the name…Mitch. Was this the Mitch who was part of Mase's chosen family?

"Did Mase allow this? My family to see me?"

"The car's right here, Mr. Hart," Mitch said in answer.

Bray turned to his family. His mother was giving him a brave smile, but he could see the sun's reflection in the tears streaming down her cheeks. He held up his good arm and waved before following Mitch to the car.

Chapter Thirty-Two

Sam

He'd been home six weeks. After salvaging what he could in Kiev, Sam had gone to Thailand. Things there had been smooth as silk.

And yet he couldn't stop thinking about those few days. He'd spent less than a week with Bray, yet here he was almost two months later, distracted and restless.

"Just call him already," Ax said without lifting his eyes from his computer monitor.

When they were Stateside and had any free time at all, Ax had one singular focus. It was the mission that had led Ax to join their little group.

Sam had nothing but respect for what Ax was trying to do. They gave him time and resources to keep searching. They all pitched in when and how they could. Ax lived in their office building, even though HC paid him a shit-ton of money.

Each contract they got was different—some paid by hour, some by contract completion. It didn't matter to

Ax. He took any job he could and either sent the cash to his family or socked the money away.

It took Sam a minute to remember that Ax had goaded him. He flipped Ax the bird. Until very recently, Sam had been with the CIA. He'd agreed to help Wade with Hart Consulting while Mase was deep undercover, but that had sort of morphed into Wade and Sam running the company in Mase's absence.

Sam's position was tenuous. The CIA had allowed him to move to HC only because they utilized them as a contractor. Sam still reported to the CIA and would for at least a year or more while they worked through the current investigation he was on.

He wasn't technically released from his position at the CIA, but they'd agreed not to give him any additional assignments. So, while he was home, he helped run Hart. While he was out of the country, he relied heavily on Wade to manage not only logistics but all aspects of HC's operations.

Their team was growing, which was good, because they had more jobs than they could handle. That was very reason Sam was heading into DC for a meeting.

"What are you bitching about over there?" Colt asked.

"I just thought Sam might not mope around so much if he gave the guy a call."

"What guy? Mase's hot brother? Fuck, I'll give him call. You got his number?"

Ax gave Sam a look. They both knew Sam had Bray's number. He just hadn't used it and he didn't plan to, either. Ax's questioning look morphed into an evil grin.

"I have his number." Ax pulled his phone out of his pocket.

"You do it and we'll have an in-depth discussion with the entire team about Kiev—specifically the safe house."

Ax rolled his eyes but put his phone away.

"We already know about that," Clay said.

All the guys in the room chuckled. Even Sam could see the humor in it now that Bray was home safe, tucked away with his family in Southern California.

"I have a meeting in DC. I'll be out the rest of the day, but you can reach me by phone."

Sam's cover was still in effect while he was Stateside. He worked for Lucien Bernard. The difference was that while on US soil, he pretended that Lucien, or rather Jazz, was a real estate investor.

That was technically his cover everywhere, but when someone allowed the mafia to pay for their hotel in Ukraine, they could only pretend so much.

The building that housed HC was in Lombardy Alley in downtown Richmond, Virginia. It was surrounded by an old brick wall and the entire place was so covered in vines that no one even knew it was there. It was the perfect place for their operation.

The four-story brick relic had been updated long before Mase had bought it. The place still looked ancient on the outside, but the inside was state-of-the-art.

* * * *

As he waited in the coffee shop on 22nd Street in the nation's capital, Sam hoped he could recruit the man he was meeting, but he wasn't sure he had anything special to offer.

He sipped coffee from his to-go cup and watched as patrons moved in and out of the tiny shop. He'd just checked his phone again and was worried he'd been stood up when the chair across from him scraped over the floor. There was a flurry of movement as a kid in a hoodie slid into the seat and scooted it forward.

"You're bigger in person than I thought you'd be," he said.

"Sin?"

He looked younger than Bray, but that could have been because he dressed like a teenager. His shirt had a pixelated character on it that looked reminiscent of Minecraft. His jeans were ancient, and his shoes were the only thing keeping the hems from dragging on the floor. Sin pulled the black hood down off his head as he sat across from Sam.

"You've got to be younger than Bray."

Sin looked like a typical high school student with his bedhead and hoodie. When his face was unobstructed, Sam saw a guy too masculine to be called pretty but too attractive to be called anything else.

His eyebrows were straight swipes of dark hair, the center low over his eyes but the tails higher, giving him almost a surprised or confused resting face. Sam knew he was anything but confused.

Sin's nose was straight, but the lines were somehow sharper than most, especially at the tip. He had a strong jawline, but not as razor-sharp as Bray's. Sam shook off the comparison.

"I'm a few years younger."

"And you're the one with the intel? You're the one who linked Mase to me and that shit-hole in Florida?"

"Yep."

"Let's take a walk," Sam said.

Sin stiffened.

"Just a walk so we can have some privacy while we talk. You can choose the direction."

"Okay." Sin nodded and stood from the table.

Sam picked up his coffee and led the way out of the shop.

"What was the link?" Sam asked as they ambled down the sidewalk.

"It took me a while to figure out that Wheeler is an alias. If I had, I would have had Bray approach you a different way. I didn't mean to push him into a shit-storm. Your alias was linked to helping Mase get a hold of some property in Richmond, Virginia."

Sam rubbed a hand over his face. His cover was as a real estate investor, but he hadn't even bought the building. When he'd realized how secure it was, he'd thought it would be a perfect safe house.

It was basically in the middle of a parking lot, like a fortress. No one could sneak up on them, the first floor had almost no windows and it had a private underground parking garage. The building had easily been renovated to become Hart Consulting.

"I wasn't a part of that deal and definitely not as my alias."

"It was the only time Mase ever touched his inheritance. I followed the money. Someone mentioned your alias in an email as having something to do with the property."

"I made up an excuse to back out of buying the property so Mase could get it. No one even knew we knew each other."

Sin shrugged. "I ran a background check on every name associated with that deal."

"A background check? My background was created by the government. It's flawless."

"That's why it took me over a week to figure out it was fake. But by then, I'd already hacked your accounts, found some intel about Mase and given your location to Bray. Mase bought that building but hadn't actually been there in years. Yet he kept in touch with you."

Sam felt like he was digging himself deeper and deeper. Did he want to know how thin the veneer of his cover really was?

"And you knew my location from?" Sam demanded.

"Your phone. And you own the building in Florida. Guess you're a slumlord?"

"I'm a lot of things. I also thought my information was secure."

"Don't sweat it. Not many would have been able to get the information—probably less than twenty people in the world."

"That's a lot of people."

"It's statistically insignificant."

"Not if one of those people works for someone I do business with under my alias."

"Not many people can afford to pay someone like me a regular salary. I get pulled in for contract jobs."

"And make more in one contract than most people make in a year?" Sam guessed.

Sin shrugged.

Sam pulled the coin out of his pocket and held it out. Sin looked down at it but gave no reaction. He looked back up at Sam.

"What about this?" Sam asked as he nodded at the coin.

"That's taken me over a year to perfect."

"What's the Latin on the back?"

"*Dum Spiro Spero*," Sin said as the corner of his mouth quirked up. "'While I breathe, I hope'."

"Hope to be found," Sam whispered.

Though Sam hadn't framed it as a question, Sin gave a slight nod.

"Do you have other gadgets like this?"

"That's classified."

A laugh burst from Sam unbidden as he shook his head.

"I can probably find out your name and who you work for," Sam said.

"I already know your name and who *you* work for."

"I'm guessing NSA," Sam whispered.

"Langley doesn't recruit dense people," Sin said.

"I'll take that as the compliment it was meant to be." Sam returned the phrase Sin had used earlier. "If you're ever looking for something new, give me a call."

Sam laid his card and the coin in his hand and held it out to Sin. He took the card but left the coin.

"I think you forgot something," Sam said. "I came here to give this back."

"No. You came here to scope me out and maybe offer me a job. I'm a contractor, so I am open for other consulting as long as it doesn't include divulging anything classified or use or expose any classified hardware."

"And in exchange, I keep the coin so you can track me?" Sam didn't think his superiors would approve of that.

"Keep it in case a certain blond-haired, blue-eyed optimist wants to find you."

Sam's chest felt tight as he closed his fist around the coin. He should give it back and walk away. And yet he put his fist into his pocket. Sam had detected something in the other man when he spoke about Bray.

"You have a thing for him," Sam said almost to himself.

"I did." Sin shrugged. "I'm not his type. Truthfully, he's not typically my type either, but who can resist falling for Brayden Hart? Not me, and apparently not you."

"I'm not—"

Sin interrupted Sam with a shake of his head. He stepped back and pulled his hood up.

"The battery lasts longer if it's stationary," Sin said. "Also, a wireless charger will recharge it." With that, he turned and walked away.

That stupid coin seemed to weigh a hundred pounds as Sam made his way home. He should flush it down the fucking toilet. He should throw it away. Then it would just guide anyone to a landfill somewhere.

He didn't do any of those things. Instead, he laid it carefully on his dresser. There was no reason for Bray to look for him. They'd both known it was a short-term affair. And yet… And yet the hope it gave Sam made him feel a little lighter, almost happy.

Chapter Thirty-Three

Brayden

Bray was finally starting to feel like himself again. The military had worked with him and had surprisingly let him move out of active duty and into IRR three months early because of his injury. Again, he wondered if Mase had gotten someone to pull some strings.

It could also have been Jazz. Meeting Jazz had been an experience. He'd looked at Bray as if he were the missing piece of a puzzle he didn't know how to fit together.

Jazz reminded Bray of Orlando Bloom in *Pirates of the Caribbean*. It wasn't just the resemblance, with the longish hair and groomed beard—it was the air about him. He was tenacious.

It had taken six hours of debrief before they'd allowed Bray to leave. Jazz, Mitch and other nameless men and women from unnamed branches of the government had asked him a million questions, recording the entire thing.

They'd warned him not to speak of any details as the mission was ongoing and classified. When he was getting ready to leave, Jazz had asked him how willing he would be to reprise his role if the need arose.

Bray's heart rate had kicked up so fast that he'd become dizzy, and a slew of butterflies had fluttered around in his stomach. He'd stuttered a little but admitted to being surprised at the request.

"You held your own. You think fast on your feet and you jumped in to save Mase," Jazz had said, but it was the last quip that had stuck with Bray. "Plus, you got the drop on Sam. I've never seen that happen."

It had taken two months for Bray to be medically cleared. During that time, he'd emailed back and forth with Mase a few times. His brother had also been replying to their mother's emails. She'd been floating around with a permanent smile on her face. Nick, on the other hand, had been grumbling about Mase's lack of response regarding their father.

Bray hadn't told him much about his conversation with Mase. They were all brothers, but that was Mase's tale to tell. Just like Bray wouldn't out Nick to their father, he wouldn't out their father to Nick. It was up to Mase to open the lines of communication.

Bray shook off those thoughts as he and Nick walked down an alley in Virginia. They'd parked in the parking structure across the street. 'Alley' was a strong term for where they were. There were small rows of shops and a somewhat-deserted parking lot behind them, across from them was another row of shops.

In the middle of the parking lot, nestled behind the first set of shops, was what Bray might have thought was a garden of some sort. Ropes of green vines covered every square inch of what he assumed was either a wall or a fence. Tall trees blocked out any view of a building beyond.

"What is this place?" Nick asked as they approached a wrought-iron gate.

They hadn't even seen the gate until their second pass around the perimeter. It was on that second time around that they'd seen the small panel with number keys and an 'enter' button.

"It's Mase's team. He asked me to come, so I came. You're here as my babysitter, apparently."

Nick rolled his eyes as Bray entered the code Mase had given him. When he pressed the enter key, nothing happened. He'd expected the gate to buzz open or for someone to talk to him through the tiny speaker holes above the keypad. He entered the code a second time then pressed the gate to make sure the lock hadn't silently disengaged.

"He's probably going to offer you a job because you told him you're out of the army. I'm just here to make sure you don't get in over your head."

"You only have to enter the code once," came a voice from the other side of the fence.

"I wasn't sure I entered it right, since the gate didn't open."

"The code doesn't open the gate."

The gate buzzed and swung open. There was a man waiting for them on the other side. The guy had both Bray and Nick a little tongue-tied. He looked like he'd just stepped off the pages of GQ magazine. He was tall, built and gorgeous. The blue of his irises was so stark against his dark eyelashes, eyebrows and hair that Bray wondered if the color was real.

"The code says you were invited to come to the party, and it also tells me who invited you," the man said as he held out his hand. "I'm Chase."

"Brayden Hart." Bray shook his hand.

"I was only expecting one visitor."

"This is Nicholas Hart. He—"

"I know who he is. I was just mentioning that it wasn't expected. Considering who you both are, I don't think it should be a problem." Chase motioned for them to step inside.

When they were both through the gate, Chase closed it and entered a code in a keypad identical to the one they'd used on the outside of the gate.

"Security measures." Chase shrugged as he moved past them toward the building.

At least Bray assumed there was a building under all the greenery. He could see a door and the outline of windows on the higher floors, with a tiny bit of brick framing them where the ivy was kept tamed, but the rest of the building was green.

"Why do I feel like *Hansel and Gretel*?" Nick asked.

"You're totally Gretel." Bray elbowed Nick.

Chase snorted a laugh.

There was another keypad at the door, along with a fingerprint scanner. Mase was consulting, mostly for the government, but Bray was still surprised by the high security.

When they walked through the front door, there was a small reception area and an older woman sitting at a desk. Her hair was mostly white, but she was beautiful, with dark, high-arching eyebrows and a welcoming smile.

"Hey, Dee. This is Brayden Hart and Nicholas Hart."

"I know who they are, *cher*. I've seen their pictures, same as you."

Chase smiled but rolled his eyes. Her accent was Cajun and the twang of it made Bray smile.

"*Bonjour,* Bray. *Bonjour,* Nick. I've been waitin' to meet Mase's baby brothers. You go get set up. We'll have a *vieller* soon enough."

"Vayay?" Nick asked.

"*Oui*. You know…a chat. We'll be old friends before you know it."

With a nod, she went back to looking at the computer monitor in front of her. Bray liked her already. Beyond Dee's desk was another door with yet another keypad. This time Chase pulled a badge from a retractable clip at his waist and scanned it. A light blinked from red to yellow. Then Chase pressed his hand to a biometric scanner. The light changed from yellow to green and there was a small click indicating the door had unlocked.

"Dee is Jazz's grandma. She's also our receptionist. Don't let her gray hair fool you. She's sharp as a tack. You'll be restricted to the first floor unless you have an escort," Chase said as he handed Bray a badge and had him scan his handprint. "I'll have a badge made for you, Nick. Wade will be available to meet with you in about ten minutes. Would you rather hang out in the library or in a conference room?"

"Library," Bray said.

"This way." Chase led them down a long hall.

Along one side were a row of empty conference rooms. Along the other were fewer doors with theater seating in two large rooms. They passed a small kitchen and dining area before coming to yet another security door. Chase used his badge again to get them through.

As the door closed behind them, Ax came around a corner, heading the same way they were. He was in athletic shorts and a soaking wet tank top that clung to every ridge of muscle on his chest and abs. He loosely gripped a towel that hung around his neck. His hair was slicked back and damp. There were rivulets of sweat making their way down his neck and temples.

If Bray weren't trying to burrow Sam out from under his skin, he might just drool over Ax, but Ax wasn't his type. At least now he knew he really did have a type. Was Sam also there?

"Well, well, well," Ax drawled as he came to a stop next to them. "If it isn't Hot Cakes. You gonna join up, Sweet Hart?"

"Not if that's my handle. Although"—Bray rubbed his chin as he pretended to think hard—"if that's my handle, then yours will have to be Prince John, prince of the johns."

Chase burst out laughing. "He's got your number, Loco," Chase said.

"Fuckin' HC. You guys are worse than a knitting club with all your gossip. And you, Hot Cakes… I should have known you'd be sniffing around here. You missing anyone in particular?" Ax winked.

"I don't see you enjoying working with assholes like this, Bray," Nick said.

"He worked with me just fine, Nickel."

Nick took a step forward, his fists clenched. Bray placed his hand on his brother's arm. Under other circumstances, Bray thought Ax and Nick might actually get along. They both had similar, teasing personalities. Then again, maybe that was why they might rub each other the wrong way.

"Later, Hot Cakes. Nice to meet ya, Nickel."

Ax sauntered past them down the hall. Seething, Nick turned and watched him go. Chase kept walking and Bray pulled Nick along.

"Make yourselves at home. I'll let Wade know where you are. He should be down shortly."

As soon as Chase closed the door behind himself, Nick turned on Bray. He was fuming mad. Bray braced himself for what was most likely to be a lecture.

"I can't believe you told that douche my nickname."

"I didn't—"

"Is he the one? The reason you got sidetracked in Ukraine?"

"Settle down. I used it as code to send a message to Mase. I wasn't spilling all your secrets or anything."

"I don't exactly have a lot of secrets, but you know I always hated that nickname."

"It's better than 'Braid'. I was so worried that would become my call sign when I joined up."

"You think 'Sweet' is any better?"

"It's better than being named after a hairstyle that's mostly used by women. And besides, at least I didn't tell anyone how you got your call sign, Dash."

"Shut up," Nick said with a half-smile on his face.

Both brothers explored the books in the library. It was filled with reference material about learning languages, different cultures and customs and laws of different countries tucked in along with books in every language.

"Like a spy reference library," Nick said.

Bray had expected to hear condescension in his tone, but there was only curiosity. The door to the library opened. A man stepped in.

The guy was huge in both height and stature. He was at least six-foot-three and could probably bench press a car. He was attractive, in a young 'Italian Stallion' kind of way. He looked like a boxer, with a nose that was crooked and a little flat at the end, but he was definitely sexy.

He was dressed in a custom suit that fit him like a glove from his wide shoulders to his narrow waist. Closing the door quietly behind himself, he sauntered forward with a slight hitch in his step.

"Bray, Nick, it's nice to meet you. I'm Wade."

Bray shook his hand but couldn't stop the wave of disappointment that swamped him at the click of the door closing. He was hoping someone would be stepping in behind him. It was too much to hope that Mase had made it home already, but Sam might have joined them.

"So Mase summoned Bray but didn't bother to show up?" Nick asked.

There was anger in Nick's words, but Bray could detect a little hurt in his voice. He knew exactly what Mase was in the middle of, but he hadn't been able to explain it to Nick. Wade, however, simply shrugged.

"What Mase is doing is classified and can't simply be cut short so he can come have coffee with his brothers. He may not be in the military anymore, but lives are still depending on his success and his sacrifice."

Nick turned to look at a row of books. Bray gave Wade a smile to try to make up for his brother's lack of manners.

"If you want to know classified information, First Lieutenant Hart, you'll either have to bump up your status in the military right quick or—"

That had Nick turning around.

"Or what? Join Mase's band of misfits?"

Bray cringed at Nick's comment. When Nick was hurt, he lashed out. Wade, on the other hand, threw his head back and laughed. It was a nice, deep, rich, honest sound.

"I like that description. It's actually very apt. 'Band of misfits'. None of us ended up being a good fit in the military, but we fit in here."

That description right there seemed to click something in place inside Bray. Being gay in the military hadn't been a good fit for him. Sure, the law was on his side, but that didn't mean his teammates had been. He'd seen some of the guys covering their junk in the shower.

He'd let it go because gay men did check out other men, but he wasn't going to attack someone because he found them attractive. It hadn't been all the guys, but the fact that he made people uncomfortable simply by existing and doing his job had weighed heavily on him sometimes.

"The job offer is for Bray, not me," Nick said.

"I didn't say anything about a job offer."

"Why else would you invite Bray here?"

"Bray did some pretty impressive footwork, even though he had no idea what he had walked into. Our entire team wants to thank him. And if he'd like to work with us now that he's a free agent"—Wade shrugged—"we'd be lucky to have him."

Bray's chest warmed at the praise. He hadn't been sure Nick had been right. He'd flubbed everything up in Kiev, but they thought he could hold his own. They thought he'd be a good fit for their team. Most of his previous teammates had been stuck with him. Here was a team of highly skilled operators and they wanted him.

"He came home with a bullet hole," Nick scoffed.

"A bullet hole that saved a life," Wade corrected.

"I'm in," Bray said.

"What life?" Nick said at the same time.

Nick grabbed the bicep of Bray's good arm and pulled him off to the side.

"Fuck, Bray. Hear their offer before you accept."

"An offer is about money. I don't care about money. I could belong here. That's more valuable to me."

"You think you can belong with a bunch of assholes like the guy in the hall?"

"It was a private joke."

Nick's eyes narrowed as they darted back and forth between Bray's. With a sigh of defeat, he let go of Bray's arm.

"Don't worry, Nick. The comp package is top of the line. It's something you'd never even dream of in the military. Now"—Wade clapped his hands then rubbed his palms together—"let's give you a tour of the building."

Chapter Thirty-Four

Sam

Sam wouldn't even admit to himself that he was avoiding the office. No one had called him on it yet, but it was only a matter of time. He didn't want it to be something they teased him about, especially in front of their newest team member.

It had been almost four months since he'd tiptoed out of that bedroom in Kiev, and he hadn't seen Bray since. They'd spent a little more than four days together. Bray should barely be a memory, yet he crossed Sam's mind in some form every single day. No one had ever gotten under his skin so fast or so deep.

Bray was in training, so if he was there, he was probably in the firing range working on his marksmanship, since he'd shot everyone in the leg in Kiev. Then again, maybe he was in one of the sparring rooms in the gym, working on hand-to-hand with one of the other guys.

Sam pictured Bray getting sweaty as he tangled with Colt or Chase. Even the thought of Bray with a sweet guy like Brody had Sam itching to press the button for the first floor instead of the second. With a shake of his head, he swiped his badge past the reader, placed his hand on the biometric pad and pressed the button for the second floor.

The first floor housed nothing that needed security clearance—not to say it wasn't secure, but they did allow guests to use it. Dee's apartment was the only living space on the first floor, since she hated elevators. The second floor was HC employees only, with a few rare exceptions—exceptions that required security clearance. The third floor was mostly unused at this point, but that would change as they hoped to expand.

The fourth floor was housing space, with different-sized apartments. Some of the guys didn't live in Virginia and stayed there while they were in town. HC had also been used as safe house space for a couple of government agencies. They could give keycard access to only the first and fourth floor, or just the fourth floor if the government agency wanted the person staying there to always have an escort. Each floor had an armory that doubled as a panic room.

When the elevator opened to the second floor, Sam made his way directly to the bullpen. Their work was often solitary, so the guys seemed to prefer the open-style office. Private little work spaces were available if anyone needed a quiet place. No one chose to have their own office, not even Sam, though he was beginning to regret it.

"Well, look what the cat dragged in," Clay said as he pushed his rolling chair back from his desk.

"Surprised it took you this long," Colt said. "I expected you to be standing guard in front of the new recruit."

"I'd make a joke about him pissing around Bray to mark his territory, but then you assholes would just make some off-color joke about me and bathrooms," Ax said.

Sam had tried to talk Mase and Wade out of offering Bray a job. He'd been outvoted. It wasn't that he didn't think Bray was capable of taking care of himself. For a typical soldier, Bray had done really well in Kiev.

Then again, Bray had had three men backing him up in Kiev and had still managed to wreak havoc. What would happen if he was without backup? Some ops called for that. The thought had anxiety clenching Sam's gut. It was a distraction they didn't need.

Ignoring all the jokes and insults flying around the bullpen, Sam pulled out his laptop. He had a little over a week until he had to be in Colombia and he couldn't avoid the office the entire time, especially since he was due to meet with Jazz.

He was going to take two 'bodyguards' with him as much as possible after the shit-show in Kiev, and that wasn't even because of the trouble Bray had caused.

Clement would have done something to try to fuck up the deal, whether Bray had been there or not. Having more people watching his six was a good thing. It also made sense. Word would spread about what had happened, and not adding security would be more suspicious.

Sam was researching what was happening in Colombia when another round of laughing and joking started up. He didn't want to turn around every time someone walked in, because eventually it was going to be Bray. But when someone called out "Woody," Jazz's call sign, Sam smiled and turned from his computer.

The smile fell from his lips when he saw that not five steps behind Jazz was Bray, looking unsure of his place. He also looked fucking amazing. His shoulder must have healed well, because he wasn't wearing a sling of any kind.

His blond hair was longer on the top, as if he'd forgotten to get it cut, but the sides were still short, so Sam figured he was finding his own style apart from a military cut. He was wearing athletic shorts and a tight T-shirt that was damp with sweat. Even seeing his bare legs had Sam struggling to control his wayward body.

"Magnum...War Room," Jazz said.

The fact that Bray was following him, along with Wade, was not a good sign. It wasn't a good sign at all. Sam blew out a slow breath before snapping his laptop shut and lugging it to the War Room.

By the time he entered, everyone else was sitting. He sat in the only open seat at the end of the U-shaped table, the seat across from Bray.

"Looks like the dust has settled in Ukraine." Jazz addressed Bray, since both Sam and Wade knew all this. "Kozak took credit for Andreiko's murder. He claimed it was a betrayal, which we knew already. He's moving up due to his loyalty. They'll probably go after Bagan for trying to usurp their territory and 'merchandise'. Mase is also moving up, especially since he was working more closely under Andreiko and knows the trafficking side of the business but remained loyal to Kozak. He'll be running day-to-day in Kiev while Kozak looks to expand into more of Europe—with our help, of course."

Sam nodded. That was probably what had helped Kozak get promoted as well, the promise of Greece that Sam had dangled in front of him.

"Kozak wants a meeting with you and Sam."

"Why? To tell us to keep our mouths shut?" Bray asked.

"I don't know and I don't care. He wants to meet in Spain. It's where he's going to be headquartered for the time being."

"I'm due in Colombia in a week," Sam said. "We don't want to ditch this either, with coke growing so fast in Europe."

"I'll go," Jazz said. "Human trafficking will always take precedence over drugs. Bottom line… People buying drugs have a choice. People being sold or cut open for organs don't."

Sam nodded, even though this wasn't news to him. Jazz turned to Bray, who seemed to be looking anywhere but at Sam, without trying to be obvious about it.

"You said you weren't sure about reprising your role as Sam's boyfriend, but I'm hoping you'll be willing since you've joined the team."

That statement confused Sam. He wasn't sure why he thought Bray would be all right with pretending to be with him again. Maybe because this was what Sam had been fantasizing about since he'd snuck out of the bedroom in the safe house several months ago.

"Can I speak with Sam privately?"

That soft request stunned him. It was brave to ask two men who outranked you to leave the room before you answered their request.

"Of course." Jazz stood.

Wade stood as well and followed Jazz out of the room. The War Room was huge, much bigger than a conference room. It could easily seat forty people between the table and the computers around the perimeter. The space felt much too large for just the two of them. When the door clicked shut, it echoed around them.

Chapter Thirty-Five

Brayden

Bray felt like such a baby. He should have just accepted the job, but he wanted to make sure Sam was all right with it first. If he'd asked Sam in front of Jazz and Wade, Sam would have complied because they were watching. Sam would hold no punches when it was just the two of them.

"I never got the chance to thank you for everything you did for me in Kiev," Bray said as he met Sam's gaze for the first time.

Sam nodded.

"I know I bombarded you. I know you could have left me twisting in the wind. You didn't, and I'm really grateful—so grateful I'll turn down my first assignment in my new job if it will make you uncomfortable."

"I would never ask you to do that."

Bray tried to swallow down the disappointment that Sam hadn't used the nickname he'd used in Kiev. He wondered if Sam even remembered.

"What if—" Bray swallowed. "What if Kozak still has the place we stayed in bugged?"

Sam licked his lips. Bray followed the movement with his eyes, his dick twitching in his pants. He knew exactly what that tongue was capable of.

"I have no doubt it will be a very similar scenario. So if you're uncomfortable—"

"I'm not. Uncomfortable, that is. Or maybe I am, but only because I'm worried you'll be uncomfortable. That last night…"

Bray didn't exactly know how to describe Sam's freak-out, so he let the sentence hang. Sam's nostrils flared and there was determination in his eyes when he spoke.

"I won't be uncomfortable. I don't get a lot of ass, remember? I'm a workaholic and my job takes me all over the world. I take it where I can get it."

The words were like ice along Bray's skin, the type of ice that was so cold it practically burned. The temptation to get up and leave was strong, but he wanted to be here. He wanted the chance to work with his brother, so he fought back.

"Are you being an asshole to get me to back off this assignment? That would be especially cruel, since I offered to do it, no harm, no foul."

Sam huffed out a laugh and shook his head.

"You're a lot braver than I ever gave you credit for. I kept thinking you were naïve, but maybe you just have balls of steel."

"How is that any sort of answer?" Bray asked.

Sam looked at him. He looked at him for so long that Bray was sure he wasn't going to get any answer at all.

"I haven't been able to stop thinking about Kiev. I'm not thrilled about that, but there it is."

The words shocked Bray enough that he opened his mouth to respond, but nothing came out.

"What I said was true, however cruel. I don't get laid a lot. Even rarer do I get to play with someone who fits me the way you do, with the same predilections."

Sam gave him a long look, as if he were looking for some sort of answer, but Bray didn't know the question.

"If that makes you uneasy," Sam continued, "or if you don't want to play again, we can always jump up and down on the bed and moan. But don't pass up your first assignment. It can be just what it was last time—a little reprieve, a little fun and games."

All Bray could do was nod. Sam stood and went to the door. He did most of the talking when Jazz and Wade returned.

Bray had a hard time finding any words. He was lightheaded. He was dizzy. He was hard as a rock.

* * * *

The trip to Malaga was night and day compared to his little adventure to Kiev. For one, they flew First Class, which was a far cry from his coach seat to Ukraine. They were already in character as boyfriends. Ax would be watching Bray *'like a hawk with no bathroom breaks'*, as he'd put it.

Mitch would be watching Sam's back. Mitch's call sign was Flash because he was such a quick draw, and that relieved Bray.

They were staying at Gran Hotel Miramar in Gibraltar, which was closer to Kozak's new base of operations and the biggest drug port on the coast of Spain.

The hotel suite was just as lavish and ostentatious as the one in Kiev, but much smaller and only had one bedroom. Kozak must have thought they were only bringing Ax, because he'd given them the suite next door, which also had only one bedroom.

Bray felt the last night he and Sam had spent together hanging over their heads. If they were in a real relationship, he would need to address it. Even though they weren't, he still wanted to talk about it.

"We should probably get some dinner then head to bed. Ax and I will take turns at the door to your suite," Mitch said.

"I call dibs on first sleep," Ax said. "Watch out for Hot Cakes there. He's good at popping up where he's not supposed to be."

"Shut up, prince of the johns."

Sam burst out laughing and Bray's chest expanded. Sam was so serious that it brought Bray pleasure when he got him to loosen up or laugh. He'd called himself a workaholic. He wanted another temporary fling. Bray wouldn't pass up the chance to be with Sam again, but he couldn't stop himself from wishing for more.

This time, he knew how hard it would be for him to walk away and how easy it would be for Sam. If Bray hadn't needed to talk to Mase, he would have sat waiting in that safe house for Sam to return. He would have made a fool of himself, so it was probably for the best.

By the time they ate and showered, separately, it was almost nine p.m. local time. Bray lingered in the shower. He was unsurprised to find Sam on his laptop, his back against the headboard.

In a way, this trip was more awkward than the last, because now Bray knew what it was like to be with

Sam. He knew what he wanted but he didn't feel like he could ask for it. He found himself wishing he had a little liquid courage like he'd had the first time.

"We need sleep, B. If you're going to dilly-dally, you won't get to come." Sam didn't look up from his laptop until the sentence hung between them.

Bray licked his lips. His heart kicked up at the use of that nickname and he hurried to the bed. He dropped the boxers he'd been wearing and slid under the covers next to Sam, who set his laptop on the nightstand.

He was glad he couldn't say things like, "I missed you," even though it was true. It would just make him seem more pathetic when Sam walked away this time.

"We've had a long day. I need to get off and so do you. What do you want, B?"

What does he want?

"I know we need to get to sleep. If I get to pick, I just want vanilla tonight."

"Vanilla, huh?"

Sam slid down so they were both lying on the same pillow, facing each other. Bray looked at Sam's full lips and licked his own.

"You want my mouth, B? You want me to blow you, or do you want sixty-nine?"

"I want to taste your mouth," Bray said. "I want to frot until I come all over your chest and I want to suck on your tongue while I do it."

Sam's eyes fluttered closed as he groaned. They hadn't kissed much the last time they'd been together. This time, Bray was looking at it like a smorgasbord. He was going to try to tick off some his bucket list items of Sam fantasies, all the things he wished they'd had time to try in Kiev.

Bray rolled on top of Sam. They both moaned when their dicks pressed against each other. Sam's was leaking just as much as Bray's. That had Bray smiling as he leaned in and captured Sam's mouth.

Bray spread his legs and pressed his knees into the mattress at Sam's hips to give himself more leverage as he began to hump in earnest. Sam thrust up against him but grunted in frustration when he couldn't get enough purchase.

Their movements became hurried and frantic. Bray was already close to the edge. Just as he felt himself building to the crest, the world toppled and Sam rolled them so Bray was on the bottom. He almost laughed at Sam being such a staunch top, but he sucked on Sam's tongue instead.

"Fuck, I'm already close," Sam panted.

"Me too. I need harder…just harder."

Bray felt Sam's cock start to spurt, his jizz helping their cocks glide more fluidly against each other. Bray was almost there. He was so close. He just needed the tiniest bit more pressure. Trying to find purchase himself, Bray grabbed onto Sam's ass and thrust up against him until he finally went over as well.

It wasn't until Bray let his head fall back onto the bed that he realized how tightly clenched Sam's entire body was and where his hands were. He had a hand on each of Sam's ass cheeks, and as he'd been pulling to get more leverage, he'd pulled Sam's ass cheeks apart.

Bray's gaze snapped up to Sam's. If he had to name an emotion Sam was feeling from the look in his eyes, he'd guess scared or confused, with maybe even a little surprise mixed in. Bray dropped his hands to the bed.

When he opened his mouth to apologize, Sam pressed a finger to his lips. Bray had forgotten someone was listening in. The only sound in the room was their panted breaths echoing off the walls. After what seemed like an eternity, Sam lifted his hand from Bray's mouth and hopped off the bed. He didn't say a word as he hustled to the bathroom and shut the door.

Chapter Thirty-Six

Sam

Fuckity, fuck, fuck, fuck. Sam paced back and forth in the bathroom a few times as the water ran in the sink. He was waiting for it to warm up so he could play the caring lover and go clean Bray up. But on the inside, he was panicking.

Bray's fingers near his hole had cut his orgasm short. His body had gone stiff as a board, but he hadn't had even an echo of a flashback like he'd had in the safe house.

Was he finally moving past what he'd done as a stupid teenager? Was it simply time, or was it Bray's sweetness that had him giving more than he ever thought he could?

He ran a washcloth under the warm water and went back into the bedroom. He wouldn't find his answers tonight, so he cleaned Bray off and ignored the apology blaring from those blue eyes.

They started the night out like they had every night in Kiev, Bray on his side of the bed and Sam on his. As Bray's breath began to even out, Sam found himself anticipating the migration across the bed he knew was coming. Even though he was exhausted, he wasn't able to find sleep until Bray had nuzzled against him. Sam turned so he was the big spoon. He wrapped an arm and leg around Bray and let sleep take him.

* * * *

"What time is your meeting?" Bray asked as they ate breakfast on the private balcony.

"Not until two. Then we're supposed to meet Kozak for dinner at seven."

"Let's go for a walk along the beach. You have time."

Sam knew what was coming. It was going to be the most epic apology, the one that seemed to be bursting from all of Bray's pores. He was such a sweet kid. He might be a soldier who could do what needed to be done, but Bray would never hurt someone emotionally – *or sexually*, a voice whispered.

"Sure," Sam said.

He'd let Bray say his piece. It would make him feel better. After breakfast, they headed for the beach, Mitch and Ax in tow. As security detail, the two hung back.

Bray kept looking back at them. When he determined they were far enough away so they couldn't hear, he started in. Sam mentally psyched himself up for the questions he didn't want to answer – the questions he wouldn't answer.

"I did a little research," Bray started.

That statement caught Sam by surprise, but he didn't say anything, just let Bray continue.

"I obviously didn't know I liked to play sub in the bedroom. I've never...at least I don't know if it will always be something I want, but I get off when we do it."

"I know you do." Sam smirked.

Bray shook his head, but there was a smile on his lips. "I read about hard limits."

Sam's footfalls stuttered a little in the sand.

"I thought we should probably discuss hard limits. I mean, I'd like to know how to avoid...sending you to that place."

Sam was floored. He'd had men try to touch his ass before. They'd assumed it was a control thing when he'd backed off. It was a little bit of a control issue, but not to control the scene. It was about controlling his reaction.

"At first I thought it was all ass play," Bray rushed on. "But then you let me...and I liked it and I thought you did, but then you said 'red' and I...I don't know what happened, but I don't want to pull up your bad memories. I was thinking we could make some good memories. I know they won't replace the bad ones..."

"It was a long time ago," Sam heard himself saying. "I thought I'd moved past it."

"I get it. I just seem to lose myself a little when we have sex. I knew about your ass but, well...it's kind of irresistible."

Bray's cheeks were pink from the admission and Sam felt honored that he would be so honest.

"I'd like to know your hard limits," Bray said. "I don't want to send you reeling every time we have sex. We don't exactly have time for me to try to learn on my own, so I'd like you to tell me."

Bray's face betrayed how important it was to him. He was willing to try to discover Sam's idiosyncrasies on his own, but was asking because they didn't have much time together?

"I actually do like swatting your perfect little ass. But it also keeps you where I need you."

Bray's blush spread from his cheeks to his neck, but he seemed pleased that Sam truly enjoyed playing with him. Whoever actually got to keep Bray would be one lucky bastard.

"But the rimming… You liked it at first."

"I liked that all the way through. Shocked the hell out of me. But when your fingers—"

"That's what did it? It seemed like you'd enjoyed the beginning, but I wasn't sure if you'd been enjoying it at all or if it was just at the end that freaked you out."

"I enjoyed it. Believe me, I enjoyed it."

"I'd like to do that again. What if you tied my hands behind my back? Then you would know I couldn't use my fingers. Would that help you relax?"

The thought had Sam getting hard in the middle of a public beach. The thought of Bray on his knees, hands tied behind his back, was hot enough on its own. The idea that he wanted to be bound too so Sam could relax was overwhelming.

"I think that might work," Sam admitted.

"I can see you at least like the idea." Bray smirked and looked pointedly at the bulge in Sam's pants.

They were supposed to be in Spain for four days but only three nights. That was all they had left. A little voice whispered that they might be able to have more, but Sam was too chicken-shit to ask for it. Bray was experimenting, but Sam didn't want to be a project. He didn't want Bray to feel the weight of having to 'fix' him.

Chapter Thirty-Seven

Brayden

When Bray woke up in Sam's arms that last morning, he felt a heart-sick desperation. He clung to a sleeping Sam. He didn't want this trip to end. They'd been able to sightsee and even spend some time playing in the ocean.

The meetings with Kozak had gone well. Bray had felt Kozak's gaze on him constantly. He guessed it was morbid curiosity, but the weight of his stare made Bray uncomfortable. He felt like he was being dissected.

The nights had made it all worth it, though. Bray had made Sam come with only his tongue, and the memory of that made him smile. He'd found a work-around for Sam's issues and now he wanted their time to last beyond Spain. He wanted Sam indefinitely.

The request had been on the tip of his tongue, but he couldn't ask Sam while they were being monitored. Then Sam had distanced himself as they lay in bed. He'd given Bray short, one-word answers as he'd worked on his laptop. Bray squeezed Sam a little tighter at the memory.

He wanted to have Sam one last time, but he couldn't bear to watch Sam pull away again, so he gently snuck out of bed to get first dibs on the shower. While he washed himself, Bray had visions of Sam coming in, pressing him against the tile and fucking him. He lingered with his fantasies longer than he should have but finally turned off the water.

As he snuck out of the bedroom, Bray asked himself some serious questions. Would he be able to work with Sam in the future? Would he be able to pretend to be Sam's boyfriend again if needed? He worried the answer to both might be no.

He'd taken this job to try to help his brother. He'd also selfishly taken it hoping he'd get to be a part of Mase's life when he returned to the States. But that could be years in the future.

Was it worth torturing himself? And what if Sam started dating someone else? What if Sam started dating another one of the guys they worked with? This whole thing was a mess of Bray's own making.

When he walked into the living room, Ax was there setting up breakfast on the balcony—breakfast for four. He and Sam had been having breakfast every morning just the two of them. Was this change Sam trying to avoid being alone with him?

Bray had just helped make his wish come true by sneaking out of their bed, not that they could have a real discussion about their relationship—or lack of relationship, as it were.

"You should be glowing after last night," Ax winked.

Bray's face burned, but he couldn't force a smile.

"Hey, hey. What's going on, Hot Cakes?"

Bray did smile at that nickname. He shook his head because he couldn't force the words past his clogged throat. He'd become friends with Ax. They'd sparred together, joked with each other. But he couldn't betray Sam's confidence, even if they hadn't been monitored.

"He's a tough nut to crack," Ax said quietly. "I've known him more than a year and I've never even seen him cut loose with the guys, let alone date or take some time for himself."

"You don't cut loose either," Bray said.

"I have my reasons."

Bray couldn't tell Ax that Sam had his own reasons too, so he just shrugged. Ax opened his mouth but shut it again when Mitch stepped out onto the balcony with them.

"What am I missing?" Mitch asked.

"Bray said he thinks the Niners will beat the Patriots this year."

"Blasphemy," Mitch said.

Bray smiled at the venom in Mitch's voice.

"I said they have a chance. They have a good team this year." Bray shoved Ax for using the opportunity to haze him in front of Mitch.

"Who has a good team?" Sam said as he stepped out onto the balcony.

"The Niners," Mitch scoffed. "Your boyfriend thinks they have a chance."

Sam stiffened but didn't say anything. Ax gave Bray's shoulder a squeeze as he moved to sit at the table.

"Sam wouldn't know a Niner from a Raider," Ax teased. "He's useless talking football."

"It's like a foreign language," Sam admitted. "I grew up playing soccer."

"You're built like a linebacker. You totally should have played defense in high school ball," Mitch said.

"Too violent for my parents," Sam said quietly.

"Soccer's no pillow fight," Ax said.

Bray was grateful to Ax for keeping the mood light.

* * * *

It was protocol to go through debrief separately. Debriefs were company policy, but this was more formal since they were consulting for multiple government agencies. Jazz and Wade were there, along with the nameless men and women asking a million questions.

Bray had been called in first, probably because he was the newest member. He was heading back to the small office where the other team members were waiting their turn to be questioned. He was just about to round the corner when the words being spoken registered. His feet froze to the floor.

"I was just saying be careful about shitting where you eat. I don't get you, Magnum. You're the one who voted against him joining HC, then you turn around and hook up with him?"

"How do you know who voted which way? We don't ask for feedback on candidates from the team until we've agreed privately to offer a position, and our votes are *supposed* to be confidential." There was suspicion in Sam's voice.

"*Pfft*. We all know," Mitch said. "Even if he hadn't taken a bullet for him, Mase would have approved him. Jazz was thinking about offering him a job after the first debrief when he was still injured. The only one who voted against him was the one screwing him."

Bray was going to lose his lunch all over the floor. Sam hadn't wanted him to join the team? Even with the other guys on board, Sam had voted against him? And yet he'd been more than willing to fuck him in Spain.

He had to get out of there. His heart was beating so hard with anxiety and fury that he was worried he was going to have a heart attack. Even though his mind told his feet to run, they stayed rooted to the floor.

"So you screwed him then screwed him over? Fuck, Magnum, he's a sweet kid. That's cold," Ax said.

"He's also the boss' brother," Mitch said.

"First of all, Mase isn't my boss or anyone's boss really. We're employee-owned, for fuck's sake. Second, us being boyfriends unfortunately became part of the cover in Ukraine and you can blame this douche over here for that," Sam said.

"Me and my big mouth," Ax grumbled. "Between you and Hot Cakes, I'm never going to hear the end of the Ukraine op."

"Look... You don't owe me an explanation. I was just telling you to be careful. If Mase had to choose between you two..." Mitch let the sentence hang.

"I've known Mase almost seventeen years. I was there for him when his 'family' wasn't. He and I are just as much brothers as he and Bray."

"Doesn't that make you and Bray brothers too? That's sick, man," Ax said.

His comment seemed to break the tension in the room. Bray could hear them chuckling. He knew they weren't laughing at him, but it felt that way all the same.

"The op is over and so is the cover," Sam said.

"I just hope Bray knows that," Mitch said.

"I just hope *you* know that," Ax said.

"Fuck you, Ax." Sam said the harsh words with no anger.

"I'm just trying to make sure we have a nice, drama-free work environment. You guys might be nice to look at, but I wouldn't risk my job over it," Mitch said.

"No one's risking their job, for fuck's sake," Sam said. "We're adults. We both know what a no-strings hookup is. Last thing I need is some kid with hero worship thinking I'm something I'm not."

"You just contradicted yourself. First you said he was an adult, then he's a kid. But in both scenarios, you're an asshole," Ax said.

Bray didn't want to hear any more, so he made sure his footfalls were loud enough that the other guys would hear him. When he turned the corner, they all looked up and gauged his face to figure out how much he'd heard. Bray gave his best impression of a smile.

"Sam, you're up," he said.

Sam hesitated before standing. Bray couldn't stand the sight of him, so he looked at Mitch.

"You're on deck," he told Mitch.

"Bray—" Sam started but was interrupted by the ringing of Bray's phone.

Bray didn't want to know what he was going to say, so even if it hadn't been Nick's ringtone, he would have answered. He picked up his phone from the table where he'd left it while in his debrief and pressed the button to accept the call as he moved past the other men and out of the office.

"Hey. Everything okay?"

"You on the job?" Nick asked.

"I'm back. Just finished my debrief. I have the rest of the weekend plus two days of R-and-R that come after an op."

"Then you should probably head west."

Bray wasn't certain what that meant. Was the end near? Sometimes Nick got worked up over nothing. Then again, even if it was just Nick needing some support, Bray would fly out for that as well.

"Let me pack a bag and I'll head to the airport," Bray said.

"Let me know when your flight lands. Either Mom or I will pick you up."

"I'll text you."

"All right."

After ending the call, Bray turned around and headed toward the stairs, but bumped into Ax. He didn't want to see pity in Ax's eyes so he pushed past him.

"Where you off to?" Ax asked as he followed.

"Home."

"Don't go, Bray. Sam's just got his head up his ass."

"I'm not going because of Sam. I'm going to see my family."

"All right. Let me know how you're doing. I'll be in NorCal, so let me know if you need anything."

Bray looked up at Ax. There was no pity there, just understanding. He took a deep breath. He appreciated having a friend, an ally, in Ax, even if they did pick at each other a little. They were almost like, well…like brothers.

"Thanks, Ax. For everything." Bray darted his eyes back to where Mitch was still sitting.

Ax gave Bray a pat on the shoulder and he was grateful it didn't feel at all like a pat on the head.

"As the great Dolly Parton said, *'He doesn't know whether to scratch his watch or wind his butt.'*"

A startled laugh burst from Bray. He'd been choking back tears a moment ago, for two different reasons, and now he was laughing. He'd have to think about that statement a little, and he wasn't sure why a guy like Ax would be quoting Dolly Parton. It gave him something else to think about as he packed a bag and headed to the airport.

Chapter Thirty-Eight

Sam

When they had to ask him the same question three different ways, Sam knew he'd be summoned later by Jazz. He could see it in his friend's eyes. He'd felt nothing but hollow when he'd seen Bray come around the corner.

He'd held his breath until Bray had smiled—or had at least tried to. Sam's gut had roiled and tightened when Bray had acted like nothing had happened. He would have much preferred to have been called out.

Lying in bed with Bray in Spain, Sam had received an email from Mase asking how his brother was doing. While Sam's heart rate was still slowing from the orgasm he'd just shared with Bray, Mase had been worried about him. He'd wanted to know if Sam thought he was enjoying himself, if he was a good fit.

Sam had felt like the worst friend in the world at that moment, because he had no intention of replying that he'd slept with Bray...again. He'd tell Mase in person, not over the phone or by email. He deserved the chance to punch Sam in the face if he so chose. While Bray was lying naked in his bed, Sam had been emailing Mase to tell him his brother's first op was going as smooth as glass.

Even with the email from Mase, his guilt hadn't overridden his want. He'd been forming words in his mind about how to ask Bray to continue what they'd started.

Thoughts had been rolling around in his head as he'd tried to go to sleep. He'd been tempted to ask Bray to try to date for real but had settled on offering to continue experimenting. It wasn't easy to find someone a person trusted enough to try new things. He didn't want Bray ending up in a precarious situation because Sam had introduced him to power exchange.

Sam had decided to offer as soon as they got back to HC, until he'd woken to Bray sneaking out of bed that next morning.

There had been a distance between them as they'd traveled home. He had wondered if Bray was reconsidering everything due to Sam's past. They hadn't had a moment alone to talk before the debrief, then he'd gotten defensive when Mitch had come after him.

Normally Sam would have rolled his eyes and laughed or told Mitch to mind his own business. But he hadn't done that. He'd gotten a severe case of verbal diarrhea, and from the look on Bray's face, he'd heard every fucking word.

"Mr. Fletcher?"

Sam shook himself out of his reverie. He'd missed another question. With a deep breath, Sam did his best to put Bray out of his mind and move through his debrief.

By the time he was finished with his interrogation, Bray was nowhere in sight. Sam couldn't remember all the bullshit he'd spouted after Mitch had blindsided him. He'd made it seem like he hadn't wanted Bray in the first place, which was a lie.

He'd wanted Bray from the moment he'd laid eyes on him. He never would have done a thing about it if they hadn't been in the scenario they'd found themselves in, and he definitely wouldn't have made the first move. That didn't mean he wasn't attracted.

After his little speech, there was zero possibility that Bray would be willing to play, even if he had to pretend to be Sam's boyfriend again.

Sam hadn't wanted Bray on the team. He'd almost abandoned his post in Kiev when he'd found out Bray had run, and he'd been temped again when Bray had been wounded. He'd only known Bray for less than a week at that point. His emotions were even more fucked-up now.

After he'd had time to think about it, Sam was glad Bray had joined HC. He had a group of elite operators watching his six.

It wouldn't erase the sight of Bray hog-tied on a dirty mattress in the basement of a club owned by a drug dealer, but he wouldn't have to worry that the kid was out there doing some kamikaze bullshit all on his own.

Sam tried to convince himself to be glad he'd snuffed out any feelings Bray might have had for him. He should also be happy he'd disabused Bray of any notion that he was some type of true-blue hero.

"He heard us," Ax said as he matched his stride to Sam's.

"No shit. I saw that sorry excuse for a smile."

Sam didn't know what Ax was so torn up about. All he'd done was defend Bray, the way Sam should have.

"Where is he? Upstairs?"

He wouldn't take everything back. Most of what he'd said was true, but he did owe Bray an apology. He shouldn't have talked about any of that behind Bray's back. He should have shut the conversation down from the start.

"Gone," Ax said.

"Gone where?"

Ax shook his head. Sam wasn't sure if that meant he didn't know or that he just wasn't telling. When their eyes met, Sam saw nothing but disappointment in his friend's gaze.

If he knew which room on the fourth floor Bray had been assigned, he would have gone up there to see if he'd left anything behind. But Sam wouldn't abuse his position to find out Bray's room assignment or to add access to the room onto his keycard.

He turned to leave, but before he stepped out of the private workspace they'd been using as a waiting room, Ax grabbed his wrist.

"If you're not going to apologize and at least try to give him what he deserves, leave him alone…for good."

"Now you sound like his brother."

"Yeah, well, maybe he needs it. Mase isn't here and I have a feeling Bray would let you trample on his heart a few more times before he finally gave up."

"Who said anything about his heart?"

"That kid's face is an open book, and when he looks at you, there're only hearts and stars."

Sam grumbled under his breath about hearts and stars.

"You got 'em in your eyes when you look at him too, only you try to cover it up with lust."

"I've spent less than two weeks total with him. There are no hearts."

"They were dancing across your face after one day—hell, after hours. Before you even had him in your bed, you were tearing after him to make sure he was safe and out of Kozak's clutches."

"I was saving Mase's brother." Sam ground his molars together. He liked Ax—he truly did—but the guy didn't know when to shut up.

"*Pfft*. I call bullshit. *I* was saving Mase's brother and I didn't break cover. You rushed in and got on your knees in front of the kid to check all his boo-boos."

Sam wanted to argue. He wanted to be able to blame Bray's kidnapping on Bray alone. But it was on Sam too. In that moment, Sam had shown a weak spot. Andreiko hadn't been in the room, but likely Kozak had told him what had happened and Andreiko had used it against him.

"You just proved my point. Bray doesn't think before he acts. He follows his heart, not his head."

"Bullshit," Ax said. "He sure had his head on straight when he kicked you out of the way and locked himself in a car. He would have been able to get away."

"From one guy. Bagan had dozens."

"Sam, listen to yourself. You're talking about 'what ifs'. Bray assessed the situation. The car was empty except for him—whether that was because it was us or because Bagan's men are stupid doesn't matter. He got it right."

"They would have shot through the window," Sam pointed out.

"He was crouched low. He knew what might have been coming. You know what your problem is, Sam?"

"I'm sure you're going to tell me."

"You're a selfish asshole." Ax said.

"I never denied that."

"Yeah, well, your selfishness doesn't just affect you. It's affecting Bray. You fucking voted against him?"

"He's a distraction," Sam argued.

"To you. Not to anyone else but you."

"He isn't trained."

"He is now. He's taken to it like a duck to water. Considering he got the jump on you when he wasn't trained as an operator, imagine how well he's doing now."

Sam's only response was to clench his teeth at the thought of Bray in hand-to-hand combat with some unsub.

"He's here because he wants to be, Sam—because he's good at what he does and he wants to work with his brother. You tried to take that away from him because it made *you* uncomfortable. You think Mase doesn't feel protective? You think he's not worried about the same things you are?"

Sam blew out a breath as the words began to penetrate.

"He put that aside to assess what was best for Bray," Ax continued. "You can damn sure bet he took Bray's desires into consideration. You only thought of yourself and how it would affect you. You didn't give one thought to Bray's happiness. So I guess you're right. You're *not* in love with him."

With one last snort of contempt, Ax turned to leave. Sam reached out and grabbed his arm before he fully turned away.

He'd told himself he hadn't wanted to risk being distracted by Bray. He'd told himself they'd be a distraction to each other. But that showed zero trust in Bray. And the truth was that even if Bray wasn't there, he was a distraction. And Sam was a selfish asshole just like Ax had accused him of being.

His only concern had been denial. Denial that he was feeling all these mixed emotions about Bray, denial that he wanted more.

He'd told himself that it was in everyone's best interest to turn Bray away, but it had only been serving his own. Sam hadn't fully realized how selfish that choice was until Ax had said it out loud.

"Is he coming back?" he asked, hoping for an actual answer this time.

"He packed up and went to the airport. I don't know his travel itinerary."

Sam rolled his eyes and walked back into the bullpen. He'd have to wait until Wade was out of debrief meetings to see if Bray had contacted him. Unless…

Chapter Thirty-Nine

Brayden

"I'm surprised to find you in here."

Bray turned away from the window he'd been staring out of. His father's study had a lot of good and a few horrible memories. He and Nick had played on the floor in front of the desk for hours. Their dad wasn't one of those who kept the kids out of his office. Bray smiled. Their mom wouldn't have stood for that anyway.

His parents had been raised very differently. Russell Hart came from a lot of money. Their mom came from a middle-class family. Dad was used to getting what he wanted and he wasn't above throwing around his weight, or his money, to get it.

They'd hidden in this room for hide and seek. Their dad had laughingly shooed them out for making faces while he was on conference calls. Their mom had sometimes taken it over when she'd been planning some sort of charity event.

But it was also the room where Mase had come out to their father. Bray had heard raised voices and snuck down to listen. It was the room where Bray had come out to his father, expecting slight displeasure but not anger at Mase.

Bray looked at his father. He was barely recognizable. He walked with a cane. He'd probably lost forty pounds in the last year since the first stroke. His left side was weak. His speech was a little slurred. He looked eighty-six rather than sixty-six.

"There are good memories in this room as well as bad," Bray admitted.

It took his dad a long time to join him at the window. Bray felt for his dad. Yes, there was some bigotry there, but it had cost him his entire family. He'd been completely alone after Nick had walked away.

"He's not going to give me a chance to apologize, is he?"

"Would you? After all this time, after what you did when he turned eighteen, would you come back?"

His dad closed his eyes and looked away. Bray had such a fucked-up relationship with his father. It was much like this room—great memories and horrible ones.

"I guess I'm not surprised he told you."

"Does Mom know? Does she know you named her in whatever you sent?"

His dad huffed out a bitter laugh, but it sounded wrong since his mouth didn't open all the way anymore.

"It's why she left. Before that, she thought he and I were both just being pigheaded. I canceled his phone. She was pissed and thought he did it. I thought I was protecting you. I thought I was protecting everyone."

"You were pissed Mase wasn't rolling over," Bray said.

"I'm not saying that wasn't part of it. It was definitely the reason I sent that document. But I…I expected him to burst into my office and throw those papers in my face. I expected him to show up here and demand to talk to me. I didn't expect him to call my bluff."

"But when I came out to you, you blamed him."

"I didn't blame him."

"You said that even from halfway around the world, Mase was cursing the family."

"I saw everything clicking in your head. In less than an instant, you closed yourself off to me. It wasn't Mase who cursed me. It was what I did to him."

"Thinking my being gay is a curse is a pretty asshole move for a parent."

Russ let out a surprised laugh that sounded a little garbled.

"I never expected you to call me an asshole to my face. Mase, definitely, Nick, maybe, but you…never."

"You didn't exactly fight me when I stopped talking to you."

"How could I fight? You wouldn't answer my calls and your mom was in full mama-bear mode. She wouldn't let me near you. She and the lawyer took out a restraining order."

"What?"

Gil had been Bray and Nick's stepdad for ten years and their dad still wouldn't say his name. Gil wasn't one of those shark lawyers. He was an estate attorney. He created trust funds for wealthy families in Orange County. He was sweet and mild-mannered and loved their mom with everything in him.

"You were still a minor. She had full custody. Said she wasn't going to let me run you off as well."

Bray couldn't exactly blame her. That was her worst fear, that she'd lose Bray and Nick like she'd lost Mase. She mourned him like he was dead, even as she continually tried to reach out to him whenever she found a route to do so.

Nick had held her at arm's length for a while when he'd been in college, but that hadn't lasted too long. Then Nick had found out what their dad had been keeping from him. Nick had walked away too, but that hadn't lasted long either.

"I don't think of it as a curse. I don't know that I ever did. It's not something I understand."

And unfortunately, people fear what they don't understand. And they fuck up. That was why he was able to forgive their father. Looking back, maybe he had understood the gravity of his mistake after Mase, but his comments had still hurt and Bray was still angry on Mase's behalf.

But time was short. The doctors had his father on a host of meds, including blood thinners, but he'd been on those before the second stroke, and the third. Apparently those were some sort of mini strokes called TIAs, but the doctors were still concerned. The second had been months ago, just before Bray had set out to find Mase. The third one had been three days ago.

"I have a letter for him if… It's in my will that you deliver it to him. I just wanted you to know. If he won't hear me out."

"Dad, I don't want to talk about this."

"I tried sticking my head in the sand. It lost me my family. Even after your mom married the lawyer, I still somehow thought we might all come back together. It wasn't until I was sure I was going to die that I knew it was up to me to make things right."

"If it comes to that, I'll give him the letter." But he wouldn't make Mase read it.

"That's all I ask."

They both looked out of the window in comfortable silence for a few moments, until the day nurse came to make sure his dad ate lunch and took his medicine. Nick pulled Bray aside before he made it to the kitchen.

"Since you're working for Mase, maybe he can give you some extra time off to stay with Dad," Nick said. "I'm not re-upping, but I still have a little over a month left of active duty. They're not being as generous with me and letting me move to inactive early," Nick grumbled.

"First of all, I was useless to them and they didn't know if I'd be medically cleared until after I would have moved to reserves anyway. Secondly, I don't work for Mase specifically. Hart Consulting is employee-owned, and though Mase has controlling shares, Wade is the one who's really running things, since he doesn't really do a lot of ops, and nothing undercover."

"So you won't even ask?"

"I'll ask, but I'll go through the chain of command. I'm not going to go crying to Mase, who might not see my email for days anyway. He's still on an op in Europe."

Nick clenched his jaw but nodded. He wanted to ask about Mase—Bray could sense it—but he remained stoically quiet. The silence stretched out so long that he was sure Nick was done talking, so he turned to leave.

"How are they treating you?"

Bray smiled. Despite Sam being a grade-A asshole, he liked everyone he'd come into contact with. No one had really hazed him. No one treated him like he didn't belong there. They didn't treat him like the boss's brother. Well, Mitch might think of him like that, but he'd never acted like it.

"They're treating me like I belong there—not like Mase's kid brother but like one of the guys."

Nick nodded but didn't say anything.

"They're looking to grow. They're trying to get Max."

"Max Freeman? They can't afford him. Kid's a genius."

"You'd be surprised. I'm not sure he can back out of any of his current contracts, but he's considering consulting for them if it doesn't compromise any of his other…projects."

Nick licked his lips but couldn't seem to get the words out.

"I'll send you the application details. I won't know if you apply unless you tell me. I'm still on my six-month probation. Since I'm not technically a full employee yet, I get no say about new candidates."

"I'll think about it. It might be nice to put down roots after moving all over the place."

Bray nodded. That was what he'd been looking for too, but he'd have to man up and face Sam. He should have confronted Sam at the time but having an audience had made Bray freeze.

Add to that the room full of VIPs waiting on Sam down the hall and Bray had needed to let it go. Now he'd have to find a way to talk to Sam, or there would always be an elephant in the room.

Chapter Forty

Sam

Sam sat in his rental car outside the mansion that was apparently Mase and Bray's childhood home. He'd considered waiting through his R&R to see if Bray would come back so he could apologize, but that felt like the coward's way. Their R&R would have taken them through Tuesday, since they'd returned on Saturday morning, but Sam hadn't even lasted twenty-four hours before he'd been boarding a flight.

He wasn't sure what to offer Bray to get him to return to HC. He wasn't even sure Bray had quit, but he was probably considering it after what he'd overheard. Sam would never forgive himself if Bray walked away before getting time with Mase.

After staring at the 'house' for almost an hour, Sam walk up the long driveway. The Hart home was in a gated community. Sam had been able to get past that barrier easily enough, so Bray had no idea he was coming and couldn't shut him out. Steeling himself, Sam knocked.

A woman in scrubs answered the door. She looked him up and down. Her eyes seemed to catch on the tattoo along his bicep peeking out of the sleeve of his T-shirt.

"May I help you?" she asked.

"I'm here to see Bray."

"Mr. Hart isn't in at the moment. If—"

"Who was it, Janet?"

An older man came hobbling around the corner, his gate slow and unsteady. His left leg seemed to drag as he used a cane to propel himself forward. There was no doubt that the man was related to Mase and Bray. There was gray in his hair, but it was the same deep blond as Bray's. He was a tall man but hunched a little.

"It's someone looking for Brayden, Mr. Hart."

The man stopped his forward progress and looked up. The guy was definitely Bray's father, but Sam did his best not to let his hatred show. Sam had assumed Bray would be staying with his mom.

"Let him in," the man said.

"But, Mr. Hart—" the nurse started to protest.

"Won't you join me in my study? I was just about to have a drink."

"Very funny," the nurse said as she stepped aside, allowing Sam to enter.

"I didn't say what I'd be drinking. I'd offer you one, but it'll be a foul-tasting thing that's supposed to help me gain weight."

His words were slow and slightly slurred. Sam didn't know what to say to that, so he said nothing and followed as Mr. Hart continued along his original path to a room down the hall. The silence between them was awkward and uncomfortable. Bray's father was out of breath by the time he turned a knob and opened the door to a large office.

Unsure what to do, Sam stood by the door until the man made it to the desk and collapsed into the large leather chair behind it.

"Sit, sit." He waved his hand at the luxurious, overstuffed leather chairs opposite him as Sam moved into the room.

Mr. Hart could almost be mistaken for Bray's grandfather, but Sam was pretty sure that whatever illness the man was suffering from had aged him.

"So you're Bray's…"

It took everything in Sam not to roll his eyes. If the guy had a daughter, he wouldn't stumble over the word 'boyfriend', but because he only had sons, he couldn't seem to get it out.

"Boyfriend? And what if I am?"

"Then I'd like to know your name."

"Sam."

"He told you about our stilted past?"

"Bray and Mase both told me how you—"

"Mase?"

The man's eyes lit up like a child looking at a pile of unwrapped presents under the Christmas tree when he said Mase's name. Mr. Hart's Adam's apple bobbed.

"How is he?"

"Mase? He's great."

Sam wished he could tell the bastard that all Mase's dreams had come true, but he wouldn't lie. He didn't know how much Bray had already told him, but his loyalty to Mase held strong.

"Is he… Is he happy?"

"Sure. He built a new family from the ground up. He and I, along with a bunch of other guys, are like brothers."

Sam didn't want to say too much, because Mase wouldn't want his dad to be privy to what was going on in his life, but he would make it clear that Mase wasn't alone.

"I'm glad he has a support system."

That answer threw Sam off kilter a little. The guy was obviously sick and was the *'life or death'* in Bray's message to Mase, but Sam wasn't sure if that meant he deserved a chat with his oldest son.

"So are you Bray's boyfriend?"

"I'm surprised you got the word out," Sam said.

Mr. Hart's eyes flared with surprise, but there didn't seem to be any anger there. He opened his mouth to respond but the nurse interrupted them.

She brought in a tall glass with what looked like a milkshake and set it on his desk with a stern look before turning and leaving the room. Sam bit back a smile as he pictured Bray's dad dumping it into a plant or something to get rid of it and totally getting caught doing it.

"You can call me Russ," he said when the door closed.

"I'm not sure I can, Mr. Hart."

"Bray's never brought a boyfriend home before, not that I can blame him. Nick hasn't either, so I'm unused to the word. I didn't mean any offense."

Sam nodded.

"I know you can't have known Bray that long. How long have you known Mase?"

"Since boot camp."

Russ nodded and looked out of the window. Sam didn't want to feel any pity or sympathy for the man who'd kicked his kids to the curb without a cent when he'd found out they were queer. He stood to leave. He'd come back when he was sure Bray was home.

"You don't have to leave. I'll stop asking about him if it makes you uncomfortable." There was a plea in Russ Hart's voice, but Sam tried to close himself off anyway.

"I'll come back when Bray's home."

"He'll be back any moment. He and Nick are at brunch with their mother. It's a Sunday tradition when they're home."

As if speaking about him conjured him, Sam heard the large front door open and close. Nick called out for his father. Sam broke out into a cold sweat when he heard multiple sets of footsteps on the hardwood in the hallway.

The door opened and Nick stepped in, followed by Bray and a small, beautiful woman who had to be Bray's mom. They all stuttered to a stop when they saw Sam. Bray's mom made her way to Russ and asked if he was giving Janet any trouble. She eyed the drink on his desk.

Russ flattened his lips but picked up the glass and began slurping it through the straw until Mrs. Hart gave a satisfied smile. Then she turned her gaze on Sam, who tried not to squirm. Apparently, he could easily deal with mafia and drug lords, but moms made him uncomfortable.

"What are you doing here, Sam?" Bray asked.

There was no inflection to his voice. Definitely not a good sign.

"Unless… Is Mase—"

"Everything at HC is fine," Sam quickly cut in, not wanting to cause worry. "I do need to speak with you, though. Just for a moment."

Bray looked at each person in the room before reluctantly nodding. Sam was pretty sure Bray wanted to tell him to go to hell but didn't want the whole scene to play out in front of his family.

He followed Bray silently through the house. They went through a bunch of large, overly decorated rooms before Bray opened a set of French doors that lead to a patio with more square footage than Sam's childhood home.

Bray walked to a staircase at the back of the patio. He didn't turn or signal Sam in any way as he trotted down the steps. Sam followed.

They ended up on a stretch of private beach that either belonged to the gated community or to Bray's father individually. It took Sam a minute to realize that Bray wasn't stopping. He continued at a quick pace down the beach, so Sam hurried to catch up. When he finally did, Bray turned on him.

"Why are you here, Sam?"

"I came to apologize."

"Fine. You've done what you came to do, now you can leave," Bray said the words to Sam, but his gaze was out on the horizon.

"Don't you want to know what I'm apologizing for?"

"You're apologizing because I heard everything. If I hadn't heard, you wouldn't apologize for all the asshole things you said and did."

Bray still wouldn't look at him. Sam wanted to refute his words, but they were at least partially true—but not for the reasons Bray thought.

"I'm here to apologize for not stopping that conversation in the first place. I never should have talked about anything that should stay between us. It all got blurred because it was part of an op, so everyone at HC seems to think they can have an opinion on it."

"Bullshit. You're one of those guys who's only sorry if he gets caught."

"If that were true, you and I would still be fucking."

"What does that even mean?"

"Bray…please look at me."

Finally, Bray turned to face him. There was fire in his eyes. His nostrils flared as he put his hands on his hips. He probably wasn't going to listen, but Sam had to try anyway.

"If my only concern was getting caught, you and I would still be sleeping together."

Bray shook his head and said, "You got what you wanted in Spain, then you acted like I wasn't even there."

"What are you talking about? You're the one who snuck out of bed at dawn-o-thirty and wouldn't look me in the eye."

"I was sick of you putting distance between us as soon as the cum cooled."

"Bray, you slept on top of me every single night. There wasn't much distance."

"That last night you wouldn't even look at me."

"That last night, I'd just gotten an email from your brother asking me how you were adjusting, asking me if I was watching your back. I'd just fucked you and Mase is asking me if I'm looking out for you."

"I don't need looking after. I don't want special treatment."

Sam looked at the mulish frown on his mouth. He wanted to kiss it right off Bray's face. The look reminded Sam of a spoiled child. It was unfortunately pretty adorable on a man as gorgeous as Bray.

"Bray—"

"What are you saying here, Sam?"

"I don't want you walking away from HC because of me."

"I won't."

That stopped Sam short. Maybe he was projecting his feelings, because Sam sure as hell would have a difficult time being around Bray and pretending he felt nothing.

"So you'll be back at work on Wednesday?"

"Not Wednesday. I did ask for some time off."

"Bray—"

"I realize I haven't worked there long, but Nick has to go back and finish out his active duty. He's got a month left before he can move to Reserves or IRR. I'm going to try to be available for my dad as much as possible until he's done. I told Wade I'll be available for West Coast ops. He mentioned maybe helping out in San Francisco."

If Bray was working SFO, it would be with Ax. Why did that make Sam's gut burn?

"Look, Sam. I forgive you, okay? It wasn't the funnest moment to have after my first op, but I'm the one who started things between us. I have to take responsibility for that as well. I was also willing to continue things. That's on me too. You can go with a clean—"

"Was?" Sam blurted.

"What?"

Bray's face scrunched in confusion. It took Sam a moment to realize he'd said the word aloud—the word he hadn't been able to get past to hear the rest of Bray's speech.

"You said 'was *willing to continue*'."

"Okay." Bray drew out the word.

Sam had lost his chance with Bray, just as he'd figured out what he wanted.

Chapter Forty-One

Brayden

Bray didn't know what Sam's goal was in picking apart what he'd said. He was trying to take responsibility for his part in this mess. If he stayed on with HC as he planned to, he'd have to see and even possibly work with Sam.

He couldn't let Sam wallow alone in guilt. Some of it rested on Bray's shoulders as well. He had been the one to back Sam into a bit of a corner in Kiev.

"You were willing to continue things…but now you're not."

Sam sounded so much like the men who questioned him in the debriefs, as if nothing could be misconstrued. Everything needed to be spelled out.

"Are you asking me to continue fucking you on the down-low, or are you just clarifying?" Bray asked.

"Our fucking was never on the down-low," Sam scoffed.

Memories of things they'd done flooded Bray's mind. He tried to shake them off before he had a tent forming in his jeans.

"We aren't compatible," Bray said.

"If that's incompatible, I'd like to see what you consider compatible."

"Sexually compatible, sure, but emotionally…" Bray shook his head.

He needed someone who would talk to him, open up to him. He wanted a real relationship, not just sex. Sam wasn't willing to give him those things.

"We're not looking for the same things," Bray finally said.

"That was true," Sam replied.

Bray's heart cracked in two.

"I sure as hell wasn't looking for a relationship," Sam said. "I know for a fact that I never expected Mase's kid brother to stumble into my life and tempt me beyond all reason. I'm not sure what makes you so sure we're not compatible. You seem to tie me up in knots and have me running around in circles."

"Stop," Bray said a little too loud. "Stop being an asshole just to turn around and say something sweet. Pick one or you're going to make me dizzy with all the back and forth."

"I'm not trying to be an asshole. I'm trying to be honest here. I wasn't looking for you, but that doesn't mean I don't want you. Bray, I've…I've never told anyone about what happened to me—not Mase, not Kota, not Jazz or Mitch or Wade. But I'm going to tell you."

Bray sucked in a breath.

"I told you my folks kicked me out when I was sixteen. But I couldn't join up even with parental permission until I was seventeen. I thought... Well, I thought my 'boyfriend' who was older would take me in. I didn't know he was married with a kid on the way. The kicker was that he pursued me, yet I felt like a home wrecker when I yelled at him in front of his pregnant wife and punched him in the face."

Sam shook his head as if he still couldn't believe it. Bray fisted his hands to keep from reaching out and comforting him. He needed to hear the whole story.

"I had a hundred and twenty bucks to my name, no real job prospects and no place to live. I couch surfed a little, but when my friends' parents found out why I'd been kicked out, I had fewer and fewer places to go. I, uh, I'd lived a pretty sheltered life. I didn't exactly have a lot of job skills. I started looking at ads for roommates. Most of them were still way out of my price range, but one guy..."

Sam took a few breaths as he looked out at the waves crashing on the sand.

"One guy said I could pay a different way. I had just under six months until my birthday. I had a plan, but I had to get through those six months. I saw the army as my salvation and I just kept my eye on the prize as I got my GED and worked as much as I could."

Bray's heart lurched and his stomach plummeted at what Sam was saying. He'd had to...

"It's like once you give up a little control, it's all taken away from you. Rent turned into more, turned into letting his friends use me, turned into guys with fetishes for young boys showing up. I guess he posted some ad somewhere."

"What? That's... That's like—"

"Like a prostitute? Yeah, I know."

"I was going to say child abuse or trafficking. You were still a kid."

"I felt used and dirty. I didn't like it, but I had nowhere else to go. I hated my life and myself, but I felt so much shame because I let it happen."

"A sixteen-year-old with no financial support doesn't *let* anything happen. Adults aren't supposed to take advantage of a child. They're supposed to protect children."

"We both know that isn't always what happens. When I was finally seventeen, I lit out of there in the middle of the night. He didn't want me moving out."

"Sam…" Bray whispered the word.

He wasn't sure why Sam was telling him all this. Was it tit for tat? Hell, it didn't even matter. Bray's heart twisted for sixteen-year-old Sam. When Sam saw Bray reaching for him, he stepped back and continued talking.

"After being so totally out of control, I think I took it back with a vengeance. Before that, I… Well, I always preferred topping, but I enjoyed bottoming on occasion as well. Afterward, I couldn't even touch myself that way. I went to a therapist when I was in college and I thought I'd made peace with it for the most part—or at least made peace with the fact that I didn't want that to be part of my sex life anymore. Because I never even considered…never wanted that to be a part of it until you."

"Sam."

Again, Bray didn't know what to do with this confession. Sam didn't want comfort, so Bray wasn't sure what he did want.

"No one's ever guessed anything happened except you."

"Is this your way of telling me you think we're emotionally compatible?" Bray asked.

"I guess it's my way of telling you I'm just selfish enough to realize you're good for me. I could probably be good for you if I put more effort in. I…I want to talk to Mase, but—"

"What the hell does Mase have to do with any of this?" Bray circled his hand between the two of them as if to prove his point.

"I just need to talk to him about what's going on. He's pretty protective of you. When he thought you were in love with me… Well, it was the first time he ever punched me for real, not sparring."

"The gut punch surprised you, huh? Jazz said it was rare for someone to get the drop on you."

"It is—and apparently specific to your family. I'm sorry about all that shit with Mitch. You're right that I wouldn't have apologized if you hadn't overheard—not because I didn't feel bad, but because at that point it would have been about making you feel bad to make myself feel better."

"Why did you vote against me?"

"Oh, B, that's such a loaded question."

Bray felt his throat close at the use of the nickname Sam had given him.

"I didn't want you putting yourself in more danger," Sam continued. "You almost gave me two heart attacks in Kiev. The bottom line is that every reason I had for voting against you was selfish, and for that, I am truly sorry. I know you're capable. I know you'll be a valuable member of the team."

"So is this you asking me to be your boyfriend?" Bray asked.

Sam chuckled. "Just as soon as I ask your brother's permission."

"Why do you need Mase's permission?"

"Because more than anything in the world, he wants a relationship with you, and I won't fuck that up. I came here to make sure I hadn't already done that. I was all set to try to stay out of your way, but then you had to go and talk about San Francisco ops, which means you'd be working with Ax and…" Sam rubbed the back of his neck.

"You're jealous? Even if we're together, I'll still need to work with Ax."

"But then we'd be together and Ax would keep his hands off you."

"Ax doesn't want me and I don't want him. It's like you and Mase. I see him like a brother."

Sam shrugged.

"Samuel Wheeler, what am I—?"

"Fuck," Sam said then started laughing.

Bray didn't know what was happening. He was a little worried about whether Sam's laughter was a good or a bad thing.

"What's so funny?" Bray demanded.

"I've slept with guys who didn't know my name, but I've never asked one to be my boyfriend."

Sam fell into another fit of laughter. Bray was elated. Sam *was* asking him to be his boyfriend. But…

"Wait, what? Sam's not your name?"

"Wheeler. It's my alias." Sam had to pause to catch his breath. "Sam's real, but it's not Samuel. My full name is Samson Fletcher."

"I've never had sex with a guy when I didn't know his name." Bray frowned.

"You have now." The words burst out of Sam before he started laughing again.

Bray couldn't help but smile. After all, he did kinda know Sam, even if he hadn't known his name. He didn't find it as funny as Sam. With Sam laughing so hard, eventually Bray joined in, laughing more at Sam's mirth than the actual situation.

"What are we doing here, Sam?"

"I was going to be all selfless and give you up so you would stay at HC, so you and Mase could build a relationship. Just like all my well-laid plans, you blew it all to hell."

"So I'm good for you," Bray clarified.

"Yeah," Sam admitted. "Definitely."

"Okay. Now we're getting somewhere. Then, yes." Bray nodded.

"Yes?"

"Yes, I'll be your boyfriend. It'll have to be long distance for the next few weeks. That will give us time to get to know each other a little better outside the bedroom and—"

Sam groaned, which made Bray laugh. He pulled Bray to him and kissed him until they were both breathless.

Epilogue

Six months later
Brayden

"What the fuck have you been telling your brother about me?" Ax grumbled.

"Which brother?"

Bray smiled at the question, because he now had two brothers he spoke to regularly again. Mase was still in Kiev, but he was getting ready to come back to the States. He'd still be undercover, but Bray would be able to see him under the guise of being Sam Wheeler's boyfriend.

"The cranky-ass one."

That would be Nick. He and Ax seemed to be butting heads more than getting along. Nick was getting ready to assist on his first op. He'd requested to work on the West Coast, so he was going to help Ax in San Francisco.

Bray had been working mostly with Sam and it had been better than he'd ever imagined it could be. Inside the bedroom or out, undercover or in real life, he and Sam had made something real from something fake. Bray knew how rare that was.

"I didn't tell Nick anything about you. Maybe if you stopped calling him Nickel, he'd like you more."

"I call you Hot Cakes and you still like me."

"I think you're incorrigible. Nick thinks you're an asshole. You have to allow for both those things."

"Aw, you think I'm adorable?"

Bray rolled his eyes and grumbled that Ax heard what he wanted to hear.

"That's not what you said last night," Sam said as he sat down next to Bray and slung his arm over his shoulders.

"I said incorrigible, not adorable." Bray enunciated both words slowly.

"Same difference." Ax waved a dismissive hand.

"It's a huge difference," Sam argued. "They're not synonyms. Incorrigible means hopeless, as in no hope for getting my boyfriend to think you're adorable."

Nick walked up and set his hip on Bray's desk, on the opposite side to Ax. He narrowed his eyes at Ax and crossed his arms.

"You just want to keep saying 'boyfriend'." Ax rolled his eyes. "We get it. It's been six months. We're over it, move on."

"Are you ready?" Bray asked Nick.

"If he doesn't fuck it up, I'll be fine." Nick pointed his chin in Ax's direction as he spoke.

"Hey," Ax replied. "I haven't fucked up an assignment yet."

Sam opened his mouth but Ax was already talking over him.

"No, no. Don't thank me for bringing you and Hot Cakes together. Just make me the godfather of your first born and we'll call it even."

Sam chuckled and shook his head.

"Everyone lived. Nothing was fucked up and you guys got to live happily ever after."

"You and your ego could take up this whole building," Nick said.

Bray was one hundred percent sure there was some sort of chemistry between his brother and Ax, but he kept that to himself. They'd have to work it out on their own. He didn't mention it to Sam, because another couple of operators dating wouldn't necessarily be a good thing.

He and Sam had had their bumps in the road. Sam had tried to pull rank a few times and keep Bray from what he viewed as dangerous jobs. After some pretty bad fights and some pretty stellar makeup sex, they'd decided that Sam would have no say in Bray's assignments. They left that up to Wade.

"Time to head out, B," Sam said as he stood.

"Aw, you two are so cute," Ax said. "Just remember… I'm the reason you two are together."

"I think we'll take credit for our own relationship, thanks," Sam said as he patted Ax on the head like a child.

"I threw you two together—" Ax said.

"By mistake, because you have a big mouth," Sam interrupted.

"And I made you jealous enough to actually do something about it," Ax continued.

Sam shook his head and took Bray's hand, leading him from the bullpen. They'd been living together for two months. Bray had been looking for an apartment, but Sam had kept calling it a waste of money since they spent every night together.

* * * *

"What's with the rush?" Bray asked as they stepped over the threshold to their apartment.

"It's our six-month anniversary," Sam said.

"Are we going out?"

"Nope. We're staying in."

The salacious smile on Sam's lips had Bray's body humming. They found their groove in the bedroom, though they still experimented pretty regularly.

"I have a surprise for you," Sam whispered.

Sam sauntered toward their bedroom, taking off his clothes as he went. Bray smiled as he followed the trail of discarded garments down the hall.

By the time Bray made it to their bedroom, Sam was in nothing but boxers as he started pulling things out of 'the drawer'. It was where they kept all their playthings. The idea of a new toy or a new scene had Bray's cock throbbing in his pants.

"Lie down on the bed," Sam said without looking up.

Bray was naked and spread out on the mattress in probably two seconds flat.

"Hands and knees or starfish?" Bray asked.

"Starfish."

Bray squeezed his thighs together. Starfish meant he got tied to the bed. After a moment, Sam tossed a bottle of lube by Bray's hip. Bray licked his lips. He had a love-hate relationship with edging. He loved the orgasm it brought on but hated the frustration it caused along the way. Sam loved edging him.

Bray wondered if Sam had bought them a new dildo, maybe a bigger one or some vibrating wand he'd been making noise about. He didn't care as long as Sam touched him.

Sam quietly and efficiently bound Bray's hands to the leather cuffs they left attached to the bed. He was surprised when Sam left his ankles free. It meant it wasn't an edging session, because Bray would be able to get traction to hump up into Sam's hand.

Sam seemed on edge. Bray had assumed it was because he was turned on, but now he seemed…different. Not quite his confident self.

"Talk to me," Bray pleaded.

Sam took a deep breath.

"I love you," he said before placing a blindfold over Bray's eyes.

Bray relaxed back on the bed. Sam placed a tender kiss at the corner of his mouth before backing away. The soft scuff of bare feet on carpet was all Bray heard until the rustle of Sam's boxers hitting the floor.

Some of Sam's weight shifted onto the bed near Bray's feet. He heard and felt Sam move around but he had no clue what was happening. Then there was the familiar snick of the lube bottle opening and finally Bray's groan as Sam grasped his cock and tightly stroked up and down with a strong hand.

Since his legs were free, Bray did what Sam would normally punish him for. He bent his knees and placed his feet flat on the bed. He pumped up into Sam's tight grasp. Instead of pressing his hips into the bed, Sam chuckled.

Bray felt small touches of skin on skin and dips in the mattress as Sam climbed over him, his legs on either side of Bray's hips. *So it's going to be a frotting session?*

Bray hummed his approval. He loved having Sam's weight on him.

Then Bray felt something. It was something warm pressing to the tip of his penis. It took a moment for it to register, but when it did, he fought his restraints harder than he ever had.

"Sam. No. Red."

"Red?"

"Yes. If you're going to force yourself to do this, then red. Red, red, red."

Sam pulled the blindfold off. Bray looked down but what he saw only turned him on more. Sam was poised over him. Bray's cock was kissing Sam's tight pucker and Sam was hard. Well, mostly hard.

"Still red?" Sam asked.

Bray shook his head.

"I need the words, B."

"Green all the fucking way unless your dick wilts—but no blindfold. I need to see your face."

"A lot of men flag a little upon entry."

Bray smirked. Sam made it sound like a military op.

"You don't have to do this," Bray said, even though his cock was throbbing with want.

"I know. I want to, and that makes all the difference in the world."

Sam had been going to therapy again. He'd said he might want to try bottoming in the future, but this seemed too soon. Bray had been sure it would take more than a few months.

"Typical Dom," Bray said. "Bottoming from the top."

Sam smiled as he pressed himself against the tip of Bray's erection. After that, Bray's thoughts scattered.

No way was he capable of carrying on a conversation when his dick was being strangled with warmth.

"Fuck. So fucking tight."

Bray closed his eyes and concentrated on remaining completely still.

I will not thrust. I will not thrust. I will not thrust.

He repeated it to himself over and over for what seemed like hours until Sam's ass cheeks finally pressed against his thighs. Bray gave in and arched up, pressing the last few millimeters of his erection inside Sam's ass.

"Fuck," Sam groaned.

"Yeah," Bray sighed. "That was a good fuck, right?" Bray's opened his eyes to assess Sam's reaction.

Sam nodded.

It was like nothing Bray had ever felt before. Then again, he was bare inside of Sam and he'd never had sex without a rubber before—well, at least not while topping…or rather topping from the bottom. It was incredible. *So. Much. Heat.*

Sam rolled his hips and Bray groaned. He was already breaking out into a sweat, trying to keep himself as flat on the bed as possible. Sam continued to experiment and it was killing Bray. He squeezed his eyes shut to keep from coming when Sam's tight hole clenched around him. Warm lips brushed over Bray's cheek and his jaw.

"Open up, B. You didn't want the blindfold. Let me see what's going on in that head of yours."

"Too tight. Concentrating. Can't. Move."

"What? Why can't you move? I left your legs free so you could have leverage."

Bray's eyes popped open and he tugged hard on the restraints. He wanted to arch up and kiss Sam, but he didn't have enough give. What he saw just made his cock throb inside the vise that was Sam's ass.

"You have no idea how good this feels. I want to be able to do it again," Bray ground out through gritted teeth. "If I fuck up now, it might send you back a few steps."

"You think I don't know how this feels? Hi, I'm Sam. I'm addicted to Brayden's ass and riding it bareback."

Bray tried to laugh but ended up groaning.

"Did you just make a joke? You choose this point in our relationship to start joking? I'm trying not to come before we even get started. It's been so long since I felt an ass gripping me and it's never been this hot, this tight. Fuck, Sam. I have to move."

"We'll talk after we come. For now, just fuck me, B."

Bray couldn't hold back anymore. He planted his feet and started arching up. Sam gasped. Bray was too far gone to get anxious about Sam's reactions. If Sam didn't like it, he'd have to pull himself off Bray's dick, because he couldn't stop now.

After a moment, Sam began to meet Bray's thrusts. He watched as Sam's cock began to fill and grow. He wished he could jack him off in time with his hips, but Sam wasn't ready for that yet.

He'd been sure Sam couldn't handle this, but the cock in front of him, pointing to the ceiling, proved otherwise. Sam did something, some move that made his ass even tighter. Bray humped up at a different angle that had Sam shouting. He used that angle again and again as he pegged Sam's prostate.

Sam leaned down and stuck his tongue in Bray's mouth. He held Bray by his hair and fucked his mouth like Bray was fucking his ass. It was almost perfect.

One day, one day soon, Sam would climb on him with no restraints and Bray would be able to run his hands over the pecs and biceps he loved. He'd be able to touch and lick Sam's tattoos while buried deep inside him, just like he did when they cuddled in bed. This, this was a step in the right direction. It was a sign that Sam trusted him, that they were moving forward.

Bray changed the angle of his hips a little more, sliding down the bed just an inch. It gave him a little more leverage and a better angle to peg Sam's sweet spot.

"Fuck," Sam shouted as he tore his mouth away. "I can't… I'm going to…"

The back of Sam's cock had been running up and down Bray's abs, but now, hot spurts of jizz landed on his skin. That and the tight spasms strangling Bray's cock had him shooting as well. And when he remembered that he was bare inside Sam's ass, a second wave of pleasure shot through him, causing him to spurt even more of himself deep inside the man he loved.

Sam was supporting his weight on the mattress as he panted. Bray's hands were still tied to the bed. Sam had come hands-free. That was the hottest thing Bray had… Fuck. He'd missed it.

"I need to see that next time," Bray panted. "You coming hands-free. That's the hottest thing I've ever not seen."

Sam chuckled as he collapsed onto Bray.

"Now who's making jokes at an inappropriate time? I can barely breathe or think and you want me to untwist that mind-fuck you just said?"

Sam reached up to unbuckle the restraints. He gently rubbed and kissed each of Bray's wrists. Bray wrapped himself around Sam like a monkey.

"Best. Anniversary gift. Ever," Bray whispered.

"Yeah?"

"Oh yeah. And this was only six months. What do I get for one year?"

Sam shook his head but laughed.

"I'll have to think about it."

"I just don't want you to push yourself. I mean, I've always leaned a little toward bottoming. You don't have to try to do this all the time."

"I liked it, B. Obviously. I'm not saying I want it every day, but sometimes, and eventually, hopefully without the restraints."

"Mm-m. That'll be a new fantasy for me if we're on different assignments, me inside you and getting to play with your nipples, stroke your cock."

Sam covered Bray's mouth with his hand.

"Stop it. You're going to make me hard again. You forget I'm older than you."

"And yet your recovery time is about the same as mine," Bray said.

"Well, that's because you and my dick are writing checks my body can't always cash. Give me at least thirty minutes before you start all the dirty talk."

"Fine. But how did you… I mean how did you know you were ready? Did you…?" Bray broke off with a groan as he pictured Sam using a dildo to fuck himself.

"I've been working my way up with my hands and some butt plugs. I didn't want to try it with you if I couldn't even get myself stretched out. I was actually wearing a butt plug the last part of the day at work. I wanted to make sure I was really stretched before I tried taking your girth-y cock."

"Oh, fuck." Bray was already hard again. "You were wearing a plug at work? Walking around, stretching yourself for me. *That's* the hottest thing I've ever not seen."

Sam laughed.

"You're going to have to show me," Bray whispered. "Maybe I'll have to pull it out with my teeth so I can fuck you with my tongue, since I'll still need my hands tied behind my back."

"Fuckin' kid," Sam grumbled as he thrust his again-steel-hard cock against Bray's hip.

"You love it," Bray teased.

"I love you," Sam said as he rolled Bray to his back and shut him up the way Bray liked, with his mouth.

Want to see more like this?
Here's a taster for you to enjoy!

Treasure Trove Antiques: The Lucky Cat

L.M. Somerton

Excerpt

Sometimes there were advantages to being vertically challenged. Landry, his ass sticking out from under a seventeenth-century folding card table, paused to contemplate other occasions when his five-feet-six-inch stature had been of benefit. Not when attempting to get served at his favorite leather bar, though getting squished between all those black-clad hunks was always bearable. He snorted. Not when reaching for his preferred brand of chips at the market, which were always on the top shelf. Put there, he was sure, by the snotty assistant manager as revenge for Landry turning down his offer of a quick blow job in the staff restroom. *As if.* Never at family meals when he got to sit between his older twin brothers like a blond munchkin between two extras from *Vikings*. He reversed, wiggling his back end to avoid a willow-patterned platter balancing on a brass coal scuttle. His knees ached and he'd banged his elbow on a cast-iron fireguard, but he had rescued the battered cannonball making an escape attempt beneath teetering piles of stock.

"Well, there's a pretty sight."

"Hey!" Landry went for indignant rather than flattered. He tried to get up too soon and banged his head on solid, woodworm-free oak. "Fuck me!" He finally made it to open air and scrambled to his feet, rubbing his already messy hair into further disarray.

"Is that a request?"

Landry looked up…and up…into a pair of twinkling pale-blue eyes. The customer, because that was who Landry guessed the newcomer must be, was drop-dead, my-ass-is-yours gorgeous and he was grinning. Well, smirking.

"Funny man. What can I help you with, *sir*?" Landry gritted his teeth and remembered that Mr. Lao, his boss, would swat him like a bug if he snarked at a potential patron. *Though, on this occasion, it might be worth it to mess with the man.*

"Another leading question."

Landry rolled his eyes. Black hair, blue eyes and a stubbled, chiseled chin did not equate to a free pass. "The massage parlor is three doors down, just before St. Peter's. You can get a full-body whatever then confess all in the space of an hour." He made an ineffective attempt to brush dust from the knees of his ripped black jeans. Blue Eyes reached into his jacket and produced a wallet, which he opened to display a Seattle PD badge and ID card.

"Gage Roskam. Is your boss around?"

Landry was more turned on than intimidated by the badge. Cop plus handcuffs equaled sexy time. Every cop he'd ever met had had a 'don't fuck with me' attitude and a natural bent for control—just the type of man Landry liked to mess with. He batted his lashes. "And what makes you think I'm not the boss?"

"You're not a sixty-eight-year-old Chinese guy by the name of Jian Lao?"

"Very observant, Officer. All that training paid off." Landry put an extra bit of swing into his hips as he walked toward the cash desk at the rear of the shop.

"Putting your tax dollars to work, brat."

"Hey! Aren't you supposed to call me sir, what with you being a public servant and all?"

"In your dreams, and you should show more respect for law enforcement."

"Gonna make me?"

"You're lucky I'm on duty or I'd bend you over the nearest flat surface and give you the spanking you're begging for."

"Is that line in the big bad cop manual?" Landry scuttled behind the cash desk, relieved that it reached to his waist and therefore hid his burgeoning erection. "Because I don't think it's very professional."

"I use language appropriate to the situation." Gage grinned. "I can give you my badge number if you wanna make a complaint. Then again, if you'd like to engage in a deep and meaningful conversation about your attitude, you can use this number." He grabbed a pen from a pot next to the cash register then scribbled his number on the top sheet of the pile of wrapping tissue.

Landry nibbled on his lower lip. He got propositioned a lot but there was something about Gage that appealed to him. He might as well have had 'Dominant' tattooed across his forehead, and that pushed all Landry's submissive buttons. He'd also called Landry out on his snarky attitude, which had the dual effect of stimulating Landry's intellect as he decided on the most appropriate retort *and* giving him the urge to drop to his knees. He resisted the latter option.

"Now you're the one who's dreaming. Mr. Lao isn't here." Landry checked his watch. "And as he headed out to lunch with a bunch of cronies from his bowling club, I don't expect him back any time soon. So is there anything I can help you with that won't involve me getting arrested?"

Gage gave him an intense look, which made Landry squirm and wish he'd put on a looser pair of pants that morning. "Fine. I have some pictures I want you to take a look at." Gage pulled out his phone.

"How kinky are they?" Landry asked. "Because I think you should know there's some stuff I'm just not into."

"Only *some* stuff? You do surprise me. Are you into receiving stolen goods?"

"No! Of course not." Landry bristled. "Treasure Trove Antiques is a reputable establishment. Mr. Lao doesn't buy anything without checking out its provenance and I don't buy anything at all because Mr. Lao won't let me yet. I can't tell the difference between Ming dynasty and tourist trash made in some underground sweatshop in Kowloon, though he is trying to teach me. I'm kind of his apprentice."

"If I show you a bunch of pictures, would you know whether you have the items in stock?"

"That I can do." Landry couldn't help but preen a little. "Mr. Lao has trouble remembering what day of the week it is. He relies on me to be able to lay my hands on anything the customers are looking for, and in this place..." He gestured at the cavernous space piled high with row upon row of stock. "That's nothing short of miraculous."

"Then is there somewhere we can sit, because this may take a while?"

"I'll have an extra-large, skinny, vanilla latte and a brownie."

Gage sighed. "You're lucky I'm a patient man. Where do you suggest I go for those?"

"Now that depends." Landry tapped a finger against his lips. "You don't look like a Starbucks man, but there's one down the block if that floats your boat. The café next door is a small independent place and there's not much I wouldn't do for a regular supply of their baked goods."

"What does a Starbucks man look like? No, don't tell me. I don't need to know."

"My cooperation is contingent on provisions."

"So you're telling me you accept bribes?"

"Absolutely. So long as they involve chocolate. Or coffee. Preferably both and in large quantities."

"I'll be five minutes. Don't go anywhere."

"Perhaps you should cuff me, Officer." Landry blinked.

"It's Detective, and don't tempt me." Gage strolled toward the exit. Landry kept his gaze glued to the man's ass, wishing that his jacket didn't cover it quite so well. He licked his lips and pushed the heel of his hand against his erection.

"Down boy. Behave. You're going to get me into so much trouble... Not that I wouldn't enjoy engaging in a little crime and punishment role play with Detective Roskam."

A carved, Middle Eastern table not far from the cash desk would allow Landry to keep an eye on the register while he helped out Mr. Hot Detective. He dragged a couple of sturdy 1930s chairs down an aisle, setting them behind the table. He also directed the battered Anglepoise lamp on one corner of the cash desk toward the table to give a bit more light, because Mr. Lao kept the place in semi-darkness in the hope that some of the customers wouldn't look too closely at what they were buying.

There were a few people browsing the aisles and Landry rang up a purchase for a young couple who'd found a pressed-glass art deco vase for a parent's birthday. He'd just finished wrapping it, having been careful to preserve the sheet of tissue with Gage's number on it, when Gage returned carrying a cardboard tray of coffee and a paper bag. Landry eyed them, happy to see they came from the café next door. He wished his departing customers well then made a grab for the bag, poking his nose inside to find two sizeable brownies, double chocolate chip cookies and two white chocolate and blueberry muffins.

"Color me impressed," Landry muttered around a mouthful of brownie. "Oh my God, this is so good."

"Anyone would think you hadn't been fed for a week." Gage set the coffees on the table. He slipped off his jacket and hung it on the back of one of the chairs.

Landry couldn't help but admire the way his shirt pulled tight across his broad chest. *The man is fit! I would pay good dollars to take a peek beneath that cotton.* "Hey, don't judge. I woke up late because I forgot to set my alarm and didn't have time for breakfast. Normally I'd sneak next door, but Mr. Lao went out before I got the chance and I can't leave this place unattended. He has spies everywhere and he'd know, even if I only locked up for five minutes. There's a kettle in the back but he only keeps tea. Tea! The man is deranged. He thinks coffee belongs in satanic rituals. There's something seriously wrong with him. He bought the kettle in England when he was there on a buying trip and now he gets tea sent over every few months because he fell in love with some brand he can't buy here."

"Have you finished?" Gage sat down, adjusting the chair so he could stretch out his legs, crossing them at the ankles.

"Why, do you have somewhere more interesting to be?" Landry pouted.

"I'm pretty sure I could find somewhere less frustrating to spend time." Gage handed over one of the coffees. "Here's your concoction."

"I suppose you think it's unmanly to drink anything but strong black stuff." Landry removed the lid of his cup and breathed in the sweet aroma. "You should try this. It might improve your temper."

Gage took one of the cookies from the bag. "I'm plenty sweet enough for you."

"Is that so? And what makes you think I'm interested in sweet men?"

"I'd guess that's the last thing you're interested in, or need. A brat like you requires a firm hand."

From Gage's tone, Landry guessed he'd be more than happy to provide that hand. "And there you go again with the inappropriate comments. Don't you have some pictures to show me?"

"We can pick up the discussion about your need for discipline later, when I'm off duty." Gage put his phone on the table. "Swipe left. Stop if you see something you recognize. It's a work phone, not personal, so don't get excited."

An array of antiques danced in front of Landry's eyes as he scrolled through Gage's extensive gallery of pictures. Oil paintings followed porcelain followed furniture and jewelry. "I don't recognize anything…" Landry kept scrolling but much of the inventory was far too high-end for Mr. Lao. "Some of this stuff is absolutely gorgeous. The boss comes up with some great pieces, but this is way beyond his budget.

Wait…" Landry went back to the picture of a gold and amethyst necklace. Dating from the early 1900s, it looked familiar. "This one… The lighting isn't great but I think we might have this. Oh God, is the boss in trouble?" His heart fell. Mr. Lao had been good to him.

"Can you lay your hands on it?" Gage asked.

"Sure. Just give me a minute." Landry shoved his chair back. Most of the decent jewelry was kept in a locked cabinet in the far corner of the store, behind two bookcases full of first editions. Mr. Lao always stashed stock that might tempt a smash and grab in the least accessible parts of the shop. Shimmying his way between teetering piles of furniture, Landry took the cabinet's key from his pocket. The necklace was on the bottom shelf, nestling on the black velvet lining of its leather-covered box. Seeing it again, Landry knew it was identical to the one in the picture. He took it from its place, relocked the cabinet then dragged his feet a bit getting back to Gage. "Here it is."

"That's the one." Gage pushed the box back to Landry before taking a huge bite of muffin. "These aren't bad."

"Not bad? What are you talking about? I just outed my boss as a jewel thief and all you're interested in is a muffin." Landry grabbed his coffee and took a long swig, wishing it contained a splash of rum.

"A small test of your honesty."

"You're making no sense whatsoever." Landry felt like stamping his foot but made do with scowling.

"I seeded the photographs with legal items from the various shops I've been visiting. If you hadn't picked it out, I would have suspected your motives. A colleague of mine took a picture of the necklace a few days ago."

Landry gaped. "You… You… Pain in the ass! You could have given me a heart attack."

Gage chuckled. "It was worth it to see your face. Did you know your earlobes go pink when you're nervous?"

"They do not!" Landry pulled on one soft lobe. "And quit looking at my ears, you freak." He sat down, groping in the paper bag for a cookie. "After that, you owe me coffee and baked goods every day this week."

"Wanna see me again, huh?"

"You can just drop them off." Unaccustomed to the shy, awkward feeling he was experiencing, Landry picked at the chocolate chips in his cookie.

"I don't think so. We need to go out on a date so I can explain to you how relationships between Dominants and submissives work."

"I haven't seen you around the local scene… How did you find out?"

"Research. You'd be surprised how much I know about you."

"Have you been following me?"

"On and off over the last few weeks. The department has been keeping tabs on antique store staff across the city. I took a special interest in you after hearing about some of the places you frequent. Fond of leather and latex, aren't you?" Gage lifted his coffee in a toast.

"I… Maybe?" Landry scuffed the toe of his sneaker against the parquet flooring. "Are you really a Dom, or just playing?"

"Through and through the genuine article."

Landry pictured Gage in full leather regalia. His mouth dried and his cock jerked. He didn't know where to put himself.

"What time do you close on Saturday?"

"You're the detective. You work it out."

"I hope you enjoy standing, because by the time I'm done with your rebellious ass, you won't want to sit on it. I'll pick you up here at closing time." Gage pushed his chair back, not waiting for a response. He strolled through the store like he owned the place.

Shell-shocked, Landry watched him go, wondering what had just happened. He shook his head. "No way he's gonna show." He grabbed the bag of leftover treats to take back to the counter along with his half-finished coffee. "More's the pity."

Sign up for our newsletter and find out about all our romance book releases, eBook sales and promotions, sneak peeks and FREE romance books!

About the Author

Rae has been secretly penning romances since high school. It started with short stories that grew into full-length novels. When she received her first Kindle and had thousands of books at her fingertips, she became a little distracted from writing. Then one day she read a book that she would have written a different way. She began writing again and hasn't stopped since.

When she's not writing, Rae can usually be found reading, walking along the beaches of Half Moon Bay, or taking her geriatric dog to the vet, yet again.

Rae loves to hear from readers. You can find her contact information, website details and author profile page at https://www.pride-publishing.com

www.ingramcontent.com/pod-product-compliance
Lightning Source LLC
Chambersburg PA
CBHW020213260626
47156CB00002B/362

* 9 7 8 1 8 3 9 4 3 9 7 8 0 *